50 Dinosaur Tales

And 108 More Discoveries From the Golden Age of Dinos

By Sabrina Ricci
With Garret Kruger

50 Dinosaur Tales: And 108 More Discoveries From the Golden Age of Dinos

This book is a blend of fiction and fact.

All rights reserved. No part of this book may be reproduced, scanned, transmitted, or distributed in any form or by any means without permission.

Copyright © 2019 Sabrina Ricci and Garret Kruger

Published by I Know Dino, LLC

iknowdino.com

Cover Image by P. Trusler [CC BY-SA 4.0 (http://creativecommons.org/licenses/by-sa/4.0)], via Wikimedia Commons

ISBN 978-1-62200-033-3

Dedicated to all our podcast listeners, and all dinosaur enthusiasts.

For Dinosaur Enthusiasts

Are you really into dinosaurs? Sign up to the *I Know Dino* mailing list for news, updates, and special offers on all upcoming dinosaur books.

iknowdino.com/subscribe

Contents

Africa	1
Ledumahadi mafube	2
Sefapanosaurus zastronensis	6
Spinosaurus aegyptiacus	10
More Dinosaurs From Africa	14
Antarctica	22
Asia	24
Bayannurosaurus perfectus	25
Caihong juji	29
Changyuraptor yangi	33
Corythoraptor jacobsi	37
Datonglong tianzhenensis	42
Deinocheirus mirificus	46
Fukuivenator paradoxus	50
Halszkaraptor escuilliei	54
Kulindadromeus zabaikalicus	58
Qianzhousaurus sinensis	62
Qiupanykus zhangi	66
Serikornis sungei	70

Tongtianlong limosus	74
Yi qi	78
Zhenyuanlong suni	82
More Dinosaurs From Asia	86
Australia	128
Diluvicursor pickeringi	129
Kunbarrasaurus ieversi	133
Weewarrasaurus pobeni	137
More Dinosaurs From Australia	141
Europe	143
Dracoraptor hanigani	144
Morelladon beltrani	148
Ostromia crassipes	152
Torvosaurus gurneyi	156
More Dinosaurs From Europe	160
North America	175
Anzu wyliei	176
Aquilops americanus	180
Arkansaurus fridayi	184
Borealopelta markmitchelli	188
Dakotaraptor steini	193
Daspletosaurus horneri	197
Dynamoterror dynastes	201

Galeamopus pabsti	205
Nanuqsaurus hoglundi	209
Probrachylophosaurus bergi	213
Rativates evadens	218
Regaliceratops peterhewsi	222
Spiclypeus shipporum	228
Tototlmimus packardensis	232
Yehuecauhceratops mudei	236
Zuul crurivastator	240
More Dinosaurs From North America	244
South America	271
Chilesaurus diegosuarezi	272
Dreadnoughtus schrani	276
Gualicho shinyae	280
Isaberrysaura mollensis	284
Lavocatisaurus agrioensis	288
Murusraptor barrosaensis	292
Notocolossus gonzalezparejasi	296
Sarmientosaurus musacchioi	301
Tratayenia rosalesi	306
More Dinosaurs From South America	310
Resources	330
Index	376

About 384
More *I Know Dino* Books 385

Introduction

Thank you so much for purchasing this book. We're all dinosaur enthusiasts here, and it's amazing to live in the golden age of dinosaurs, where paleontologists are continuously learning about new dinosaurs and new facts about already known species. Between 2014 and 2018, more than 150 dinosaurs were named!

Garret and I have been doing the *I Know Dino* podcast for over four years now, and every day we're inspired by our wonderful, enthusiastic audience. We love learning about dinosaurs, and we love sharing our knowledge with you. That's why we decided to create one big dinosaur book, covering the discoveries from the last few years. To do that, we've combined our stories from the Top 10 Dinosaur series, and added new stories and facts from dinosaurs discovered in 2018.

Because we're including so many dinosaurs, we thought it'd be fun to sort them by the continent where they were found. In some cases, this was tricky. A few of the dinosaurs found in Russia were from Europe, while others were from Asia. The dinosaurs in this book are organized into two groups: those that we wrote short stories about and those that have lists of facts, all arranged alphabetically.

As we mentioned in our Top 10 Dinosaur series, we may never know exactly how dinosaurs lived and behaved. But we still have fun imagining scenes of dinosaurs eating, fighting, and playing. This book is a mix of imagination and research, combining fictitious scenes of 50 of the dinosaurs that made recent headlines with a list of facts about each one to help paint a broader picture. And, if you are interested in staying up to date on new discoveries or learning more about the dinosaurs in this book, check out the *I Know Dino* podcast.

Please enjoy.

– Sabrina

Africa

Ledumahadi mafube:
"A giant thunderclap at dawn"

Ledumahadi mafube, courtesy of Nobu Tamara via Wikimedia Commons

It's good to be alive. *Ledumahadi mafube* looks at her surroundings. There is enough vegetation everywhere, so she can always eat her fill. She's one of the largest animals around. No real threats for her to worry about.

Ledumahadi is a sauropodomorph about 14 years old and an adult in her species. She is about 13 ft (4 m) tall at her hip and weighs around 26,000 lb (12 tonnes). Her toenail alone is bigger than many of the animals that live in the area.

She's large and stout, especially her front legs, so *Ledumahadi* walks on all fours. However, she likes to stand in a peculiar manner by flexing her limbs instead of using her legs like columns. This gives her a sort of crouching position, which looks a little awkward but is perfectly comfortable.

Ledumahadi walks. It's a hot day. The land is very flat, so she can see far into the distance. Something glimmers. *Ledumahadi* sees water, which reminds her that she is thirsty. She takes quick steps and soon finds herself standing on the shore.

There is not much water, and *Ledumahadi* can see the rocks at the bottom, but she doesn't mind. She plants her feet firmly in the ground and bends her legs, lowering herself to the cool liquid. She laps it up greedily. Once she has her fill, she looks for her next activity.

Not too far away is a tall conifer. Most of the leaves have been stripped away by other animals, except for the top of the tree. Fortunately, *Ledumahadi* is immense, so she knows that she can easily reach the top for a tasty snack.

Ledumahadi makes her way to the tree. Standing at the base is a small *Heterodontosaurus tucki*. It's only about 5 ft (1.5 m) long, and most of the length is in its tail. *Heterodontosaurus* gives *Ledumahadi* a curious look. *Ledumahadi* doesn't pay the little dinosaur much attention and stands up on two legs. She leans on the trunk of the tree with her two forelimbs and stretches her long neck. She opens her mouth and bites a mouthful of leaves. As she chews, she looks down.

Heterodontosaurus is staring at her, watching her eat. It looks hopeful, waiting for some of the leaves to fall to the ground.

No such luck.

Ledumahadi is hungry and efficient. She keeps her mouth closed as she eats, so she does not lose any of her food.

Heterodontosaurus keeps looking at her, expectant. It opens and closes its mouth, to signal hunger.

Ledumahadi finishes chewing. She sees a large branch full of leaves, but it's nearly out of her reach. *Ledumahadi* grabs the few leaves within her range and pulls them back. She clips the leaves with her teeth, and the branch swings back into place.

The movement startles a small lizard in the tree. *Ledumahadi* watches it run from her branch, down the trunk, and onto the ground.

Heterodontosaurus lunges and picks up the lizard in its mouth almost as soon as it's on the ground. Then the pint-sized animal darts away so fast that *Ledumahadi* doesn't see where it goes.

No matter. *Ledumahadi* moves her head back to the top of the tree and continues to eat.

Facts

- *Ledumahadi mafube* was a sauropodomorph that lived in the Early Jurassic in what is now South Africa.
- *Ledumahadi* was quadrupedal but had flexed limbs instead of columnar arms and legs (like its later sauropod relatives).
- *Ledumahadi* weighed 12 tonnes and is one of the earliest known giant sauropodomorphs.
- The genus name *Ledumahadi* means "a giant thunderclap" in Sesotho.
- The species name *mafube* means "dawn" in Sesotho.

Find out more in the I Know Dino *podcast, episode 201, "Dracorex."*

Sefapanosaurus zastronensis: "Cross lizard"

A thin layer of fog covers the area around *Sefapanosaurus zastronensis*, making the hard dirt under his feet cold. *Sefapanosaurus* shivers, takes a few gentle steps on all fours, and then rises up onto two legs. He uses his long tail to help balance.

The sun is just rising, and *Sefapanosaurus*' stomach is growling. He stretches his long neck and scours the area for food. Lucky for him, it's not far.

A few feet in front of him is vegetation, and *Sefapanosaurus* reaches out and grabs at it with his hands. On both his thumbs are claws, which he flexes as he shoves plants into his mouth. He is medium sized and, if he needs to, he can use his claws to defend himself.

After devouring a few bites, he glances at the stones below him, looking for the smoothest ones. A ray of sunshine slices through the fog, glimmering against a particularly round stone.

Eager, *Sefapanosaurus* scoops up the rock and swallows it whole. Then he picks up another. And another. These gastroliths will help him to digest his breakfast. *Sefapanosaurus* has weak teeth, so he relies on the stones to grind up his food.

Satisfied, *Sefapanosaurus* returns his attention to the vegetation and picks off the choicest, most tender leaves he can find. Now that he has some food in his belly, he can afford to be picky.

He continues to enjoy his meal. When he is full, he moves to a warmer spot. By now the sun is making its way through even more of the fog. *Sefapanosaurus* heads towards a less damp spot, near a tree, and gets comfortable.

One of his favorite pastimes is to nap, especially after eating. He takes a quick look around to make sure no predators are nearby. Enough brush surrounds him that he should be able to hear anyone who approaches him.

Feeling safe, he closes his eyes. But he doesn't fall asleep right away. Smaller, harmless animals are starting to wake up, and *Sefapanosaurus* can hear them. He enjoys the sounds they make—faint squeaks and grunts, as they scamper around him in search of their own breakfast.

Sefapanosaurus senses that he is being watched. He lazily opens one eye on his small skull and sees a small, furry animal staring at him. *Sefapanosaurus* snorts, and the animal scurries away.

Sefapanosaurus closes his eye again, relaxed. He continues to listen to the sounds around him.

Then he senses he is being watched again. This time he opens both eyes. The furry animal is back, but this time with a friend.

Annoyed, *Sefapanosaurus* lifts his head. Both animals squeak and duck for cover under some nearby brush.

Sefapanosaurus lowers his head and closes his eyes again. He starts to fall asleep, but then he feels a flicker on one of his legs. Startled, he jumps up and flashes his thumb claws, ready for a fight.

He sees a blur of two tails—the same furry animals from before. *Sefapanosaurus* shakes his head to wake himself up, knowing he won't be able to take his nap here.

He shuffles along, keeping an eye out for a quieter place to sleep.

Facts

- *Sefapanosaurus zastronensis* was a sauropodomorph that lived in the Late Triassic in what is now South Africa.
- *Sefapanosaurus* was discovered in the late 1930s, in the Elliot Formation in South Africa. The partial skeletons of four individuals were housed at Wits University and at first thought to be the fossils of *Aardonyx*. Closer studies in 2015 showed the bones were of a new dinosaur genus.
- One interesting feature of *Sefapanosaurus* is the cross-shaped talus bone in its ankle.
- The genus name *Sefapanosaurus* means "cross lizard."
- The species name *zastronensis* is in honor of Zastron, the town near the Elliot Formation where *Sefapanosaurus* was found.

Find out more in the I Know Dino *podcast, episode 32, "Fukuiraptor."*

Spinosaurus aegyptiacus: "Spiny lizard"

Spinosaurus aegyptiacus, courtesy of ДиБгд, via Wikimedia Commons

The water is murky. Sand and grit stir it up, making it difficult for the giant predator with the 6-foot-tall sail on his back to see. He lowers his mouth into the water, his high nostrils allowing him to breathe easily while the pits on his snout feel for pressure and sense for fish swimming nearby.

Nothing moves, or at least nothing worth attempting to catch. The large theropod—*Spinosaurus aegyptiacus*—wades into the water. Tired from balancing his long head and neck with his short back legs, *Spinosaurus* relaxes as he submerges like a crocodile, flexing his flat, webbed feet in the water.

The river is shallow, but *Spinosaurus* paddles quietly, looking for easy prey. An unsuspecting sawfish passes by. It is 25 feet long with jagged teeth.

Spinosaurus knows the sawfish will be hard to catch, but the thought of a big meal is enticing. He opens his mouth and tries to rake in the fish with his teeth. Needle-like teeth line the sides of his upper jaw, with more teeth behind them and interlocking teeth at the end of his snout. *Spinosaurus* tries to bite down with his powerful jaw, but his teeth are not serrated, so he cannot just rip apart the sawfish.

The teeth land in the wrong place, near the sawfish's narrow rostrum, which has sharp teeth along it, like a saw. The sawfish struggles, its teeth digging into *Spinosaurus*. *Spinosaurus* shakes his long, narrow head and tries to at least stun the sawfish, so he can eat it without the struggle.

But the sawfish proves to be too strong, and *Spinosaurus* is forced to let go. The sawfish swims away as fast as it can while *Spinosaurus* tends to his wounds. The cuts aren't too deep, and *Spinosaurus* is not that hurt, but he feels the sting of defeat in the pit of his empty stomach.

Back on the surface, *Spinosaurus* keeps only his nostrils above water while he paddles towards land. Only his sail and two large eyes can be seen.

A pterosaur lands at the edge of the water and stops to take a drink. *Spinosaurus* spots the potential meal. Still hungry, *Spinosaurus* decides to scare and confuse his prey.

Spinosaurus raises his sail to create a shadow in the water, arching his back for effect. It works.

The pterosaur continues to sip but more cautiously. *Spinosaurus* slowly moves towards his prey. When he gets within biting distance, he opens his jaws and snaps down quickly. But not quickly enough.

The pterosaur flaps its wings and, with a surge of adrenaline, manages to get away, though not without a souvenir. When the pterosaur fights its way out of *Spinosaurus*' jaws, it rips out one of *Spinosaurus*' teeth.

The pterosaur is badly wounded and dripping blood, which only makes *Spinosaurus* hungrier. He lunges out of the water and runs for the injured prey, using his arms as legs. When he gets close, he reaches out with his blade-like claws, grasping for the pterosaur.

But his stumpy back legs and front-heavy top get in the way. *Spinosaurus* stumbles and the pterosaur flees, escaping for good this time. Stomach growling, *Spinosaurus* returns to the water where he lies in wait for an easier kill.

Facts

- *Spinosaurus aegyptiacus* was a spinosaurid that lived in the Late Cretaceous in what is now North Africa.
- *Spinosaurus* had a sail that it may have used for thermoregulation, to create shadows to find prey, or to attract mates.
- *Spinosaurus* was first discovered in 1912, but the first *Spinosaurus* fossils found were destroyed in World War II.
- New fossils were eventually found, and *Spinosaurus* was redescribed in a new study published in 2014.
- The genus name *Spinosaurus* means "spiny lizard."

 Find out more in the I Know Dino *podcast, episode 195, "Gryphoceratops."*

More Dinosaurs From Africa

Afromimus tenerensis

- *Afromimus tenerensis* was an ornithomimosaur that lived in the Cretaceous in what is now Niger.
- Scientists found tail vertebrae, ribs, and part of the right leg, but no skull or foot.
- Ornithomimosaurs were theropods that look somewhat similar to modern ostriches.
- The genus name *Afromimus* means "Africa mimic."
- The species name *tenerensis* refers to Tener, which is Tuareg for the area where the dinosaur was found.

 Find out more in the I Know Dino *podcast, episode 158, "Camarasaurus."*

Chenanisaurus barbaricus

- *Chenanisaurus barbaricus* was an abelisaurid that lived in the Cretaceous in what is now Morocco.
- *Chenanisaurus* was about 23 to 26 ft (7 to 8 m) long, similar to its relative *Carnotaurus*.
- Like *Carnotaurus*, *Chenanisaurus* had a deep, short jaw. It may have used a hatchet-style attack on its prey.
- The genus name *Chenanisaurus* comes from the Sidi Chennane phosphate mines where the dinosaur was found.
- The species name *barbaricus* refers to the Barbary Coast, an old term that used to include Morocco.

 Find out more in the I Know Dino *podcast, episode 123, "Barapasaurus."*

Eucnemesaurus entaxonis

- *Eucnemesaurus entaxonis* is a prosauropod that lived in the Triassic, in what is now South Africa, and was found in the Elliot Formation.
- *Eucnemesaurus entaxonis* is the second species in the genus *Eucnemesaurus*, after *Eucnemesaurus fortis* (named in 1920).
- *Eucnemesaurus entaxonis* was discovered in 2003 but not described until 2015.
- Scientists found a partial skeleton of *Eucnemesaurus entaxonis*, including part of the pelvis, right leg, and vertebrae from the tail, hips, and back.
- The genus name *Eucnemesaurus* means "good tibia lizard." The species name *entaxonis* refers to the inner digits of the hand or foot carrying most of the dinosaur's weight.

Mansourasaurus shahinae

- *Mansourasaurus shahinae* was a titanosaur that lived in the Late Cretaceous in what is now Egypt.
- *Mansourasaurus* was about 30 ft (9 m) long and weighed 5 to 6 tons.
- *Mansourasaurus* is more closely related to titanosaurs in southern Europe and East Asia than South America, which helps show that the continent of Africa was not as isolated as previously thought.
- The genus name *Mansourasaurus* refers to Mansoura University, where the dinosaur was found.
- The species name *shahinae* is in honor of Mona Shahin for her contributions to the university's paleontology program.

 Find out more in the I Know Dino *podcast, episode 167, "Xenotarsosaurus."*

Meroktenos thabanensis

- *Meroktenos thabanensis* was a sauropodomorph that lived in the Triassic in what is now Lesotho, South Africa.
- *Meroktenos* was originally classified as another sauropodomorph, *Melanorosaurus*, in 1993, until scientists did an anatomical comparison of the two genera and found enough differences that *Meroktenos* could be its own genus.
- The specimen found may have been a juvenile.
- The genus name *Meroktenos* means "femur animal." Originally only the right femur was found.
- The species name *thabanensis* refers to the Thabana Morena area in Lesotho, where *Meroktenos* was found.

 Find out more in the I Know Dino *podcast, episode 63, "Concavenator."*

Pulanesaura eocollum

- *Pulanesaura eocollum* was a sauropodomorph that lived in the Jurassic, in what is now South Africa, in the Elliot Formation.
- Scientists think *Pulanesaura* is one of the earliest sauropods or sauropodomorphs with a horizontal neck.
- *Pulanesaura* walked on all four legs and had teeth indicating that it ate tough foods. It also had a small head. These characteristics may have contributed to sauropods eventually growing so large.
- *Pulanesaura* was probably 26 ft (8 m) long and weighed 5 tons.
- The genus name *Pulanesaura* means "rain maker." Naude Bremer, who used to own the farm where the fossil was discovered, nicknamed his daughter Panie, "Pulane." It was also very rainy when paleontologists were excavating the bones. The species name *eocollum* means "dawn neck."

 Find out more in the I Know Dino *podcast, episode 39, "Brachiosaurus."*

Shingopana songwensis

- *Shingopana songwensis* was a titanosaur that lived in the Cretaceous in what is now southwest Tanzania.
- Scientists found about 10 percent of the dinosaur's bones, and many of them had holes bored into them by insects (possibly termites or ants). This probably happened after the dinosaur was buried.
- *Shingopana* was about 26 ft (8 m) long and weighed about 5 tonnes.
- The genus name *Shingopana* means "wide neck" in Swahili.
- The species name *songwensis* refers to the Songwe area where the dinosaur was found.

 Find out more in the I Know Dino *podcast, episode 150, "Antetonitrus."*

Antarctica

Morrosaurus antarcticus

- *Morrosaurus antarcticus* was an iguanodontian that lived in the Cretaceous, in what is now Antarctica, in the Snow Hill Island Formation.
- Scientists have only found parts of the right hind leg of *Morrosaurus*.
- Paleontologists think *Morrosaurus* was medium sized. They also think *Morrosaurus* may have been a runner.
- The genus name *Morrosaurus* is in honor of El Morro, where the bones were found.
- The species name, *antarcticus*, is in honor of Antarctica, the continent where the dinosaur was found.

Asia

Bayannurosaurus perfectus: "Bayannur lizard"

Bayannurosaurus perfectus is having a lazy day. Yesterday she had a feast after finding an unclaimed area of vegetation not too far from where she sleeps. Today she woke up late. The sun has been in the sky for a few hours already and is keeping her warm.

Bayannurosaurus moseys back to her feasting spot. She's pretty large—about 30 ft (9.1 m) long. When given the choice, she prefers to walk on all fours.

She keeps a slow pace. She's still not in any hurry. To her side, she notices a small animal following her. It's only about 3 ft (1 m) long but not a threat. *Bayannurosaurus* stops and turns to take a better look. The smaller animal also stops and, for a moment, the two stare at each other.

The smaller animal is quite colorful with long filaments on its tail and a beak. *Bayannurosaurus* recognizes it as a *Psittacosaurus*. They're both herbivores, which could be a problem, but the *Psittacosaurus* is kind of cute, so *Bayannurosaurus* decides to tolerate the smaller dinosaur for now.

Bayannurosaurus lets out a soft snort to indicate to *Psittacosaurus* that the two of them can be around each other in peace. To her surprise, another *Psittacosaurus* appears. This one is a little smaller than the first.

Bayannurosaurus bobs her head and continues her leisurely stroll to her patch of vegetation. The *Psittacosaurus* follow closely behind.

Bayannurosaurus reaches her destination and looks around for the perfect spot. The first *Psittacosaurus* wastes no time and rushes past *Bayannurosaurus*. She watches, fascinated, as *Psittacosaurus* crops a piece of the plant with its beak. With its mouth full, it looks satisfied.

The second *Psittacosaurus* is more guarded and keeps its eyes on *Bayannurosaurus*.

Bayannurosaurus sees some tender leaves in a tree near the first *Psittacosaurus*. She takes a few steps, still on all fours. When she gets to the base of the tree, she stands on her two back legs. Now she can almost reach the leaves.

Bayannurosaurus uses the spikes on the ends of her thumbs to balance herself on the tree. Then she stretches her neck and grabs hold of her prize with her teeth. When her mouth is full, she drops back down to four legs and moves to a shady spot.

Once she is comfortable, *Bayannurosaurus* uses her dental batteries to crush and grind her food. Each *Psittacosaurus* watches her, looking confused. *Bayannurosaurus* is amused and thinks that they must be juveniles.

Bayannurosaurus is not that hungry, but she is getting sleepy. She can also tell that both *Psittacosaurus* want more food. An idea comes to her. She stands on two legs and walks back to the tree. She digs her thumb spikes into the bark again and grabs a mouthful of leaves.

The *Psittacosaurus* watch her as she gets back on the ground. *Bayannurosaurus* walks a few steps toward them and releases all the leaves from her mouth. Both *Psittacosaurus* scarf down the food.

Bayannurosaurus returns to the tree a few times to retrieve more leaves for the hungry young dinosaurs. They look pleased.

Bayannurosaurus lies in the shade. Before she closes her eyes, she nods to both *Psittacosaurus*. They return her nod with soft grunts, an agreement of sorts to keep watch for any predators. Happy, *Bayannurosaurus* takes her nap.

Facts

- *Bayannurosaurus perfectus* was an iguanodontian that lived in the Early Cretaceous in what is now Inner Mongolia.
- The skull of *Bayannurosaurus* was about 3 ft (80 cm) long.
- *Bayannurosaurus* was a facultative biped, which means that it was capable of walking on two legs and four legs.
- The genus name *Bayannurosaurus* refers to Bayannur, the area where the fossils were found.
- The species name *perfectus* refers to the fossils' amazing preservation.

 Find out more in the I Know Dino *podcast, episode 180, "Nipponosaurus."*

Caihong juji: "Rainbow"

Lucas Attwell 2018

Caihong juji courtesy of Lucas Attwell via Wikimedia Commons

It's time. *Caihong juji* is ready. He has finally grown into his feathers, and he must now attract a mate.

His feathers cover all 16 in (40 cm) of his body. He only weighs 1.05 lb (475 g), but he cannot fly. *Caihong* can, however, dance.

The sun will set soon, and the lighting is golden and perfect. *Caihong* has been waiting all afternoon for this moment. He staked out a branch in his tree that morning, making sure the branch was at a height that would not overshadow other vegetation. He has been visiting this branch for weeks to make sure that female *Caihong* visit from time to time, and to make it known that this is his territory.

Caihong hops from one side of his branch to another. He lightly shakes his feathers, so they catch the light. Most of his body is iridescent black and shimmers. The feathers on his arms and legs are long and symmetrical, while the feathers on his tail are asymmetrical and fan out.

Caihong's head and neck are more colorful, with a mix of blue, green, orange, and red. He also has a crest on his head, which juts out in front of his eyes and makes him more appealing to a female *Caihong*.

Something lands on the branch next to *Caihong*. He jerks his head and sees her. He's been waiting for so long that he almost forgets what he needs to do to woo the female *Caihong*. Then his instincts kick in.

Caihong puffs up his chest to feature the blues and greens on his neck. Then he struts back and forth on his branch to give the female the best view of his shimmering body and to show off his balance.

The female *Caihong* doesn't seem too impressed, but she doesn't move away either. *Caihong* raises his arms as high as he can to display the red and orange feathers on his wings. He pauses for a moment to see the female *Caihong*'s reaction. She's watching him.

Caihong hops from side to side, keeping his arms outstretched. He stops again to make sure that his intended mate is still interested. She continues to look at him. Good.

Caihong stops hopping and takes a bow, spreading out the feathers on his tail. Then he shakes them, so they look as if they're waving to the female *Caihong*.

It works. The female *Caihong* sidles up to him. She takes another look at his tail feathers. Then, in unison, they hop from side to side on their branch, a signal that she has accepted his offer to mate.

The timing is just right. The sky has now turned yellow, orange, and red to complement *Caihong*'s feathers. The lighting illuminates the nearby tree branches, giving the pair of *Caihong* a path to follow.

Caihong wastes no time. He makes a gurgling sound to let his partner know to follow him. The two take off and glide from branch to branch.

Facts

- *Caihong juji* was a small paravian theropod that lived in the Late Jurassic in what is now China.
- *Caihong* had a bird-like body and feathers, but it probably did not fly.
- Scientists compared the structure and shape of *Caihong*'s feathers with modern bird feathers and found that they were mostly black with red, orange, green, and blue neck feathers.
- The genus name *Caihong* means "rainbow" in Mandarin Chinese.
- The species name *juji* means "big crest" in Mandarin.

Find out more in the I Know Dino *podcast, episode 166, "Minmi."*

Changyuraptor yangi: "Long-feathered robber"

Changyuraptor yangi courtesy of Emily Willoughby via Wikimedia Commons

The breeze feels cool and refreshing, ruffling the feathers on *Changyuraptor yangi*'s body. Gliding through the dense trees is the most natural thing in the world, and *Changyuraptor* relishes the tall obstacles, using the feathers on her legs and tail to turn quickly and avoid colliding with branches.

The view is beautiful. Below, *Changyuraptor* can see other animals stuck on the ground. A terrible way to live, she thinks. One of those animals is *Yutyrannus*, busy ripping open its prey with its sharp, menacing teeth. *Yutyrannus* is a fearsome predator, also covered in feathers. *Changyuraptor* is glad that the tyrannosaur cannot fly.

Changyuraptor moves higher into the air and turns to get a view of the volcanoes. They are large and menacing. But, in the sky, *Changyuraptor* feels safe. Nearby is a lake. *Changyuraptor* salivates at the thought of the fish and frogs that live in the water.

But the wind is blowing in the right direction, and *Changyuraptor* decides to ignore the potential prey for now and stay in the sky. The day is warm and sunny, and she would rather spend time in the air. She lowers herself back among the trees, taking care to twist and turn.

Changyuraptor spreads out her full 21-foot (6.4 m) wingspan and brushes past a tree with long branches and thick, bundled leaves. The edges of the leaves scrape against *Changyuraptor*, but she doesn't mind. She continues to glide around the trees.

From the corner of her eye, *Changyuraptor* sees a sudden movement. A small lizard scurries up a conifer tree. *Changyuraptor* salivates. Lunch.

She swivels and dives towards the lizard, using her tail feathers to slow down at the last second and land on the ground, near the trunk of the tree. But the lizard is also quick and jumps away before *Changyuraptor* has a chance to catch her prey.

Frustrated, *Changyuraptor* decides to move on. She grabs onto the tree and pulls herself up, climbing further and further until she reaches nearly the top. She hops over to a slightly taller tree next to it and continues to climb. *Changyuraptor* is a great climber and enjoys the exercise. It's almost as good as flying.

Up here, *Changyuraptor* sees a small bird, flying at a slow speed, not too far away. Her stomach growls, and she jumps and heads towards the bird. The bird hears *Changyuraptor* and starts to move faster. But *Changyuraptor* is determined not to miss another meal. Using all four of her wings, *Changyuraptor* quickly catches up to the bird and attacks.

The bird tries to find cover in the trees, but *Changyuraptor* is too nimble. After just a few seconds, *Changyuraptor* has her lunch. Satisfied, she lands and rips into her prey. The meat is warm and, after *Changyuraptor* gets her fill, she walks briskly to a nearby tree and begins climbing.

When she reaches the top, she notices a *Yutyrannus* walk by. Good choice, *Changyuraptor* thinks. It is always safer to be higher up.

Facts

- *Changyuraptor yangi* was a dromaeosaur that in the Cretaceous period in what is now northeastern China.
- *Changyuraptor* had long leg feathers that looked like a second set of wings.
- *Changyuraptor* is not a bird but is instead a non-avian dinosaur that could probably fly and/or glide.
- Paleontologists still don't know exactly how *Changyuraptor* moved through the air. But *Changyuraptor* could probably turn and brake fast through dense trees.
- The genus name *Changyuraptor* means "long-feathered robber."

 Find out more in the I Know Dino *podcast, episode 22, "Changyuraptor."*

Corythoraptor jacobsi: "Cassowary-like crested thief"

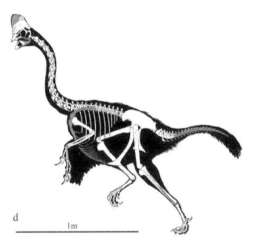

Corythoraptor jacobsi courtesy of Junchang Lü, Guoqing Li, Martin Kundrát, Yuong-Nam Lee, Zhenyuan Sun, Yoshitsugu Kobayashi, Caizhi Shen, Fangfang Teng, and Hanfeng Liu via Wikimedia Commons

Finally, the rain has stopped and the sun is shining. Springtime. Time for *Corythoraptor jacobsi* to find her mate—or actually mates.

Normally, she feels shy, but now is the time of year for her to find a number of males who will incubate her eggs. She needs to lay eggs at multiple nests and make sure they are all cared for.

Like all the oviraptorids in the area, *Corythoraptor* is drawn to the largest body of fresh water. The atmosphere is relaxed, though there are too many animals around for *Corythoraptor*'s taste. She's used to being alone, prefers it even.

Today, however, she does not have that luxury. She holds her head up high so her potential mates can notice her long neck, which is twice as long as her back. It also allows the light to bounce off the large, colorful crest on the top of her head.

The water is surrounded by all types of oviraptorids. *Corythoraptor* walks slowly, looking for signs of her own species, the ones with a similar crest.

She spots a *Ganzhousaurus nankangensis* first, and she keeps walking. His beak is far too curved.

Next she sees a *Jiangxisaurus ganzhouensis*, a dinosaur with much too small of a beak and a tail that is too fluffy. Such a show-off, *Corythoraptor* thinks.

She turns her head, and someone catches her eye. He's facing away and sitting down, so she can only see his back. But he has a similar coloring to her, and his tail looks about right—just long enough and not too fluffy.

Corythoraptor pauses for a moment, considering her options. Should she signal to him that she's interested or wait to get a better look at him?

Before she has a chance to decide, the male stands up. *Corythoraptor* is disappointed. He's much smaller, and he's not a male *Corythoraptor*. He's a *Nankangia jianxiensis*—she can tell by the size of his small crest.

Corythoraptor walks away, annoyed. But she keeps her head high, just in case. Everywhere she looks, she sees oviraptorids, but none of them *Corythoraptor*. Instead, she sees a *Banji long*, with a striped crest; a *Tongtianlong limosus*, with a dome-shaped crest; and a *Huanansaurus ganzhouensis*, with a crest so small that it looks almost nonexistent.

None of them are right for her.

Corythoraptor makes a full lap around the water and still sees no signs of other *Corythoraptor*. The sun is getting low in the sky, and *Corythoraptor* thinks about leaving. She can try again tomorrow.

Then she hears it: a low, rumbling sound, barely detectable. *Corythoraptor* perks up. She knows that sound.

Corythoraptor runs toward the sound,

feeling hopeful. She reaches the spot where the sound originated and is rewarded. It's coming from a male *Corythoraptor*—a tall one, taller than her 5 ft (1.6 m) build, with a gorgeous, almost red crest.

Corythoraptor returns his call. He looks at her and gives his approval. She wastes no time and signals for him to follow her. She walks away to where she has already determined her first nest should be.

Facts

- *Corythoraptor jacobsi* was an oviraptorid that lived in the Cretaceous in what is now Guangdong Province in China.
- The fossils were found near the Ganzhou Railway Station, and the specimen is mostly complete (only missing the tail, part of the crest, and a few other small pieces).
- *Corythoraptor* is housed in the Jinzhou Paleontological Museum, in Jinzhou, Liaoning Province, China.
- The genus name *Corythoraptor* refers to the dinosaur's "cassowary-like crest," which was 6 in (15 cm) tall.
- The species name *jacobsi* is in honor of Professor Louis L. Jacobs, who mentored three of the authors who named and described *Corythoraptor*.

Bonus fact: When cassowaries mate, female cassowaries have multiple male cassowaries incubate their eggs, and they take care of the chicks for nine months.

 Find out more in the I Know Dino *podcast, episode 141, "Ohmdenosaurus."*

Datonglong tianzhenensis: "Datong city dragon"

The morning is peaceful, quiet. *Datonglong tianzhenensis* takes advantage of this time and enjoys a breakfast of horsetails.

She puts all her weight on her four limbs and grinds up the bristly plant in her dental battery. Each of her tooth sockets contains two teeth, a unique feature that helps her eat.

No one else is around, and food is plentiful. *Datonglong* is pleased at finding this spot. With her large body, she needs to consume a lot of food each day, and she prefers to eat alone so as not to fight over resources.

The sun has been up for a couple hours, and it gently warms her back. *Datonglong* closes her eyes for a second. When she opens them again, she notices a large animal approaching.

It's a sauropod (much larger than *Datonglong*,

a hadrosauroid), so *Datonglong* is wary. The sauropod moves slowly, its head towering above *Datonglong*, but it either doesn't notice or care about *Datonglong*.

Datonglong takes a few steps to the side, never taking her eyes off the intruder. She continues to grind her food.

The sauropod keeps moving, but *Datonglong* decides to stand her ground. Soon the sauropod is within striking range, and *Datonglong* can clearly see its long, thick tail. The giant blocks out the sun, so *Datonglong* no longer feels the warmth.

Not that *Datonglong* is thinking about the sun anymore. One blow from the tail could be disastrous. Still, the sauropod seems not to see *Datonglong*.

Datonglong grabs another horsetail and keeps a close eye on the sauropod. She doesn't want to give up her spot, and right now the sauropod doesn't perceive her as a threat.

Then, *Datonglong* hears a sound behind her. She turns and sees three theropods. They do not appear to be stalking her, so they must have stumbled onto her breakfast site by accident.

But *Datonglong* is aware of her vulnerability. She's too close to the sauropod, who could easily injure her, and she's too out in the open, with nowhere to run from the predators should they decide to attack.

The sauropod finally seems to take notice of its surroundings, and it plants its feet firmly in the ground to face the potential threat. *Datonglong* takes a few steps to the side, careful not to startle the giant.

The theropods each cock their heads, sizing up *Datonglong* and the sauropod. The largest theropod takes a step toward *Datonglong*. In response, the sauropod rears up: a warning.

The theropod stops, tips its head again, and then changes its mind and walks back to the other two theropods. They cackle at each other, and then go back the way they came.

The sauropod gets back on all fours and looks down at *Datonglong*. *Datonglong* looks toward the theropods, who have disappeared. Feeling safe again, she grabs another piece of horsetail with her mouth and starts grinding it up.

The sauropod stops paying attention to *Datonglong* and starts walking, once again leaving *Datonglong* in peace.

Facts

- *Datonglong tianzhenensis* was a hadrosauroid that lived in the Cretaceous in what is now China.
- *Datonglong* has a unique feature: two teeth in each tooth socket. This creates a pattern of ridges on the grinding surface of its dental battery.
- The only part of *Datonglong* that has been found so far is its right dentary (about half its jaw plus teeth).
- *Datonglong* is from the Upper Cretaceous in the Huiquanpu Formation. It was found in the Tianzhen County in the Shanxi province of China, which is a little west of Beijing.
- The genus name *Datonglong* comes from "Datong City," and the word "long" means "dragon" in Chinese. The species name *tianzhenensis* refers to the county where the dinosaur was discovered.

 Find out more in the I Know Dino *podcast, episode 72, "Bagaceratops."*

Deinocheirus mirificus: "Terrible hand"

Deinocheirus mirificus, courtesy of FunkMonk (Michael B. H.) via Wikimedia Commons

The sun is hot on *Deinocheirus mirificus'* back. The morning had passed quickly and uneventfully. *Deinocheirus* wades in a shallow stream, partly to find food, but mostly to cool himself down. His hoof-like claws on his toes keep him from sinking in the mud.

The dinosaur lowers his head towards the water and, with his duck-like bill, *Deinocheirus* sucks up the soft plants that hide at the bottom of the stream. His round, flat beak is covered in keratin, which strengthens it. *Deinocheirus* uses his big tongue inside his deep, lower jaw to push the vegetation down his gullet. *Deinocheirus* has no teeth so, to help grind up his meal, *Deinocheirus* picks up a couple of smooth stones and swallows them whole. These gastroliths will help him digest food over time.

A small fish swims near *Deinocheirus* to pick at the plants. Not wanting to miss an opportunity, *Deinocheirus* reaches out for the fish with his 8 ft (2.4 m) long arms. The fish tries to dart out of the way, but *Deinocheirus* uses his claws to catch the prey. The giant dinosaur has a weak bite, so he cannot simply take a chunk out of his meal. Instead, *Deinocheirus* scoops up the fish from his hands with his tongue and swallows.

Now, after a light snack and a chance to cool down, *Deinocheirus* wades out of the water and looks for more vegetation to eat. At 35 ft (10.6 m) long and weighing 6 tons, he lumbers out of the water on his two muscular legs and heads for a patch of trees full of fresh, mouth-watering leaves.

Deinocheirus pulls down the branches with his claws and plucks off his food. With his long, ostrich-like neck, he can reach almost all of the vegetation. As he eats, *Deinocheirus*' tail feathers wag happily. He is so engrossed in his food that he almost doesn't see the hungry *Tarbosaurus* approach.

But he hears the carnivore growl and, though *Deinocheirus* is not the brightest dinosaur, he understands that he is in danger. Instincts kick in, and *Deinocheirus* looks around for an escape route. But *Tarbosaurus* is too close and *Deinocheirus* has too large a stomach and cannot run, so he must find another way to defend himself.

Deinocheirus decides to make himself seem bigger. He lifts his large, horse-like head and straightens out his s-curved back, to better emphasize the sail-like structure that lines his vertebrae. He grunts to show *Tarbosaurus* that he is not afraid.

Tarbosaurus takes a closer look at *Deinocheirus*, sizing him up. Puffed up, *Deinocheirus* looks much bigger than *Tarbosaurus* originally thinks. Eventually, the carnivore decides that it is not worth the effort and backs away.

Deinocheirus waits for the predator to skulk out of sight, and then resumes eating. Wanting to spice up his diet, he chooses to dig for the next meal, using his blunt claws to root for food in the ground.

The fish and the plants are not enough for *Deinocheirus*, and he wants to eat as much as he can before the sun sets and he must settle in for the night.

Facts

- *Deinocheirus mirificus* was an ornithomimosaur that lived in the Cretaceous in what is now Mongolia's Gobi Desert.
- *Deinocheirus* was originally discovered in 1965. But, for 50 years, all scientists knew about *Deinocheirus* was that it had giant, 8-foot-long arms.
- *Deinocheirus* had spines like *Spinosaurus*; truncated, hoof-like claws on its feet; an ostrich-like neck; a flat, duck-like bill; a large lower jaw; tail feathers; short claws on its hands; bulky, tyrannosaur-like hind legs; and sauropod-like hips.
- *Deinocheirus* has been compared to Jar Jar Binks from *Star Wars* because it looks so strange.
- The genus name *Deinocheirus* means "terrible hand."

 Find out more in the I Know Dino *podcast, episode 10, "Deinocheirus."*

Fukuivenator paradoxus: "Paradoxical hunter of Fukui"

Fukuivenator paradoxus, courtesy of Nobu Tamura via Wikimedia Commons

Hiding in the shade of a large tree is a sapling with tender, small leaves. *Fukuivenator paradoxus* opens his mouth and lets out a low sound to alert his sister: food.

She runs over to him, careful to keep the big claw on each of her feet up so as not to touch the ground. When she reaches him, she bends down and stretches her long neck to reach the small sapling. *Fukuivenator* lets her take the first bite, and then grabs a few leaves with his teeth. His mouth is full of different kinds of teeth, some of them with flattened ends so he can grind up the plant matter. The leaves are a treat—easy to chew and swallow.

The two theropods continue to enjoy the sapling together, but the young tree does not yet have many leaves. Stomach still growling, *Fukuivenator* looks around for a supplement to their meal.

The two siblings are still young, not yet fully grown, and consuming as much food as possible is important. They are similar in size, about 8 ft (2.4 m) long, and weigh about 55 lb (25 kg).

Fukuivenator walks away from the tree and the sapling. The area is thick with vegetation, which means it's a good spot for digging a nest. His sister follows, and they both take slow, deliberate steps. If there is a nest, they must watch out for any protective adults.

Everything around them is still and quiet. *Fukuivenator* feels something with his foot. He stops moving, and his sister comes closer. At their feet is a pile of brush, leaves, and dirt. A good sign.

Fukuivenator jerks his head around, looking for any hints of the parents. He has a well-developed sense of hearing, which he also relies on to sense danger.

His sister starts digging at the pile gently with her toe, while *Fukuivenator* keeps a lookout. It doesn't take long for her to uncover their treasure: a clutch of eggs.

Fukuivenator carefully fits one of the eggs into his mouth, using his teeth to keep it in place. His sister does the same. They give each other a quick glance, then start running in the same direction, careful not to crack the eggs. Now that they have their snack, they don't want to risk being caught.

The wind feels good as it weaves through *Fukuivenator*'s feathers. He and his sister run on a familiar path, to where they typically go to rest. *Fukuivenator* doesn't bother to look back—his ears are on alert, and so far he hasn't heard anything suspicious.

They keep moving until they reach their spot. It's secluded and surrounded by large rocks. *Fukuivenator* ducks under some branches with thorns, safe. Only then does he lay the egg down.

He cracks the shell with his teeth and laps up the inside. His sister does the same. They each eat their eggs sloppily and greedily so as not to risk another animal from stealing from them. Their slurping sounds are the only things that break the silence.

Facts

- *Fukuivenator paradoxus* was a coelurosaurian that lived in the Cretaceous in what is now Fukui, Japan.
- The team who discovered *Fukuivenator* found a nearly complete skeleton, the most complete non-avian dinosaur found in Japan.
- *Fukuivenator* looks similar to dromaeosaurs because it has a big claw that sticks up on one toe and a similar head and body shape. But it also has common features of *Archaeopteryx*, ornithomimosaurs, troodontids, and other maniraptorans.
- *Fukuivenator* has heterodont teeth, which means it has multiple kinds of teeth. Some of its teeth are flattened in a way similar to herbivores. *Fukuivenator* evolved from carnivores, so it may have been an omnivore.
- The name *Fukuivenator paradoxus* means "paradoxical hunter of Fukui," and the dinosaur got its name because it has an interesting combination of features and is an example of mosaic evolution.

 Find out more in the I Know Dino *podcast, episode 69, "Microraptor."*

Halszkaraptor escuilliei: "Halszka thief"

The sun has reached the highest point in the sky and is beating down on *Halszkaraptor escuilliei*. It's not a problem for her though since she lives near a large body of water.

The water shimmers, as if inviting her in. *Halszkaraptor* makes her way to the edge, taking careful steps with her raptor-like feet. She keeps her sickle claw on each foot off the ground and moves, almost as if on tiptoes.

With each step, her long neck and tail sway with her. She keeps her short wings tucked to her sides for now.

Halszkaraptor is not that large, only about 18 in (45 cm) tall and 20 in (50 cm) long. On land, she's not much to look at, and she's more of a target. But, in water, she's quick and graceful and a threat to fish.

Halszkaraptor steps into the water and immediately feels more relaxed. The water is almost like a second skin, and its coolness is refreshing. She splashes around for a few moments. Then she feels a hunger pang.

She prepares herself, and then immerses her whole body into the water. *Halszkaraptor* opens up her wings and uses them to propel herself. Her body naturally straightens out, so she becomes like an arrow, shooting through the water. She beats her wings to keep moving.

Soon she sees a school of fish. She swims to the middle of the group, opening her mouth wide, her jaws full of teeth, ready. Without losing any momentum, she catches one, clamps her mouth down so it can't get away, and moves to the surface. She can feel the fish wriggling between her teeth, so she bites down harder.

When she reaches the surface, she opens her jaws and jerks her head upward, tossing the fish up in the air. It spins around for a few seconds, and she catches it in her mouth again. This time, she's ready to eat. The fish goes in head first, and she swallows it whole.

The total experience is satisfying, and *Halszkaraptor* is ready to do it again. She goes back underwater and heads in the direction of where she found fish. By now they will have moved, so she may have to find a different school to hunt. But *Halszkaraptor* doesn't mind. One fish is enough to take her mind off food, and now she's looking for entertainment.

She finds it with another *Halszkaraptor*. It's another female, also in search of fish. *Halszkaraptor* swims over to the other female, and then propels past her as a friendly gesture. The other *Halszkaraptor* seems to like it and moves her wings to gain speed.

The two of them take turns passing each other in the water. Eventually they come upon a school of fish and give each other a knowing look. *Halszkaraptor* swims to one side, and her friend swims to the other. Together they confuse the fish, who all move in different directions. It becomes a free-for-all, and both *Halszkaraptor* and her friend are able to easily catch one fish each in their jaws. They both swim to the surface so they can eat their meals and do it again.

Facts

- *Halszkaraptor escuilliei* was a dromaeosaurid that lived in the Cretaceous in what is now Mongolia.
- *Halszkaraptor* had a swan-like neck and raptor-like feet and was semiaquatic.
- The *Halszkaraptor* specimen was pretty complete, and scientists used the European synchrotron (a massive, powerful X-ray) to scan the bones and ensure that it wasn't a fake.
- The genus name *Halszkaraptor* is in honor of Halszka Osmólska "for her contributions to theropod palaeontology."
- The species name *escuilliei* is in honor of François Escuillié, who returned the poached holotype of *Halszkaraptor* to Mongolia. (The fossils were smuggled from Mongolia to Japan to Britain to France before being returned.)

 Find out more in the I Know Dino *podcast, episode 160, "Scutellosaurus."*

Kulindadromeus zabaikalicus: "Kulinda River running dinosaur"

Kulindadromeus zabaikalicus, courtesy of Tomopteryz via Wikimedia Commons

Wind slices through *Kulindadromeus zabaikalicus'* feathers as he runs as fast as his two small legs can carry him. Although *Kulindadromeus* is only 5 ft (1.5 m) long, the little dinosaur is known in his habitat for his speed.

The wind feels good. But, after a few minutes, *Kulindadromeus* slows down and stops to take a drink from the river near where he lives. From the edge of the water, he has a good view of one of the many volcanoes in the area. They are all active, but *Kulindadromeus* has adapted to life near the volcanoes and knows how to get away when necessary.

He takes a few steps into the water and splashes around. The water weighs down the feathers on his arms and legs, but *Kulindadromeus* doesn't care. The day is warm and the extra insulation is a burden, at least for now. When night falls, the down feathers will be more welcome.

After his thirst is quenched and *Kulindadromeus* has cooled down, he leaves the water and searches for food. Vegetation lies only a few feet away, but it is tough plant matter. Fortunately, *Kulindadromeus* has sharp ridges in his teeth to help him chew. He bites into his lunch with gusto, loudly chewing with his mouth open.

The vegetation is rough, but the scales on *Kulindadromeus*' hands, ankles, and feet help protect the dinosaur and prevent cuts. *Kulindadromeus* also has scales on his tail, which he uses for balance while he bites off vegetation.

Sensing another dinosaur, the bristles on *Kulindadromeus*' head and back stiffen. *Kulindadromeus* takes a break from his lunch and turns around.

A female *Kulindadromeus* awaits him. Though *Kulindadromeus* is still a juvenile, he is old enough to know how his kind mates. Wanting to impress the female, he uses his short arms to show off his impressive, soft feathers.

The female, who is also young, seems to approve. Slowly she approaches *Kulindadromeus* but is interrupted when the nearby volcano erupts. The eruption is sudden, and ash and lava spew out thousands of feet into the air, accompanied by a deafening roar. Ash and dust form a large, dark cloud that starts to roll towards the dinosaurs.

Kulindadromeus can see rocks falling. He quickly looks over to the female, and they give each other a curt nod before taking off. Lava could start flowing at any moment, and it is best to get away as far as possible.

Kulindadromeus flaps his arms, but he cannot fly. Instead, both *Kulindadromeus* and the female *Kulindadromeus* run as fast as they can. Behind them, the smoke and ash gobble up everything, covering it in darkness.

The two run for miles, not stopping to look back. They head uphill when they can. Eventually, they can no longer run, and they collapse. Luckily, the volcano's eruption is relatively small, and they are out of harm's way.

After stopping to catch his breath, *Kulindadromeus* looks over at the female. She feels him staring, and she looks back at him. He raises his arms, so she can once again see his impressive feathers.

Facts

- *Kulindadromeus zabaikalicus* was a neornithischian that lived in the Jurassic in what is now eastern Siberia.
- *Kulindadromeus* is one of the few herbivores found to have fossil feathers, which makes some scientists believe that all dinosaurs could have had feathers, or at least the potential for feathers.
- The area where *Kulindadromeus* was found had a lot of volcanoes. Fossil feathers are rare, and they may be preserved in *Kulindadromeus* because the dinosaur specimens fell to the bottom of the nearby lake and were covered in ash.
- *Kulindadromeus* could not fly, but it may have used its feathers for insulation or display.
- The genus name *Kulindadromeus* means "Kulinda runner." *Kulindadromeus* was found near the Kulinda River.

 Find out more in the I Know Dino *podcast, episode 12, "Kulindadromeus."*

Qianzhousaurus sinensis: "Pinocchio rex"

Qianzhousaurus sinensis shuffles through the lush trees along the edge of a body of water. At 29 ft (8.8 m) long and weighing 1,800 lb (363 kg), she is one of the fiercest and most threatening dinosaurs in the area.

At first glance, she doesn't look too threatening, with her comically long, thin snout covered in tiny horns. But the other inhabitants know better. Nearby, an oviraptor busies itself by crushing a mollusk in the water. Soon it senses *Qianzhousaurus*, and it jerks its head up, leaves the mollusk, and runs in the opposite direction.

Qianzhousaurus grunts, flashing her long, narrow teeth. The oviraptor is too far away to see. Not discouraged, *Qianzhousaurus* takes softer steps, keeping an eye out for a quick meal.

Soon *Qianzhousaurus* spots a small lizard. She starts to stalk her prey, careful not to alert it to any danger.

When *Qianzhousaurus* is within striking distance, she traps the lizard with her feet. The lizard reacts too late and tries to wriggle free, but *Qianzhousaurus* is strong and heavy.

Salivating, *Qianzhousaurus* crushes her prey and leans down to take a bite. She swallows a small chunk, and then takes the rest in her teeth, tilting her head back so that the carcass falls into her mouth. It's a small piece of meat, but it's warm and easily slides down *Qianzhousaurus*' gullet.

Still hungry, *Qianzhousaurus* glances around, looking for another easy target. A sauropod catches *Qianzhousaurus*' eye, but *Qianzhousaurus* knows that she does not have a strong enough bite to take down such a large creature. *Qianzhousaurus* feels the sauropod eyeing her, watching her, but it's too far away to get into a fight.

Qianzhousaurus turns her eyes in a different direction. She hears a splash from behind and rotates to see the source of the sound.

Another oviraptor.

Qianzhousaurus thinks she has a chance of catching this one, but she knows she will have to be quick. From the corner of her eye, she sees another *Qianzhousaurus*, joining her in the hunt. *Qianzhousaurus* makes brief eye contact with her kin, giving her approval.

The two predators chase after the oviraptor, who is slowed down by the water. *Qianzhousaurus* and her partner move along on either side of their prey. Scared, the oviraptor looks from side to side, judging which way to go next.

Qianzhousaurus braces herself. If the oviraptor heads in her direction, *Qianzhousaurus* will need a burst of speed to take it down.

The oviraptor leaps out of the water and dashes as fast as it can in front of the other *Qianzhousaurus*, who is not prepared and stumbles.

Qianzhousaurus lets out a roar and runs through the shallow water towards the oviraptor, nearly knocking over the other *Qianzhousaurus*.

She is fast and almost catches up to the oviraptor. But the oviraptor is just a little bit faster. As a final attempt, *Qianzhousaurus* stretches out her neck and chomps at the oviraptor, hoping to reach it with her long snout. But all she gets is a mouth full of feathers.

Frustrated, *Qianzhousaurus* stops and spits them out. She will have to find another meal.

Facts

- *Qianzhousaurus sinensis* was a tyrannosaurid that lived in the Cretaceous in what is now China.
- According to the study's leader, Junchang Lu from the Chinese Academy of Geological Sciences in Beijing, the *Qianzhousaurus* skeleton was so complete because, right after it died, dirt buried it, which protected it from water and air eroding it.
- *Qianzhousaurus* had a snout 35 percent longer than other dinosaurs of its size. *Qianzhousaurus* got its nickname, "Pinocchio rex," because of its snout.
- Scientists do not yet know what *Qianzhousaurus* used its nose for, but they plan on using computer models to see how *Qianzhousaurus* used its snout. Modern animals with long snouts, like crocodiles, use them to catch fish.
- The genus name *Qianzhousaurus* comes from Qianzhou, the ancient name for the Chinese city Ganzhou, where a nearly complete *Qianzhousaurus* specimen was found.

 Find out more in the I Know Dino *podcast, episode 19, "Qianzhousaurus."*

Qiupanykus zhangi: "Qiupa claw"

Qiupanykus zhangi is a mysterious little animal. She's one of the smaller dinosaurs in the area, weighing only about 1 lb (0.5 kg). Yet her home is also home to much bigger animals, including ankylosaurids, dromaeosaurids, and ornithomimids. But they don't usually pay attention to *Qiupanykus*. She's almost too small to notice.

Though she is small, *Qiupanykus* has a long tail and long legs. She can run fast if she needs to. She also has two short arms, and each arm has one large claw. To use her arms, *Qiupanykus* must bend all the way forward, so her snout also touches whatever her claws touch.

Qiupanykus finds herself by a nest full of large eggs. The eggs look tasty, but *Qiupanykus* knows that it would take her far too long to attempt to eat one. She's not sure how she would open it. She would have to roll one egg out of the nest, try to drop it from somewhere, and hope that would crack the shell so she could lap up the yolk. In her experience, nests full of eggs do not stay unguarded for long.

Instead, *Qiupanykus* opts to continue her quest for food. The nest is near a shoreline, which means there are plenty of potential things to eat. *Qiupanykus* walks along the water, looking around for her next meal.

Then she spots it: a termite nest. A feast. The large mound stands tall, overlooking the water. Inside, *Qiupanykus* knows that her lunch awaits.

Qiupanykus steps lightly to avoid alerting the termites. She pauses for a moment at the base. The mound is pretty sturdy; however, the walls are porous. *Qiupanykus* positions herself against the mound so that her arms can easily reach. Then she uses her claws to break open the nest. At first, she only has a small hole, so she uses her claws to make the hole larger.

She sees the termites scrambling inside. Wasting no time, she puts her head into the mound and pushes out her tongue. Her tongue is long and sticky, and soon she's slurping up dozens of termites at a time. They are crunchy and satiating.

Qiupanykus eats as many termites as she

can. She doesn't know when she might eat so well again. Time passes quickly, and *Qiupanykus* notices that the sun is getting lower in the sky.

Reluctantly, she shifts her weight, so she's no longer leaning on the nest. It may be for the best. The termites are well aware of the danger and many have moved underground, making it harder for *Qiupanykus* to eat them.

She continues to move along the shoreline, heading home. Her burrow is not that close, and *Qiupanykus* wants to get home before the sun sets or else she may end up as someone else's meal. The sky starts to turn colors. She picks up the pace.

Eventually, *Qiupanykus* makes it home. She spots the small opening to her burrow. Before she enters, she looks around and listens. Nothing seems out of the ordinary.

Satisfied, *Qiupanykus* runs into her burrow, so she can warm up and go to sleep.

Facts

- *Qiupanykus zhangi* was an alvarezsaurid that lived in the Late Cretaceous in what is now China.
- *Qiupanykus* was found with a broken dinosaur eggshell, likely belonging to an oviraptorosaur.
- *Qiupanykus* may have used its arms for burrowing or breaking open termite nests, or possibly to crack open eggs.
- The genus name *Qiupanykus* refers to Qiupa, the town in Luanchuan County where the fossils were found.
- The species name *zhangi* is in honor of Shuancheng Zhang, for his support in searching for fossils and fossil excavations.

 Find out more in the I Know Dino *podcast, episode 200, "T. rex revisited."*

Serikornis sungei: "Silk bird"

Serikornis sungei courtesy of Emily Willoughby via Wikimedia Commons

From far away, *Serikornis sungei* looks soft. She is covered in feathers, which give her a silky look. The feathers on her neck are wispy and bundled, while the feathers on her arms are short, slender, and symmetrical. Her hindlimbs are also covered in feathers, though these have fuzz and quills. And she has a nice, long tail, also full of feathers.

Despite all of her feathers, *Serikornis*

cannot fly. She's proud of the feathers on her legs though—they never fail to attract her mates.

Serikornis is small, about 19 in (49 cm) long, with a short head, only 2.5 in (6 cm) long. Any animal that gets close to her, however, would know that she's not just some silky, soft thing. She has sharp, serrated teeth and enlarged claws on her feet.

Serikornis uses her claws to climb up a nearby tree. She digs the claws into the trunk, to keep herself on the tree, and pulls her body further up. The best meals always hide in the trees, so *Serikornis* spends as much time as possible in the vegetation.

Serikornis clambers up to the second branch of her tree and pauses to rest. She looks around for any signs of movement. On the branch next to her is a small insect. *Serikornis* pushes off from her branch and glides over. But the insect is too quick and scurries away before *Serikornis* has a chance to catch it.

A second insect appears from beneath a leaf, and *Serikornis* tries to pounce. But the branch is thinner than she realizes, and *Serikornis* has to grab tightly with her claws so as not to fall. The insect gets away. *Serikornis* slides over to the thicker part of the branch and takes a moment to rest. She's about to give up and try another tree when she sees something sparkle: a web.

She doesn't have to look much farther to find the maker of the web. In the corner is a large, juicy-looking spider. *Serikornis* gets ready. She will have to jump and grab the spider in her teeth before it has a chance to escape.

A breeze blows through the trees, and *Serikornis* ruffles her feathers. Unfortunately, it's enough to draw attention to herself. The spider, sensing danger, uses its silk to bungee jump off the web to the ground. Once on the ground, it starts to run.

Serikornis chases after the spider. First she glides to a branch closer to the spider's web. Then she parachutes from the tree to the ground. The feathers on her hindlimbs help to slow down her fall, so she can land safely.

Once her feet hit the ground, *Serikornis* runs to the spider. The spider is fast but no match for *Serikornis*. She quickly catches up to the spider and scoops it with her mouth. She bites down on a leg, and then tilts her head up and back before tossing the spider in the air and catching it again with her jaws.

Facts

- *Serikornis sungei* was a small paravian that lived in the Jurassic in what is now Lianoning Province, China.
- The holotype of *Serikornis* was nicknamed "Silky" because its hindlimbs looked like the breed of chicken with the same name.
- *Serikornis* was covered in feathers, even on its legs, but it couldn't fly. (However, it may have glided.)
- The genus name *Serikornis* means "silk bird."
- The species name *sungei* is in honor of Sun Ge for contributions in Jurassic and Cretaceous ecology in Asia.

 Find out more in the I Know Dino *podcast, episode 151, "Deltadromeus."*

Tongtianlong limosus: "Muddy dragon on the road to heaven"

Tongtianlong limosus, courtesy of Junchang Lü, Rongjun Chen, Stephen L. Brusatte, Yangxiao Zhu, and Caizhi Shen via Wikimedia Commons

Tongtianlong limosus bends his head and picks at the insects crawling on the base of a tree. They're not his favorite food, but the tree offers some shade on this hot day. He's also next to a muddy pit, so he can cool down even more if he wants. However, he has to be careful. If he ventures too far into the mud, he could easily get stuck.

Tongtianlong pecks at his food with his

rounded, toothless beak. The insects are not too quick today, and they make for an easy meal.

From a distance, he hears a low, rumbling sound. He stands upright and cocks his head, which has a dome-shaped crest at the top. He turns his head from side to side, listening. The sound gets louder as the creature making it comes closer. *Tongtianlong* waits, unsure of what to do next. If he runs now, he will attract attention; if he stays, he risks being a target.

He decides to wait just long enough to see if there is any real threat. The growling stops, and *Tongtianlong* stiffens. Silence is worse than snarling. He should not have stayed.

From the corner of his eye, he sees the long snout of *Qianzhousaurus*, a large tyrannosaurid. *Qianzhousaurus* looks poised and ready to attack. Its mouth is open, and its sharp teeth glint in the sun. *Tongtianlong* breaks into a sprint, away from the large predator.

In his hurry, he forgets where he's heading. Five swift steps in, and he can't move anymore. *Tongtianlong* panics and flaps his wings in an attempt to get out of the mud, but it only makes it worse. The mud covers the feathers on his body, weighing him down even more.

Qianzhousaurus roars but does not pursue

Tongtianlong, once it sees that the mud is a trap. *Tongtianlong* doesn't have time to feel relief. More mud covers his body, and he starts to sink.

In desperation, *Tongtianlong* continues to flap. Mud splashes everywhere. *Tongtianlong* stretches out his arms, looking to grab something—a branch, anything. But the nearest branch is too far away. All *Tongtianlong* can see is mud. He's completely surrounded, with no way to escape.

Tongtianlong panics even more. It becomes harder and harder to breathe. He keeps his arms outstretched, unsure of what else to do. He tries to thrash his legs, but the mud is too thick and strong. It clings to him and saps his strength.

Minutes pass, but it feels like hours. *Tongtianlong* grows more tired, and he starts to resign himself to his fate. His body sinks deeper into the mud. Out of instinct, he keeps his head up high, so he can keep breathing. But the effort is taxing.

More time passes. The mud is a powerful force. It envelops *Tongtianlong* and presses down on him, crushing his lungs. In one last act of defiance, *Tongtianlong* jerks his head up again and spreads his wings, just before the mud overtakes him.

Facts

- *Tongtianlong limosus* was an oviraptorid that lived in the Late Cretaceous in what is now China.
- *Tongtianlong* was found at a construction site in Ganzhou, in southern China, after a TNT blast.
- *Tongtianlong* is estimated to be between the size of a sheep and a donkey.
- The name *Tongtianlong limosus* means "muddy dragon on the road to heaven." *Tongtianlong* refers to Tongtianyan of Ganzhou. "Tongtian" also means "road to heaven" in Chinese, a fitting name because *Tongtianlong* died with its arms outstretched and its head raised up. The word "long" means "dragon" in Chinese.
- The species name *limosus* means "muddy" in Latin, and refers to the fact that the *Tongtianlong* holotype was found in mudstone.

 Find out more in the I Know Dino *podcast, episode 104, "Archaeopteryx."*

Yi qi: "Strange wing"

Yi qi courtesy of Emily Willoughby via Wikimedia Commons

The sky is calling. The morning is warm and much clearer than the day before. Remnants of ash from a recent volcano eruption linger in the air, but no clouds are in sight. An otherwise perfect morning for gliding.

Eager, *Yi qi* begins his climb from the base of

a conifer tree. He is able to scale the tree with ease, grasping onto the trunk with his sharp toes and fingers.

About three-quarters of the way up the tree, *Yi* stops to take in the view. Below him is a forest full of ginkgo trees, conifers, and ferns, surrounded by large lakes. He can see the nearby volcanoes that stand on the edges of the lakes. *Yi* stays still, listening for any cracking or bubbling sounds that occur right before an eruption.

Nothing.

Satisfied, *Yi* scampers up to nearly the top of the tree and prepares for takeoff. He is a winged theropod but not a large animal—about the size of a pigeon and weighing only 0.84 lb (380 g).

His snout is short, with a downturned lower jaw, and he has teeth in the tip of his jaw. In his upper jaw are four front teeth on each side, large and pointing forward.

Most of his body is covered in feathers: large, stiff feathers on his hind limbs and long, slender forelimbs; thick feathers on his head and neck; and longer feathers on the rest of his body, some as long as 2.3 in (6 cm).

Thin, pliable skin stretches between his fingers and the long, pointed, rod-like bone that extends from each of his wrists. *Yi* flexes his fingers—the first finger of each hand is the shortest, and the third finger is the longest—and extends his wings. Without a second thought, he launches himself from the tree.

He spreads his arms and legs, enjoying the feeling of the air rushing past him. After a few seconds he lands on another tree, and he quickly climbs higher and launches himself towards the next tree.

Yi continues to glide from tree to tree with no particular destination in mind. He aims for taller and taller trees, so he can glide faster and for longer lengths. From the corner of his eye, he notices a pterosaur flying in his direction.

Time to hide.

Yi lands on a tree and this time scurries down before taking off. He glides in short spurts, to keep the pterosaur guessing, in case the pterosaur is after him. As he glides he looks for trees with small holes in them—dwellings of his friends.

At the next tree, *Yi* turns his head and sees the pterosaur, who is now flying faster to catch up. *Yi* panics, and then spots a small hole nearby. He jumps off and lands a couple of feet from the hole. His instincts take over, and he runs and dives inside.

The pterosaur screeches in frustration. *Yi* breathes a sigh of relief as he hears the carnivore flap its wings, away from his tree.

Facts

- *Yi qi* was a scansoriopterygid that lived in the Late Jurassic in what is now China.
- Scansoriopterygidae is a group of maniraptoran dinosaurs that could climb and fly. They tend to be very small, and they have long third fingers.
- Scientists are not entirely sure how *Yi* used its wings. It may have been able to fly, or it may have been a glider, like a flying squirrel.
- A farmer, Wang Jianrong, who lives in the Hebei Province of China, found the only known fossil of *Yi*. He sold the specimen to the Shandong Tianyu Museum in 2007, though *Yi* wasn't formally described until April 2015.
- The name *Yi qi* is the shortest binomial name for a dinosaur. The name is tied with the great evening bat, *Ia io*, for the shortest name for anything.

 Find out more in the I Know Dino *podcast, episode 25, "Allosaurus."*

Zhenyuanlong suni: "Zhenyuan's dragon" a.k.a. the poodle from hell

Zhenyuanlong suni, courtesy of Emily Willoughby via Wikimedia Commons

Thin rays of sunshine break through the thick patches of trees. The dense forest is peaceful, and *Zhenyuanlong suni* feels content, her large wings engulfing her nest and keeping her eggs warm.

Then she hears a low sound. It doesn't last long, but *Zhenyuanlong* doesn't want to take any chances, not when her eggs are due to hatch at any moment.

She turns her back to her nest and kicks dirt onto her eggs, as a way to keep them temporarily warm and to better camouflage them. *Zhenyuanlong* has taken every precaution by building her nest in between two entangled trees, so it would blend well into the background.

But *Zhenyuanlong* knows she can never be too careful. Cautious, *Zhenyuanlong* takes a couple of slow steps away from her nest, pausing to listen for any threats.

A salamander runs and brushes past her foot, but *Zhenyuanlong* does not even flinch. She is on the lookout for *Yutyrannus huali*, a large bipedal predator. At only 6.6 ft (2 m) long and weighing 44 lb (20 kg), *Zhenyuanlong* knows she is no match for *Yutyrannus*, a giant at 26 ft (8 m) long and 3,100 lb (1,400 kg). But she will also do everything in her power to protect her young ones.

She waits another moment, and then another for good measure. Satisfied, she takes one step back to her nest. In front of her is another *Zhenyuanlong*. A male.

Zhenyuanlong spreads her long wings on her thin forearms. Her arms are much shorter than her legs, and she can't fly, but her pen-like feathers, coupled with her long tail feathers, are still impressive. The tiny feathers on her head and neck bristle. She is in no mood—she just wants to get back to her eggs.

But the young male *Zhenyuanlong* doesn't take the hint. He mistakes her display as a signal of interest, and in response he opens his wings. He is about the same size, but his wings are more colorful, with hints of blue and green mixed with brown and white.

If it weren't for her eggs, *Zhenyuanlong* would have been intrigued. But she has a family to take care of, and she knows she needs to get back to them now.

She opens her mouth, revealing her sharp teeth. If he doesn't go away soon, *Zhenyuanlong* is prepared to fight. The male *Zhenyuanlong* cocks his head, unsure. He keeps his wings extended, just in case.

Zhenyuanlong takes an aggressive step forward, her eyes glinting in anger. This time the male takes the hint, and he folds up his wings and takes a few steps back before turning to leave.

Zhenyuanlong watches him go, and then closes her mouth and attends to her nest. With one arm, she brushes away the excess dirt. On the last egg, she sees a small crack. She hears a faint chirp from another egg.

Excited, she wraps her wings around her nest and watches. Nothing happens, but *Zhenyuanlong* continues to stare. She doesn't mind the wait.

Facts

- *Zhenyuanlong suni* was a dromaeosaurid that lived in the Early Cretaceous in what is now Liaoning, China.
- Compared to other dromaeosaurs that were discovered around the same time and place, *Zhenyuanlong* was very large and had shorter arms.
- *Zhenyuanlong* had complex feathers, but, since it couldn't fly, scientists are not sure what the feathers were for. It's possible that the feathers were used to attract mates, intimidate rivals, or protect eggs.
- *Zhenyuanlong* has been described as looking like a turkey, an emu, or a big chicken, with wings like an eagle or a vulture.
- Both the genera and species name for *Zhenyuanlong* is in honor of Zhenyuan Sun, who secured the dinosaur specimen for study.

 Find out more in the I Know Dino *podcast, episode 35, "Acrocanthosaurus."*

More Dinosaurs From Asia

Aepyornithomimus tugrikinensis

- *Aepyornithomimus tugrikinensis* was an ornithomimid that lived in the Cretaceous in what is now southern Mongolia.
- *Aepyornithomimus* is closely related to *Struthiomimus* and *Gallimimus*.
- The area where *Aepyornithomimus* was found is known for many dromaeosaurids. *Aepyornithomimus* is the first ornithomimid discovered there.
- The genus name *Aepyornithomimus* means "elephant bird mimic."
- The species name *tugrikinensis* refers to the Tögrögiin Shiree locality where the fossils were found.

 Find out more in the I Know Dino *podcast, episode 140, "Liliensternus."*

Almas ukhaa

- *Almas ukhaa* was a small troodontid that lived in the Cretaceous in what is now Mongolia's Gobi Desert.
- *Almas* lived alongside *Velociraptor* and *Protoceratops*.
- *Almas* had "derived features" like other Late Cretaceous troodontids.
- The genus name *Almas* refers to the "wild man or snowman of Mongolian mythology."
- The species name *ukhaa* refers to Ukhaa Tolgod where the dinosaur was discovered back in 1993.

 Find out more in the I Know Dino *podcast, episode 161, "Apatosaurus."*

Anhuilong diboensis

- *Anhuilong diboensis* was a mamenchisaurid that lived in the Middle Jurassic in what is now Eastern China.
- Mamenchisaurids are known for their incredibly long necks.
- *Anhuilong* is one of a few mamenchisaurids found in the Tunxi Basin in Huangshan, Anhui Province. The discovery shows a larger diversity of mamenchisaurids in an area where there was already a variety of sauropods.
- The genus name *Anhuilong* refers to the Anhui Province, where the specimen was found. The word *long* means "dragon" in Chinese.
- The species name *diboensis* refers to the locality where the dinosaur was found.

Find out more in the I Know Dino *podcast, episode 203, "Cedarosaurus."*

Anomalipes zhaoi

- *Anomalipes zhaoi* was a caenagnathid that lived in the Late Cretaceous in what is now China.
- Only a foot and most of the left leg of *Anomalipes* has been found.
- *Anomalipes* is estimated to have weighed around 100 lb (50 kg).
- The genus name *Anomalipes* means "odd feet."
- The species name *zhaoi* is in honor of "Xijin Zhao, a Chinese paleontologist who has made great contributions to research on Zhucheng dinosaur fossils," according to the paper in *Scientific Reports*.

 Find out more in the I Know Dino *podcast, episode 177, "Hoplitosaurus."*

Avimimus nemegtensis

- *Avimimus nemegtensis* was an oviraptorosaur that lived in the Late Cretaceous in what is now Mongolia.
- There are two species of *Avimimus: portentosus* and *nemegtensis*. *Avimimus nemegtensis* is the second named species. *Avimimus portentosus* was named in 1981.
- Scientists found a bone bed of *Avimimus nemegtensis* with adult and subadult specimens. This may mean that *Avimimus* formed groups for flocking.
- The genus name *Avimimus* means "bird mimic."
- The species name *nemegtensis* refers to the Nemegt Basin, where the dinosaur was found.

 Find out more in the I Know Dino *podcast, episode 170, "Auroraceratops."*

Bannykus wulatensis

- *Bannykus wulatensis* was an alvarezsaur that lived in the Early Cretaceous in what is now Inner Mongolia.
- *Bannykus* had transitional features, with its pointer finger as the dominant digit.
- *Bannykus* was similar to *Alvarezsaurus*, with a small head and an ostrich-like neck.
- The genus name *Bannykus* means "half claw."
- The species name *wulatensis* refers to the county where the dinosaur was found.

 Find out more in the I Know Dino *podcast, episode 197, "Achillobator."*

Beibeilong sinensis

- *Beibeilong sinensis* was a caenagnathid that lived in the Cretaceous in what is now Henan, China.
- The fossils found included a dinosaur embryo surrounded by eggs, with five eggs in a row, and a dinosaur fossil perpendicular across three of them. The embryo was curled up like it was in an egg.
- The egg with the embryo was large, around 16.5 in (42 cm) long, which made scientists estimate the adult to be about 2,400 lb (1,100 kg).
- The genus name *Beibeilong* refers to the fossil nickname "Baby Louie." The egg made its way illegally to the United States in 1995 and was featured as a drawing on the cover of *Nature* in 1996, with the name "Baby Louie." (Baby Louie was repatriated back to China in 2013 where it could finally be analyzed.)
- The species name *sinensis* refers to the fact that it was discovered in China.

 Find out more in the I Know Dino *podcast, episode 130, "Puertasaurus."*

Beipiaognathus jii

- *Beipiaognathus jii* was a compsognathid that lived in the Cretaceous in what is now China.
- *Beipiaognathus* was similar to other compsognathids in that it had fan-shaped dorsal neural spines.
- *Beipiaognathus* was different from other compsognathids because it had teeth that were unserrated and conical-shaped.
- It also had a relatively short tail.
- The genus name *Beipiaognathus* means "Beipiao jaw." Beipiao is the name of a city in northeast China.

Choyrodon barsboldi

- *Choyrodon barsboldi* was an iguanodontian that lived in the Early Cretaceous in what is now Mongolia.
- Scientists found three *Choyrodon* specimens, which included a complete skull, a partial sternum, partial hips, a left femur, and a right tibia.
- The skull of *Choyrodon* curved downward in the front with the top overlapping the bottom.
- The genus name *Choyrodon* means "Choyr tooth." The dinosaur was found near Choyr, Mongolia.
- The species name *barsboldi* is in honor of Dr. Rinchen Barsbold, a prominent Mongolian paleontologist who helped find the first *Choyrodon* fossils.

 Find out more in the I Know Dino *podcast, episode 198, "Alectrosaurus."*

Crichtonpelta benxiensis

- *Crichtonpelta benxiensis* is an ankylosaur that lived in the Cretaceous, in what is now China.
- Paleontologists found an incomplete skeleton without a skull.
- *Crichtonpelta* was referred to as *Crichtonsaurus*, but in 2014 *Crichtonsaurus* was considered a nomen dubium. So Victoria Arbour named the genus *Crichtonpelta*.
- *Crichtonpelta* may be the oldest known ankylosaurine.
- The genus name *Crichtonpelta* is in honor of Michael Crichton, who wrote *Jurassic Park*, and means "Crichton small shield."

 Find out more in the I Know Dino *podcast, episode 208, "Crichtonpelta."*

Daliansaurus liaoningensis

- *Daliansaurus liaoningensis* was a troodontid that lived in the Cretaceous in what is now Liaoning Province, China.
- The *Daliansaurus* specimen was smuggled for a while, so parts of the skull were reconstructed before the fossil was recovered and described.
- *Daliansaurus* was about 3 ft (1 m) long, with tiny serrated teeth and a sickle claw. It was probably covered in feathers.
- The genus name *Daliansaurus* refers to Dalian, a nearby city in Liaoning.
- The species name *liaoningensis* refers to Liaoning.

Find out more in the I Know Dino *podcast, episode 135, "Siats."*

Hualianceratops wucaiwanensis

- *Hualianceratops wucaiwanensis* was a ceratopsian that lived in the Jurassic, in what is now China, in the Shushugou Formation.
- The fossils of *Hualianceratops* were found in 2002, but the dinosaur was not officially described until 2015.
- *Hualianceratops*' skull was 9.8 in (25 cm) long.
- The genus name *Hualianceratops* means "ornamental hornface."
- The species name *wucaiwanensis* is in honor of Wucaiwan, the province where it was found, known as the "five color bay."

 Find out more in the I Know Dino *podcast, episode 57, "Compsognathus."*

Huanansaurus ganzhouensis

- *Huanansaurus ganzhouensis* is an oviraptorosaur that lived in the Cretaceous, in what is now China, in the Nanxiong Formation.
- The Nanxiong Formation is home to many oviraptorosaurs, with six genera found so far. They had different jaw structures, which means that they probably had different ways of feeding and could coexist.
- Scientists discovered an incomplete *Huanansaurus* skeleton, which had a nearly complete skull, lower jaws, part of the right arm, the left hand, part of the thighbone and shinbone, part of the right foot, a humerus, an ulna, and seven neck vertebrae.
- *Huanansaurus* was very bird-like and probably had feathers.
- The genus name *Huanansaurus* means "southern China lizard." The species name *ganzhouensis* is in honor of Ganzhou, where the bones were found.

 Find out more in the I Know Dino *podcast, episode 33, "Parasaurolophus."*

Ischioceratops zhuchengensis

- *Ischioceratops zhuchengensis* was a leptoceratopsid that lived in the Cretaceous, in what is now China, in the Wangshi Group of Zhucheng.
- *Leptoceratopsids* were small, four-legged, horned dinosaurs—averaging 6.5 ft (2 m) long, which is much smaller than ceratopsids—with large teeth, no horns, and short frills.
- *Ischioceratops* may end up being a junior synonym of *Zhuchengceratops* because both sets of fossils were found in the same location. However, only bones from the front of *Zhuchengceratops* were found, such as skull and jaw bones, and only bones from the back of *Ischioceratops* were found, such as the femur and caudal vertebrae (no skull). Since scientists have not found any overlapping bones between *Zhuchengceratops* and *Ischioceratops*, it is hard to know if they are the same animal or different genera.
- *Ischioceratops'* ischium, which forms the lower and back part of the hip bone, is, according to the study, "unique and presumably autapomorphic, with a robust shaft that

resembles that of a recurved bow and flares gradually to form a subrectangular-shaped obturator process in its middle portion."

- The genus name *Ischioceratops* means "ischium horn face." The species name *zhuchengensis* is in honor of Zhucheng, where *Ischioceratops* was found.

 Find out more in the I Know Dino *podcast, episode 59, "Falcarius."*

Jianianhualong tengi

- *Jianianhualong tengi* was a troodontid that lived in the Cretaceous in what is now Liaoning Province, China.
- The *Jianianhualong* specimen found was a very complete adult skeleton, with feather impressions, a skull, claws, a wishbone, and a tail.
- *Jianianhualong* is the earliest known troodontid with asymmetrical feathers, which it used to fly.
- The genus name *Jianianhualong* refers to the Chinese company, Jianianhua, which helped collect the specimen.
- The species name *tengi* refers to the woman, Fangfang Teng, who helped collect the specimen.

Find out more in the I Know Dino *podcast, episode 129, "Edmontosaurus."*

Jinguofortis perplexus

- *Jinguofortis perplexus* was a primitive avialan bird that lived in the Early Cretaceous in what is now Hebei Province, China.
- *Jinguofortis* had teeth in the front of its mouth and a pygostyle-like tail.
- *Jinguofortis* had feathers with fused bones near where the arm attached, so it most likely couldn't fly.
- The genus name *Jinguofortis* means "female warrior."
- The species name *perplexus* means "perplexing" and refers to the fact that the dinosaur has an unusual mix of bird and non-avian dinosaur traits.

 Find out more in the I Know Dino *podcast, episode 202, "Hadrosaurus."*

Jinyunpelta sinensis

- *Jinyunpelta sinensis* was an ankylosaur that lived in the Cretaceous in what is now Jinyun, China.
- *Jinyunpelta* had a tail club and many osteoderms and was about 11 ft (3.5 m) long.
- *Jinyunpelta* is the oldest known ankylosaur with a "well-developed" tail club knob and the oldest known ankylosaurid (but not the oldest known ankylosaurine).
- The genus name *Jinyunpelta* means "Jinyun shield." The pelta part of the name refers to the ostedeoderms found on ankylosaurs.
- The species name *sinensis* means "Chinese."

 Find out more in the I Know Dino *podcast, episode 172, "Sauroposeidon / Paluxysaurus."*

Koshisaurus katsuyama

- *Koshisaurus katsuyama* was a hadrosauroid dinosaur that lived in the Cretaceous, in what is now Japan.
- Not much is known about *Koshisaurus* since only a partial maxilla, teeth, and other bits of the skull have been found.
- *Koshisaurus* is different from other hadrosauroids because it had an antorbital fossa, which is an opening in the skull in front of the eye sockets.
- *Koshisaurus* is considered to be distinct from *Fukuisaurus*, a nonhadrosauroid hadrosauriform found in the same formation as *Koshisaurus*.
- The genus name *Koshisaurus* means "koshi lizard." Koshi is the former name of the Fukui Prefecture, where *Koshisaurus* was found. The species name is *katsuyama*. Katsuyama is a city near where *Koshisaurus* was found.

Laiyangosaurus youngi

- *Laiyangosaurus youngi* was a saurolophine hadrosaurid that lived in the Cretaceous in what is now Shandong Province, China.
- Scientists found fossils from five individuals, including different parts of the skull and a dental battery with hundreds of teeth.
- *Laiyangosaurus* was related to *Edmontosaurus* and may have been similar, given the resemblances in their skulls.
- The genus name *Laiyangosaurus* refers to Laiyang, the city where the dinosaur was found.
- The species name *youngi* is in honor "of the 120th Anniversary of Dr. Chungchien Young's Birth. Dr. Young is the pioneer of vertebrate paleontological research in Laiyang, and who has discovered many dinosaurs at this locality," according to the study.

 Find out more in the I Know Dino *podcast, episode 140, "Liliensternus."*

Lepidocheirosaurus natatilis

- *Lepidocheirosaurus natatilis* was an ornithischian that lived in the Jurassic, in what is now Russia.
- When *Lepidocheirosaurus* was first described, scientists thought it was a theropod, not an ornithischian.
- The reason it's now considered an ornithischian is because it had a hand with strange proportions, which scientists now think is a foot.
- *Lepidocheirosaurus* may be a junior synonym of *Kulindadromeus*.
- The genus name *Lepidocheirosaurus* means "scale hand lizard." The species name *natatilis* means "able to swim."

Liaoningotitan sinensis

- *Liaoningotitan sinensis* was a titanosauriform that lived in the Early Cretaceous in what is now Liaoning, China.
- *Liaoningotitan* had been informally named for a few years, and mounted at the Frankfurt airport, before being officially named and described in 2018.
- *Liaoningotitan* was more derived than *Brachiosaurus*.
- The genus name *Liaoningotitan* refers to Liaoning, where the dinosaur was found.
- The species name *sinensis* means "Chinese."

Find out more in the I Know Dino *podcast, episode 210, "Yangchuanosaurus."*

Liaoningvenator curriei

- *Liaoningvenator curriei* was a troodontid that lived in the Cretaceous in what is now Liaoning Province, China.
- The specimen found is nearly complete, including the skull. The dinosaur was found curled up in a fetal position, so it almost looks like an embryo, and it fits in an area less than 17 x 14 in (42 x 36 cm).
- However, the *Liaoningvenator* specimen found was at least four years old and likely still growing.
- The genus name *Liaoningvenator* means "Liaoning hunter."
- The species name *curriei* is in honor of the paleontologist Phil Currie, for his work on small theropod dinosaurs.

Find out more in the I Know Dino *podcast, episode 133, "Lesothosaurus."*

Lingwulong shenqi

- *Lingwulong shenqi* was a sauropod that lived in the Jurassic in what is now Lingwu, China.
- *Lingwulong* grew up to 57 ft (17.5 m) long and had a short neck that was only 20% of its length.
- *Lingwulong* had a long tail that was about half its body length.
- The genus name *Lingwulong* refers to Lingwu, the city. The word long means "dragon."
- The species name *shenqi* means "amazing" and refers to everyone's surprise to find a diplodocoid in the area.

Find out more in the I Know Dino *podcast, episode 192, "Ampelosaurus."*

Microenantiornis vulgaris

- *Microenantiornis vulgaris* was an enantiornithine that lived in the Early Cretaceous in what is now China.
- *Microenantiornis* was only about 5 in (12 cm) long.
- Scientists found a mostly complete skeleton, including a crushed skull with a short, sharp beak.
- The genus name *Microenantiornis* means "small opposite bird."
- The species name *vulgaris* means "common."

Find out more in the I Know Dino *podcast, episode 179, "Microceratus."*

Mosaiceratops azumai

- *Mosaiceratops azumai* was a neoceratopsian that lived in the Cretaceous, in what is now China, in the Majiacun Formation.
- *Mosaiceratops* had a narrow beak and teeth similar to *Psittacosaurus*.
- Although *Mosaiceratops* does not really resemble *Triceratops*, scientists consider it more closely related to *Triceratops* than to *Psittacosaurus*.
- *Mosaiceratops* is an example of mosaic evolution, which is the idea that evolution occurs in some parts of the body without changes occurring in other parts of the body. *Mosaiceratops* has features of basal ceratopsians, psittacosaurids, and basal neoceratopsians.
- The genus name *Mosaiceratops* means "mosaic ceratopsian." The species name *azumai* is in honor of Dr. Yoichi Azuma, from the Fukui Prefectural Dinosaur Museum, who helped organize and took part in dinosaur expeditions in China.

Nebulasaurus taito

- *Nebulasaurus taito* was a sauropod that lived in the Jurassic, in what is now China, in the Yunnan Province, Zhanghe Formation.
- Because of the discovery of *Nebulasaurus*, paleontologists now think there were a wide range of sauropods that lived in the middle Jurassic in Asia.
- Scientists speculate that *Nebulasaurus* may have had a thagomizer, or spikes on the end of its tail, because of its similarities to *Spinophorosaurus*, a dinosaur from Africa. However, a *Nebulasaurus* tail has not yet been found to confirm.
- The genus name *Nebulasaurus* means "misty cloud lizard," referring to Yunnan, the province it was found in, which means "southern misty cloudy province."
- The species name *taito* is in honor of the Taito Corporation of Japan, a company that funded the project to excavate *Nebulasaurus*.

Qijianglong guokr

- *Qijianglong guokr* was a mamenchisaurid sauropod that lived in the Jurassic, in what is now China.
- A farmer found the first *Qijianglong* vertebra in the 1990s. Then, construction workers discovered *Qijianglong* in 2006 while they were digging. They found neck vertebrae in the ground, which was still attached to the skull.
- *Qijianglong* was about 49 ft (15 m) long, and its neck was about half the length of its body. Its neck vertebrae were full of air, which made the neck fairly lightweight.
- Mamenchisaurids, sauropods known for their extremely long necks, have only been found in China. Scientists are not sure why the group never migrated.
- The genus name *Qijianglong* means "dragon of Qijiang." The dinosaur was found near Qijiang City.

Shuangbaisaurus anlongbaoensis

- *Shuangbaisaurus anlongbaoensis* was a theropod that lived in the Jurassic in what is now Yunnan Province, China.
- Scientists found a partial skull, including crests and a partial lower jaw.
- *Shuangbaisaurus* was similar to *Sinosaurus triassicus*, and some scientists consider *Shuangbaisaurus* to be a synonym.
- The genus name *Shuangbaisaurus* refers to Shuangbai, the county where the dinosaur was found.
- The species name *anlongbaoensis* refers to Anlongbao Town where it was found, which means "dragon-placing fort."

Find out more in the I Know Dino *podcast, episode 124, "Majungasaurus."*

Sibirotitan astrosacralis

- *Sibirotitan astrosacralis* was a titanosaur that lived in the Early Cretaceous in what is now Western Siberia, Russia.
- *Sibirotitan* has been called "Sibirosaurus" in the press in the years before the dinosaur was officially named.
- The species name *astrosacralis* is "an allusion to the unusual configuration of sacral ribs which radiate, in dorsal view, from the middle of the sacrum as the rays of a star," according to the official description.
- The genus name *Sibirotitan* means "titanosaur from Siberia."
- The species name *astrosacralis* means "star sacred bone."

Find out more in the I Know Dino *podcast, episode 169, "Epidexipteryx."*

Sirindhorna khoratensis

- *Sirindhorna khoratensis* was an iguanodon that lived in the Cretaceous, in what is now Thailand, in the Khok Kruat Formation.
- *Sirindhorna* was about 19.5 ft (6 m) long, 6.5 ft (2 m) tall, and weighed about 1 ton.
- *Sirindhorna* is a hadrosauroid and was found nearby two other hadrosauriforms, *Siamodon nimingami* and *Ratchasimasaurus suranareae*. However, *Sirindhorna*'s upper and lower jaws were different enough to be considered its own genus.
- The genus name *Sirindhorna* is in honor of Princess Maha Chakri Sirindhorn for supporting paleontology in Thailand.
- The species name *khoratensis* is in honor of Khorat, the informal name for Nakhon Ratchasima Province, where *Sirindhorna* was found.

Find out more in the I Know Dino *podcast, episode 64, "Kentrosaurus."*

Tarchia teresae

- *Tarchia teresae* was an ankylosaurid that lived in the Cretaceous in what is now Mongolia.
- *Tarchia teresae* is the second species of *Tarchia* described. Teresa Maryańska described the type species, *Tarchia kielanae*, in 1977.
- *Tarchia teresae* is similar in size to *Tarchia kielanae*, but certain bones in *Tarchia teresae* are not fused, and there are differences in nerve exits and proportions.
- The genus name *Tarchia* means "brainy one."
- The species name *teresae* is in honor of Teresa Maryańska.

 Find out more in the I Know Dino *podcast, episode 215, "Tarchia."*

Tengrisaurus starkovi

- *Tengrisaurus starkovi* was a titanosaur that lived in the Cretaceous in what is now Transbaikalia, Russia.
- Only three tail vertebrae of *Tengrisaurus* have been found.
- However, phylogenetic analysis shows *Tengrisaurus* to be closely related to *Rapetosaurus*, which lived in the Late Cretaceous in what is now Madagascar. This may have indicated that titanosaurs arrived in Asia by the Early Cretaceous, and may have originated in Asia, though this is a bit of a stretch.
- The genus name *Tengrisaurus* refers to "Tengri, the primary chief deity in Mongolian-Turkish mythology," according to the study.
- The species name *starkovi* is in honor of Alexy Starkov for his "generous assistance and contribution to the study of Early Cretaceous vertebrates of Transbaikalia.

Find out more in the I Know Dino *podcast, episode 129, "Edmontosaurus."*

Timurlengia euotica

- *Timurlengia euotica* was a tyrannosaurid that lived in the Cretaceous in what is now Uzbekistan.
- The holotype of *Timurlengia* consists of a braincase. Other fossils from other individuals were also referred to *Timurlengia*.
- *Timurlengia* had large inner-ear canals, which may mean it was very agile. It also had blade-like teeth for slicing through prey.
- The genus name *Timurlengia* refers to Timur Leng, the 14th century central Asian ruler.
- The species name *euotica* means "well-eared" and refers to the holotype's large inner ear.

 Find out more in the I Know Dino *podcast, episode 69, "Microraptor."*

Xingxiulong chengi

- *Xingxiulong chengi* was a basal sauropodiform that lived in the Jurassic in what is now Yunnan Province, China.
- Scientists found three individuals: two adults and one juvenile. Together they make a nearly complete skeleton.
- The *Xingxiulong* adults were about 13-16 ft (4-5 m) long and 3-5 ft (1-1.5 m) tall.
- The genus name *Xingxiulong* means "constellation dragon" and refers to the local Xingxiu Bridge.
- The species name *chengi* is in honor of the late Zheng-Wu Cheng, a significant local Chinese biostratigrapher.

 Find out more in the I Know Dino *podcast, episode 119, "Chasmosaurus."*

Xiyunykus pengi

- *Xiyunykus pengi* was an alvarezsauroid that lived in the Early Cretaceous in what is now China.
- *Xiyunykus* weighed about 33 lb (15 kg).
- *Xiyunykus* helps show the evolution of alvarezsauroids.
- The genus name *Xiyunykus* means "western regions claw."
- The species name *pengi* is in honor of local geologist Peng Xiling.

 Find out more in the I Know Dino *podcast, episode 197, "Achillobator."*

Yangavis confucii

- *Yangavis confucii* was a confuciusornithid that lived in the Early Cretaceous in what is now Liaoning Province, China.
- *Yangavis* had a 1.5 ft (50 cm) wingspan and was probably a little smaller than a pigeon.
- *Yangavis* had a "normal-sized" claw and longer arms than other confuciusornithids.
- The genus name *Yangavis* is in honor of the late paleontologist Zhongjian Yang and in memory of the 121st anniversary of his birth.
- The species name *confucii* refers to Confucius and the fact that the dinosaur is a confuciusornithid.

Find out more in the I Know Dino *podcast, episode 203, "Cedarosaurus."*

Yizhousaurus sunae

- *Yizhousaurus sunae* was a sauripodiform that lived in the Early Jurassic in what is now Yunnan Province, China.
- Scientists found a *Yizhousaurus* skeleton that was 23 ft (7 m) long.
- *Yizhousaurus* had a high, dome-shaped skull and a slender jaw.
- The genus name *Yizhousaurus* refers to the Chuxiong Yi Autonomous Prefecture of Yunnan Province, in China.
- The species name *sunae* is in honor of Professor Ai-Ling Sun, for her contribution to Chinese vertebrate fossils.

 Find out more in the I Know Dino *podcast, episode 200, "T. rex revisited."*

Zhongjianosaurus yangi

- *Zhongjianosaurus yangi* was a dromaeosaurid that lived in the Cretaceous in what is now Jinzhou, Liaoning Province, China.
- *Zhongjianosaurus* is a microraptorine, a subgroup of dromaeosauridae. It was small, weighing about 11 oz (319 g).
- *Zhongjianosaurus* looked like a modern bird except for its longer legs and tail and sickle claw.
- The genus name *Zhongjianosaurus* is in honor of Yang Zhongjian, "the founder of vertebrate paleontology in China," according to the study.
- The species name *yangi* is also in honor of Yang Zhongjian, who was involved in the creation of China's Institute of Vertebrate Paleontology and Paleoanthropology.

 Find out more in the I Know Dino *podcast, episode 125, "Omeisaurus."*

Zhuchengtitan zangjiazhuangensis

- *Zhuchengtitan zangjiazhuangensis* was a titanosaur that lived in the Cretaceous in what is now Shandong Province, China.
- *Zhuchengtitan* is the first titanosaur found in the area from the Late Cretaceous.
- Scientists found most of a humerus, which is more robust than other titanosaurs.
- The genus name *Zhuchengtitan* efers to Zhucheng, a city in Shandong Province, China, and the fact that the dinosaur is a titanosaur.
- The species name *zangjiazhuangensis* refers to the Zangjiazhuang Quarry where the dinosaur was found.

 Find out more in the I Know Dino *podcast, episode 158, "Camarasaurus."*

Zuoyunlong huangi

- *Zuoyunlong huangi* was a basal hadrosaurid that lived in the Cretaceous in what is now Zuoyun, Shanxi Province, China.
- *Zuoyunlong* was medium-sized, at about 30 ft (9 m) long.
- Close relatives include *Probactrosaurus*, which lived in the Early Cretaceous in Inner Mongolia, and *Eolambia* and *Protohadros*, hadrosaurs that lived in North America. Scientists think *Zuoyunlong* may have lived around the time hadrosauroids moved from Asia to North America.
- The genus name *Zuoyunlong* means "Zuoyun dragon" and refers to Zuoyun, where the dinosaur was discovered.
- The species name *huangi* is in honor of Mr. Huang Wei-Long "who excavated the first dinosaurs in Zuoyun County and even Shanxi Province in 1957."

Find out more in the I Know Dino *podcast, episode 160, "Scutellosaurus."*

Australia

Diluvicursor pickeringi: "Flood runner"

Diluvicursor pickeringi courtesy of P. Trusler via Wikimedia Commons

Squish, squish. Everything is wet. *Diluvicursor pickeringi* can feel the water in his toes and the soggy leaves. *Diluvicursor* hates getting wet, but he knows it can't be helped. The rain has been falling hard for hours, and he needs to eat.

The ornithopod walks with his friend, another male *Diluvicursor*, along the riverbank. The water levels are rising, and *Diluvicursor* is careful to stay as inland as possible. The problem is that the best vegetation is nearest to the water.

Diluvicursor plans to eat only enough to sustain him for the day, and then move far away from the water. The river is rushing much faster than usual, and the downpour makes it hard for *Diluvicursor* to see where he is walking.

Diluvicursor feels water coming up to his knees. He sends his friend a warning signal, and they both stop moving. The rain has caused the river to flood. He takes a few steps back. Fortunately, he's on a slope. *Diluvicursor* rotates. He sees the water surrounding them. They are trapped.

Diluvicursor tries not to panic. At 3.9 ft (1.2 m) long, weighing 6 to 8 lb (3 to 4 kg), he's not that large. He's not even fully grown, but his legs are strong. *Diluvicursor* knows that he's a good runner, and he may be able to use the muscles in his legs to swim or at least get to safety.

The rain continues, and the river is starting to look angry. *Diluvicursor* knows that he cannot stay on his island. He looks around, trying to figure out his options, and then spots a thick tree trunk in the water, making its way toward him. The tree is moving fast.

Diluvicursor has no time to think. He jumps onto

the tree trunk, his friend following close behind. The trunk is not stable, and it starts to spin. *Diluvicursor* and his friend have to run in place to stay on top of the log.

As they're running, *Diluvicursor* sees a branch floating their way. He waits for the branch to get closer, and then leaps from his trunk. The river is moving so fast that he almost doesn't make it. *Diluvicursor* has to get on all fours and grasp onto the branch.

The river whirls him around to face the rolling trunk. *Diluvicursor* looks up just in time to see his friend lose balance and fall into the water. *Diluvicursor* hopes that his friend has enough strength to swim.

Diluvicursor tries to find his center of gravity while clutching the branch. He stretches out his long tail to help and keeps his head close to the tree. He can no longer see any land, and he has no idea where the river will take him. The rain continues to pour down.

Diluvicursor waits to see what will happen. With any luck, the storm will stop, and he will be able to find a way back to shore and back to home.

Facts

- *Diluvicursor pickeringi* was an ornithopod that lived in the Early Cretaceous in what is now Australia.
- The *Diluvicursor* holotype was a juvenile.
- *Diluvicursor* is estimated to grow to about 7.5 ft (2.3 m) long.
- The genus name *Diluvicursor* means "flood runner."
- The species name *pickeringi* is in honor of David A. Pickering, who contributed significantly to Australian paleontology and who passed away while the fossils were being prepared.

 Find out more in the I Know Dino *podcast, episode 164, "Nasutoceratops."*

Kunbarrasaurus ieversi: "Shield lizard"

Kunbarrasaurus ieversi stomps through the forest, its tail thumping against trees. She can barely feel it though.

Her body is covered in armor—or, more specifically, bony deposits that form scutes and plates. She has a ring of scutes around her neck, and armor that covers her head, back, abdomen, and legs. Her tail has triangular plates and long scutes that form a row.

She walks on four legs, knowing that she could win in a fight with pretty much any predator. Her skin gives her confidence, and one of her favorite pastimes is to announce to the world her presence by being as loud as possible.

Out of the corner of her eye, she sees a flash of something, but *Kunbarrasaurus* keeps stomping along.

If anyone does dare to give her trouble, *Kunbarrasaurus* can defend herself. One swift flick of her tail, with its sharp plates, can easily break bone.

Kunbarrasaurus spots a tasty-looking tree and decides to take a break. She plucks off foliage with her parrot-like beak and chews, happy.

A piece of a branch falls onto *Kunbarrasaurus'* flat head. She shakes it to the side and looks up. A small animal with feathers and wings is high above her. *Kunbarrasaurus* grunts, but the animal doesn't notice.

Annoyed, *Kunbarrasaurus* stomps, but still the animal keeps going about its business. *Kunbarrasaurus* watches as it climbs even higher up the tree, knocking down leaves as it goes.

One leaf floats down within *Kunbarrasaurus'* reach. Not wanting to waste an opportunity, she opens her mouth and eats it. The leaf is more tender than the leaves at the bottom of the tree where *Kunbarrasaurus* can reach.

The animal is now too high for *Kunbarrasaurus* to do anything, but *Kunbarrasaurus* is no longer annoyed. She keeps looking up at the small animal, now hoping that it continues to disturb the branches and leaves in the tree.

A few more leaves fall down, and *Kunbarrasaurus* chomps at them in greed. She looks up, expecting more, but the animal is gone.

Confused, *Kunbarrasaurus* scans the area. She

sees a bit of the animal's tail peeking out from the tree next to hers. Excited, *Kunbarrasaurus* heads to the next tree, and keeps her mouth open for falling leaves.

The animal only stays for a brief time in each tree before hopping to another one. *Kunbarrasaurus* has no idea what it's doing up there, and she doesn't care.

She follows the strange creature from tree to tree for hours. It's not the quickest way to get a meal, but it is the tastiest food *Kunbarrasaurus* has eaten in a while.

Kunbarrasaurus checks to make sure the animal is still in the tree above her. This time it notices her. It stares for a moment. *Kunbarrasaurus* stares back. The animal looks nervous.

After a few seconds, the animal jumps to another tree, and then another. It moves too fast for *Kunbarrasaurus* to follow. *Kunbarrasaurus* looks down. She's lost her access to the choicest leaves.

Still hungry, she takes a few steps, looking for a different type of vegetation to eat. Then a small branch hits her on the head. *Kunbarrasaurus* looks up. Another, smaller animal with feathers and wings is in her tree.

Delighted, *Kunbarrasaurus* opens her mouth.

Facts

- *Kunbarrasaurus ieversi* was an ankylosaur that lived in the Cretaceous in what is now Australia.
- *Kunbarrasaurus* was originally thought to be a different ankylosaur dinosaur called *Minmi*. However, a recent study of the skull, using 3D scans, found there were enough differences to warrant classifying it as its own genus. (*Minmi* is about 10 to 20 million years older than *Kunbarrasaurus*.)
- *Kunbarrasaurus* has a large inner ear, similar to a turtle's. This has not been found in dinosaurs before, and scientists are not yet sure what that meant for *Kunbarrasaurus*.
- The *Kunbarrasaurus* specimen is nicknamed the "Marathon specimen" because it was found on Marathon Station. It was not as heavily armored as other ankylosaurs and may have lived in a time when ankylosaurs first deviated from stegosaurs.
- The species name *ieversi* is in honor of Ian Ievers, who discovered the holotype in 1989.

 Find out more in the I Know Dino *podcast, episode 57, "Compsognathus."*

Weewarrasaurus pobeni: "Wee Warra lizard"

Look to the right. Nothing. Good. Look to the left. Still nothing. Good. Tilt head back to the right. What's that crackling sound? Just a fellow *Weewarrasaurus pobeni* taking a step. Good.

Weewarrasaurus has been on guard for hours with her brother and sister, watching over her family's territory. The three ornithopods stand in a semicircle, ready to sound the alarm at any moment, if necessary.

The rest of her family is busy foraging for food. *Weewarrasaurus* doesn't mind. She has an important job: to keep her family safe. After her shift ends, she will be able to eat.

They are in a particularly lush area. Sweet, fresh vegetation is everywhere. *Weewarrasaurus* knows that she won't have any problem finding a snack later.

Like the rest of her family, *Weewarrasaurus* is a

small animal, and living in a group has a lot of advantages. Someone is always watching for threats, so it's safe to concentrate on finding food. If there are any threats, *Weewarrasaurus* can band together and show their strength in numbers. At night, everyone cuddles for warmth.

Most of the time, guard duty is uneventful, but it is also exhausting. *Weewarrasaurus* is on constant alert, looking in all directions and listening for any unusual sounds. Even normal sounds require scrutiny. A small splash could be her brother taking a drink or a potential predator dipping its toes into her family's usual watering hole.

To be an effective sentry, *Weewarrasaurus* must stand upright on two legs, her head held high. She likes to stand on her toes to get the best view. *Weewarrasaurus* never takes a break, not even when her legs feel tired. Her job is too important.

Weewarrasaurus hears a smacking sound. She turns her head and sees her brother chewing on a plant. He's on all fours and has used his beak to crop off a few tender leaves. *Weewarrasaurus* moves to his side and smacks him with her tail—a warning that he should respect his duties.

He flinches and stares at her for a moment, still chewing. Then he swallows and stands up straight.

Weewarrasaurus moves back to her post and looks away from him to show her disapproval. She has a reputation in the family for being a reliable guard, and she doesn't want her brother to ruin it.

Luckily, her duties are almost done for the day. The sun is low in the sky, and the foraging family members are looking full.

Weewarrasaurus looks over to her mother, the leader of their group, for a sign that they're ready to go home. Her mother notices the sun and lets out a quick grunt. Everyone stops feeding and lifts their heads. As a unit, they start to move back to their home for the night.

Weewarrasaurus quickly bends down into a quadrupedal position and heads to the nearest plant. She picks off as many leaves as she can with her beak. Once her mouth is full, she runs to catch up with the rest of the group, chewing as she goes. Her brother and sister follow.

Weewarrasaurus is satisfied. Another job well done.

Facts

- *Weewarrasaurus pobeni* was an ornithopod that lived in the Late Cretaceous in what is now New South Wales, Australia.
- *Weewarrasaurus* fossils were preserved in green-blue opal.
- *Weewarrasaurus* had teeth and a beak to eat vegetation.
- The genus name *Weewarrasaurus* refers to Wee Warra, where the holotype was found.
- The species name *pobeni* is in honor of Mike Poben, an opal dealer who first recognized the fossil when it was in a bag of rough opals he got from miners. He donated the fossil to the Australian Opal Center.

 Find out more in the I Know Dino *podcast, episode 212, "Wuerhosaurus."*

More Dinosaurs From Australia

Savannasaurus elliottorum

- *Savannasaurus elliottorum* was a titanosaur that lived in the Cretaceous in what is now Queensland, Australia.
- Only one *Savannasaurus* specimen has been found so far, and it is nicknamed "Wade." Wade was about 40 ft (12 m) long and weighed 22 tons.
- Wade is one of the most complete sauropods found in Australia. It took a decade to excavate Wade because about 40 bones were inside a boulder.
- The genus name *Savannasaurus* refers to the countryside where Wade was found.
- The species name *elliottorum* is in honor of the Elliott family for their contributions to paleontology in Australia. David Elliott first found Wade's bones, and his wife Judy and their kids helped piece together some of the fragments.

 Find out more in the I Know Dino *podcast, episode 102, "Edmontonia."*

Europe

Dracoraptor hanigani: "Dragon robber"

Dracoraptor hanigani, courtesy of David M. Martill, Steven U. Vidovic, Cindy Howells, and John R. Nudds via Wikimedia Commons

The day is almost over, and the sky is turning colors: purple, red, orange. *Dracoraptor hanigani* takes a few, deliberate steps toward the setting sun, letting his toes sink into the sand. Water gently laps his feet.

He's a young dinosaur, hungry and eager to prove himself as a hunter. But, with the light dimming, he knows that all his favorite meals will soon be tucking in for the night.

Dracoraptor's belly rumbles. He's not large, only about 7 ft (2 m) long, but he has long legs and is lightly built. He's meant to chase down small, fast prey.

He had come to the shore in hopes of finding an easy meal, perhaps some washed-up carrion. But no such luck. *Dracoraptor* continues to walk along the water, still hoping to find something, anything. He's not picky, and he has pointed, serrated teeth—perfect for ripping into flesh.

A tangy smell wafts up and into *Dracoraptor's* large nostrils. The faint scent of blood. *Dracoraptor* drools in anticipation. He stops and sniffs loudly, trying to pinpoint the source.

The sun is nearly gone from the sky. *Dracoraptor* knows he should find shelter soon—he's still too small to be safe on his own, especially out in the open and at night, when it's harder to see.

But he's so close to his food he can practically taste it. Then he sees a carcass, limp on the shore, the water partially covering its body. It's fresh, which means *Dracoraptor* must be careful. Who knows what other predators are nearby.

Dracoraptor inhales deeply again. He can detect a faint trace of another animal. He takes a couple of cautious steps and looks around. The other animal seems to have left. *Dracoraptor's* belly growls again. He runs to the carrion and tears off a piece of meat. It's warm, and blood dribbles down *Dracoraptor*'s snout. Satisfying.

Dracoraptor buries his snout into his meal, so engrossed that he doesn't notice at first the return of the other predator. He whips his head up just in time to avoid being bitten.

That other animal is an adult female *Dracoraptor*—much larger and with bigger teeth. *Dracoraptor* snarls but knows he cannot win against her. He takes a step back to show submission, but it's not enough.

The female lunges at *Dracoraptor*. *Dracoraptor* jumps back but loses his footing in the soft sand. He stumbles for a second, but that's all she needs. Using her head, she pushes *Dracoraptor* over, and he falls into the water. Before he has a chance to get up, she bites down on his neck and shakes him.

Dracoraptor tries to fight back, but he's in a weak position. He can feel the blood flowing from his body.

Eventually the adult female stops and grunts. *Dracoraptor* is too weak to stand. She goes back to the carrion and starts eating, keeping one eye on *Dracoraptor*. When he doesn't move, she appears satisfied that he won't steal any more of her meal.

Dracoraptor stays where he is until the sun goes down and darkness sets in. He closes his eyes, feeling the water washing up against him.

Facts

- *Dracoraptor hanigani* was a small theropod that lived in the Jurassic in what is now Wales.
- At 40% complete, *Dracoraptor* is one of the most complete theropod fossils found in Europe from the Jurassic era.
- An ammonite, *Psiloceras* (which was around in the Jurassic), fossilized with *Dracoraptor*. This is because *Dracoraptor* probably washed out to sea after it died and fossilized there.
- The genus name *Dracoraptor* means "dragon robber."
- The species name *hanigani* is in honor of Nick and Rob Hanigan, who found *Dracoraptor*'s skeleton and donated it to science.

 Find out more in the I Know Dino *podcast, episode 62, "Fosterovenator."*

Morelladon beltrani: "Morella tooth"

Morelladon beltrani's mouth is dry. He craves fresh vegetation, leafy greens full of water that spills out with every bite.

But he has to keep moving.

If he can't keep up with his herd, he will be left behind. And alone, he has no chance of defending himself from predators. Not even the smaller, scavenger types—at least not in his hungry state.

They have only been walking a few days, but it feels much longer to *Morelladon*. He dreads this time of year, when he and his family have to migrate. But the dry season doesn't care about his desires, and the need to find food and water is greater than the yearning to stay put.

Morelladon walks on all fours, using his forearms mostly for balance. At about 20 ft (6 m) long, a height of 8 ft (2.5 m), and weighing about 2 tons, *Morelladon* is not small. He and his herd move at a slow pace, partly to preserve their strength.

The path—the one *Morelladon* and his ancestors have taken every year for many generations—is clear. *Morelladon* knows the way by heart. He also knows they are about to enter the driest, most barren part of the journey.

At least he is prepared this year. He made sure to eat twice as much food and store more fat in the large, high hump on his back. Long neural spines, about 12 in (31 cm) long protrude from his back and hold up his hump. These humps also make it easy for *Morelladon* to spot his own kind and make sure they have no intruders accompanying them on their migration.

Saliva dribbles down the corners of *Morelladon*'s mouth as he remembers his last feast, which consisted of as many ferns and conifers as he could shove into his muzzle. That last day, he had eaten until his stomach was so full he almost couldn't move. At the time, he thought that had been enough, but now his stomach is growling.

Morelladon looks around. Others in his herd look tired and hungry too. They can't afford to stop, even for a brief rest. Not that there is anywhere suitable to stop. Everything around them is hot and dry and barren, and the unspoken rule is they only stop when it is dark, to protect themselves.

He keeps going, focusing on one step at a time. The ground is dusty. *Morelladon* tries to remember how much longer he and his herd have to keep going for the day. But the heat has gotten to him, and his memory is fuzzy. He doesn't know how many hours it's been since they started today.

Instead he concentrates on what he will find when they reach their new home: water, lush leaves, and shade. Each step will bring him closer.

Morelladon thinks of nothing else, and the hours pass quickly. Soon the sun disappears from the sky, and *Morelladon*'s herd stops. Lost in thought, *Morelladon* bumps into another *Morelladon* in front of him.

He backs away and looks around, relieved that they are taking a break. Everyone huddles together for warmth and settles in. *Morelladon* tucks himself between two others and closes his eyes. Tomorrow will be another long day.

Facts

- *Morelladon beltrani* was an ornithopod that lived in the Early Cretaceous in what is now Spain.
- *Morelladon* is related to *Iguanodon*, and it lived in the same area as other iguanodonts around the same time (125 million years ago). The discovery of *Morelladon* shows a rise in iguanodontoid diversity.
- *Morelladon*'s hump may have been used for fat storage, thermoregulation, or to attract mates.
- *Morelladon* was discovered in 2013 and named in 2015 by Juan Miguel Gasulla, Fernando Escaso, Iván Narváez, Francisco Ortega, and José Luis Sanz.
- The species name *beltrani*, is in honor of Víctor Beltrán, who helped uncover fossils at the Mas de la Parreta quarry, where *Morelladon* was found.

 Find out more in the I Know Dino *podcast, episode 58, "Saurophaganax."*

Ostromia crassipes: "Haarlem specimen"

Ostromia crassipes is small but mighty. He's about the same size as a modern crow, and he has feathers on all four of his limbs, which look like wings. But he can't fly.

Instead, he stays active on the ground, taking advantage of his claws and teeth to find food. He's not a picky eater and will eat just about anything he can fit into his mouth: insects, small reptiles, amphibians, and even mammals.

Sometimes all he has to do is open his jaws and clamp down on his meal. Other times, it takes more effort, and *Ostromia* has to pin down his food with his claws while he takes bites. Those meals are usually more satisfying, but they also leave *Ostromia* tired.

Ostromia's favorite snacks are dragonflies. He falls into a daydream, thinking about chasing one. Dragonflies are so mesmerizing, and they come in an array of colors. Sometimes they're bright blue, sometimes dark green, and sometimes even a golden yellow. And their wings—*Ostromia* likes how they shimmer in the sun.

From the corner of his eye, *Ostromia* sees a flash of light and turns his head. It's a dragonfly, flying low to the ground. It's one of the bright blue ones, and even its wings have a blue tinge. *Ostromia* salivates.

The dragonfly doesn't seem to notice *Ostromia*. Even without any apparent threats, it moves fast. *Ostromia* jerks his head around, keeping his eyes on his next meal. His body is still so as not to scare it away. Then he waits.

Sooner or later, he knows the dragonfly will stop to rest.

Fortunately, he doesn't have to wait long. The dragonfly lands on the branch of a short tree nearby. The branch is close enough to the ground that *Ostromia* can jump and catch his meal.

Ostromia wastes no time. He takes two quick hops toward the tree and swipes at the dragonfly with his claw.

The dragonfly flaps its wings and gets out of the way. *Ostromia* watches as the dragonfly hovers just out of his reach. He jumps up, trying to grab the little insect, but it flies high enough for safety.

The two play this game for a while. The dragonfly gets lower to the ground, and *Ostromia* jumps but is not quick enough. *Ostromia* doesn't mind though. He enjoys this game, and he likes to see the dragonfly's wings glimmer as they move.

The dragonfly gets low to the ground again, and this time *Ostromia* is ready. He jumps, one claw outstretched, and tears through part of the dragonfly's wing. The insect is injured and falls to the ground.

Ostromia pounces. He doesn't need to pounce, but he doesn't want to risk his meal getting away. And besides, pouncing is fun.

Ostromia opens his jaws and bites the dragonfly in half. His meal is crunchy and satisfying. Definitely worth the wait. He eats the rest of the dragonfly in a couple of quick bites, saving the wings for last.

Facts

- *Ostromia crassipes* was an anchiornithid theropod that lived in the Jurassic in what is now Bavaria, Germany.
- Originally, *Ostromia* was considered to be *Pterodactylus crassipes* when it was first described in 1857. Then John Ostrom reclassified it as *Archaeopteryx*, and it was one of 12 *Archaeopteryx* specimens. In 2017, it was reclassified as its own genus, *Ostromia*.
- *Ostromia* was bird-like, had four wings, and was similar in size to *Anchiornis*, a small paravian dinosaur that lived in the Jurassic in what is now China.
- The genus name *Ostromia* is in honor of the paleontologist John Ostrom, who identified the *Ostromia* specimen (also known as the Haarlem specimen because it's housed at Teylers Museum in Haarlem, Netherlands) as a theropod.
- The species name *crassipes* possibly means "thick foot," based on the 1857 description of the dinosaur.

 Find out more in the I Know Dino *podcast, episode 159, "Lufengosaurus."*

Torvosaurus gurneyi: "Savage lizard"

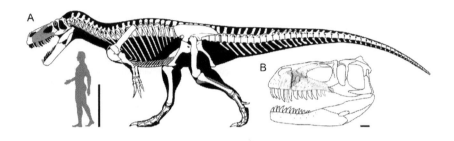

Torvosaurus gurneyi courtesy of Scott Hartman, Carol Abraczinskas, Simão Mateus, Christophe Hendrickx, and Octávio Mateus via Wikimedia Commons

The ground quivers as *Torvosaurus gurneyi* takes a step. Pebbles bounce off the earth when *Torvosaurus* takes another step. He stops to sniff the air.

Around him, *Torvosaurus* can feel the tension. Small dinosaurs scatter and run away, trying to blend in with the lush vegetation. But *Torvosaurus* doesn't care; they are too small, and *Torvosaurus* has a craving for a larger meal.

At 32 ft (9.8 m) long and weighing 4 to 5 tons, *Torvosaurus* is the largest predator in his habitat. His name, meaning "savage lizard," is accurate: *Torvosaurus* is equipped with sharp claws and 4 in (10 cm) long, blade-shaped teeth.

The air smells sweet and fresh, thanks to a large river that cuts through the middle of the vegetation. *Torvosaurus* lets his eyes wander; potential food sources are always more vulnerable when they are thirsty.

Torvosaurus is in luck. *Lusotitan* stands by the river, only a few yards away. The large sauropod is a formidable match for *Torvosaurus*, being 80 ft (24 m) long and weighing 50 tons, but *Torvosaurus* is in the mood for a challenge. He just has to be careful of *Lusotitan*'s tail.

Torvosaurus walks quickly over to *Lusotitan*. He knows *Lusotitan* can hear him coming, so *Torvosaurus* prepares himself for the fight. When *Torvosaurus* gets within a few feet of *Lusotitan*, he stops and roars as loudly as he can, showing off his sharp teeth. He also flexes his claws for good measure.

Lusotitan growls back at *Torvosaurus* and lashes its tail. Their noises attract other, smaller carnivores' attention. Behind *Lusotitan*, *Torvosaurus* sees *Allosaurus*. *Allosaurus* is too far away to attack, but *Torvosaurus* can see that *Allosaurus* is interested. *Torvosaurus* knows that, if he wins this fight, he may have to defend his kill.

For now though, *Torvosaurus* turns his attention to *Lusotitan*, just as *Lusotitan* rears up on its hind legs. *Torvosaurus* sees a chance and is quick to step forward and take a large bite out of his prey.

The fight is over almost as soon as it starts.

Lusotitan yelps in pain and gets back on all fours. The blood drips, a heavy flow, but *Lusotitan* is still too strong for *Torvosaurus*. *Torvosaurus* backs away a few steps and waits for the blood loss to take its toll on his meal.

He has to wait a while, but *Torvosaurus* doesn't mind. Dizzy and weak, *Lusotitan* eventually falls to its side. *Torvosaurus* comes closer, and *Lusotitan* tries to snap at *Torvosaurus* using its long neck. *Torvosaurus* roars and, with brute force, takes another large bite out of *Lusotitan*, this time out of the neck.

The meat is warm and already attracts other carnivores. *Torvosaurus* sees the *Allosaurus* from earlier trying to sneak in and scavenge *Torvosaurus*' kill. Angry, *Torvosaurus* runs at *Allosaurus*, biting at its heels. *Allosaurus* runs into the vegetation, far enough away where it knows that *Torvosaurus* will not follow—at least not while *Torvosaurus* is enjoying his meal.

Torvosaurus returns to *Lusotitan*'s carcass and rips out another chunk of flesh, satisfied.

Facts

- *Torvosaurus gurneyi* was a megalosaurid that lived in the Late Jurassic in what is now Portugal.
- Christophe Hendrickx, who was a PhD student at the New University of Lisbon in Portugal, discovered *Torvosaurus gurneyi* when studying what scientists thought were the bones of *Torvosaurus tanneri*, a related species that lived in North America's Rocky Mountains in the Jurassic.
- *Torvosaurus* probably hunted large prey, but may also have been a scavenger.
- The genus name *Torvosaurus* means "savage lizard."
- The species name *gurneyi* is in honor of paleoartist James Gurney, who created *Dinotopia* (published in 1992).

 Find out more in the I Know Dino *podcast, episode 10, "Torvosaurus."*

More Dinosaurs From Europe

Adynomosaurus arcanus

- *Adynomosaurus arcanus* was a hadrosaurid that lived in the Late Cretaceous in what is now Spain.
- Scientists have found and described a right scapula, neck, sacrum, and tail vertebrae, part of the pelvis, parts of the forelimbs and hindlimbs, and part of the sternum.
- *Adynomosaurus* had an unexpanded shoulder blade, which may mean that it was not as strong as other hadrosaurids.
- The genus name *Adynomosaurus* means "weak shoulder lizard."
- The species name *arcanus* means "secret" or "occult," and refers to the fact that it's difficult to classify hadrosaurs in the area where *Adynomosaurus* was found.

 Find out more in the I Know Dino *podcast, episode 217, "Nanosaurus."*

Burianosaurus augustai

- *Burianosaurus augustai* was a basal ornithopod that lived in the Cretaceous in what is now the Czech Republic.
- *Burianosaurus* is the first Czech Republic dinosaur. It was originally described in 2005 and thought to be an indeterminate species of Iguanodontidae. It was finally named (and differentiated) in 2017.
- Scientists found a left femur and other pieces of bone, and determined that the fossils found were of a young adult that may have been an "insular dwarf" at only 10 ft (3 m) long.
- The genus name *Burianosaurus* is in honor of Zdeněk Burian, a Czech paleoartist who "greatly influenced the perception of dinosaurs during most of the twentieth century."
- The species name *augustai* is in honor of Josef Augusta, a Czech paleontologist and prolific science popularizer.

 Find out more in the I Know Dino *podcast, episode 153, "Giraffatitan."*

Europatitan eastwoodi

- *Europatitan eastwoodi* was a sauropod that lived in the Cretaceous in what is now Burgos, Spain.
- *Europatitan* had air pockets in its neck vertebrae, so it probably had a long neck like *Giraffatitan*.
- *Europatitan* was known as "El Oterillo II" before it was officially named.
- The genus name *Europatitan* means "European giant."
- The species name *eastwoodi* refers to the actor Clint Eastwood. The film *The Good, the Bad, and the Ugly* was partially filmed near where the dinosaur was found.

 Find out more in the I Know Dino *podcast, episode 138, "Antarctopelta."*

Haestasaurus becklesii

- *Haestasaurus becklesii* was a sauropod that lived in the Cretaceous, in what is now England.
- *Haestasaurus* may be a primitive titanosaur.
- Originally, *Haestasaurus becklesii* was classified as *Pelorosaurus becklesii* until paleontologists determined in 2015 that it had many different traits from *Pelorosaurus conybeari*. *Pelorosaurus conybeari* is now considered to be a junior synonym to *Cetiosaurus*.
- Only a forelimb has been found of *Haestasaurus* along with a skin impression. It was the first dinosaur integument (natural covering) found.
- The genus name *Haestasaurus* means "Haesta lizard" and is named for the chieftain who started the town Hastings. The species name *becklesii* is in honor of Samuel Beckles, who found the bones in 1852.

Horshamosaurus rudgwickensis

- *Horshamosaurus rudgwickensis* was an ankylosaur that lived in the Cretaceous, in what is now England.
- *Horshamosaurus* used to be classified as *Polacanthus rudgwickensis*; before that, it was classified as *Iguanodon*. Then, in 2015, paleontologists described it as its own genus, based on differences in the armor and vertebrae.
- *Horshamosaurus* is about 30 percent longer than *Polacanthus*.
- *Horshamosaurus* had osteoderms on its body to protect it, and was a low browser.
- The genus name *Horshamosaurus* means "many spines." The species name, *rudgwickensis*, is in honor of the Rudgwick quarry where it was found.

Iguanodon galvensis

- *Iguanodon galvensis* was an ornithopod that lived in the Cretaceous, in what is now Spain.
- Paleontologists found 13 juvenile specimens of *Iguanodon galvensis*. Juvenile *Iguanodon* specimens are rare.
- The juveniles were only a few months old. Based on their length of 23.5 in (60 cm), paleontologists think adults grew up to 19.5 ft (6 m) long.
- Scientists believe these juveniles were all together when they died, so they were part of a "dinosaur nursery."
- The genus name *Iguanodon* means "iguana tooth." The species name *galvensis* is in honor of the town Galve.

 Find out more in the I Know Dino *podcast, episode 87, "Iguanodon."*

Lohuecotitan pandafilandi

- *Lohuecotitan pandafilandi* was a titanosaur that lived in the Cretaceous in what is now Spain.
- Scientists don't know how large *Lohuecotitan* was, since only a partial skeleton, including vertebrae and parts of the hips and limbs, has been found.
- However, *Lohuecotitan* is the most complete titanosaur found so far that lived in the Late Cretaceous in what is now Europe.
- The genus name *Lohuecotitan* means "Lo Hueco titan," and refers to the giant dinosaur being found in Lo Hueco, in Spain.
- The species name *pandafilandi* comes from the name of a giant, Pandafilando de la fosca vista, in Miguel de Cervante's novel, *The Ingenious Gentleman Don Quixote of La Mancha*.

Magnamanus soriaensis

- *Magnamanus soriaensis* was an iguanodont that lived in the Cretaceous in what is now Spain.
- *Magnamanus* was about 33 ft (10 m) long and weighed approximately 3.5 tons.
- The *Magnamanus* specimen found was old and had a large dental battery in its mouth, which was very worn.
- The genus name *Magnamanus* means "large hand."
- The species name *soriaensis* refers to where it was found: Soria, Spain.

Matheronodon provincialis

- *Matheronodon provincialis* was a rhabdodontid that lived in the Cretaceous in what is now Provence, France.
- *Matheronodon* was an herbivore about 16 ft (5 m) long.
- *Matheronodon* had larger-than-expected teeth, which were about 2 x 2 in (5 x 5 cm). The teeth had thick enamel on one side and worked like a pair of scissors on tough fiber.
- The genus name *Matheronodon* is "in honor of Philippe Matheron, who was the first to describe dinosaur remains in Provence."
- The species name *provincialis* means "from Provence" in Latin.

Find out more in the I Know Dino *podcast, episode 155, "Appalachiosaurus."*

Saltriovenator zanellai

- *Saltriovenator zanellai* was a ceratosaur that lived in the Early Jurassic in what is now Italy. It was the first Jurassic dinosaur found in Italy.
- *Saltriovenator* is estimated to be between 23 to 26 ft (7 to 8 m) long.
- *Saltriovenator* fossils were found at the bottom of a shallow body of water. Scientists found evidence that marine invertebrates ate some of the carcass after it died.
- The genus name *Saltriovenator* means "Saltrio hunter" and refers to the "Salnova" quarry in Saltrio, the locality where the holotype was found.
- The species name *zanellai* is in honor of Angelo Zanella, who found the fossil.

 Find out more in the I Know Dino *podcast, episode 215, "Tarchia."*

Soriatitan golmayensis

- *Soriatitan golmayensis* was a sauropod that lived in the Cretaceous in what is now Soria Province, Spain.
- Scientists found a tooth, several vertebrae, some ribs, parts of the hips, a partial femur, an ulna, a radius, and a humerus, but no skull.
- Based on the humerus, scientists think *Soriatitan* was about 43 ft (14 m) long.
- The genus name *Soriatitan* refers to Soria Province.
- The species name *golmayensis* refers to the Golmayo Formation where the dinosaur was found.

 Find out more in the I Know Dino *podcast, episode 149, "Rebbachisaurus."*

Volgatitan simbirskiensis

- *Volgatitan simbirskiensis* was a sauropod that lived in the Early Cretaceous in what is now Ulyanovsk Oblast, Russia.
- *Volgatitan* weighed about 17 tons.
- *Volgatitan* helps show that titanosaurs may have been more widely distributed than previously thought.
- The genus name *Volgatitan* refers to the Volga River, near where the dinosaur was found.
- The species name *simbirskiensis* refers to the city of Simbirsk, now known as Ulyanovsk, near where the dinosaur was found.

 Find out more in the I Know Dino *podcast, episode 212, "Wuerhosaurus."*

Vouivria damparisensis

- *Vouivria damparisensis* was a titanosauriform that lived in the Jurassic in what is now Damparis, France.
- The specimen was called the "Damparis sauropod," and it had nearly all of its bones (with the exception of the skull, most vertebrae, and most ribs).
- *Vouivria* was originally described in 1943, without a name, and had been sitting in storage at the Muséum national d'histoire naturelle in Paris, France.
- The genus name *Vouivria* refers to the old French word "vouivre," which is either a legendary winged reptile or a beautiful woman who lives in a swamp and protects a ruby.
- The species name *damparisensis* refers to Damparis.

 Find out more in the I Know Dino *podcast, episode 128, "Yutyrannus."*

Wiehenvenator albati

- *Wiehenvenator albati* was a megalosaurid that lived in the Jurassic in what is now Germany.
- *Wiehenvenator* is nicknamed "The Monster of Minden" because it was found close to the town Minden, in Germany.
- *Wiehenvenator* had very large teeth, with the longest ones measuring 5 in (13 cm).
- The genus name *Wiehenvenator* means "Wiehengebirge hunter." Wiehengebirge is the German name of the Wiehen Hills, where the fossils were found (near Minden).
- The species name *albati* is in honor of Friedrich Albat, the geologist who first discovered Wiehenvenator in 1998.

 Find out more in the I Know Dino *podcast, episode 95, "Vastatosaurus rex."*

North America

Anzu wyliei: "Chicken from Hell"

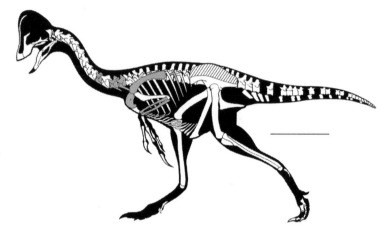

Anzu wyliei, courtesy of Scott Hartman, Lamanna MC, Sues H-D, Schachner ER, and Lyson TR via Wikimedia Commons

All around is the sound of life. Bubbling, squawking, growling, chomping, noisy life.

Anzu wyliei runs through it all, at a fast pace, avoiding the pockets of water in the wet floodplains he calls home. At 11.5 ft (3.5 m) long, and weighing 550 or so pounds (250 kg), *Anzu* is large enough to roam almost as freely as he would like. However, he does have to keep watch for *T. rex* in the area.

But today, *Anzu* is feeling carefree, enjoying the wind that ripples through his feathers on his upper arms as he moves swiftly. He holds his head up high, showing off the large, thin, bony crest that sits atop his head.

As *Anzu* runs, a female *Anzu* catches his eye. Intrigued, *Anzu* stops, using his long tail to help balance. He cocks his head at the female in a curious and an inviting way.

The female is not interested and turns her back on *Anzu*. But *Anzu* is not discouraged. He takes slow steps towards the female, careful not to scare her away. Eventually *Anzu* gets right next to her.

She continues to ignore him and uses her toothless beak to pick at some vegetation on the ground. *Anzu* does the same, using his sliding jaw joint to cut up the plants. After each bite, he lifts his head to steal another glance at her.

Then he notices a small, unsuspecting animal nearby. *Anzu* is quick to use his beak and claws to grab hold of his prey and cut into it. The prey squirms but is no match for *Anzu*. Once it goes limp, *Anzu* nudges the meat towards the female, who inspects *Anzu* more closely.

Anzu tilts his head so she can better see his tall crest. But the gesture annoys her, and she backs away, giving *Anzu* a warning sound. *Anzu* decides to take the aggressive approach and moves a step closer.

Another male *Anzu* comes from nearby and charges *Anzu*. *Anzu*, too immersed in impressing the female and not expecting competition, is caught off guard as the other male knocks the wind out of him. *Anzu* quickly recovers and switches from mating to fighting mode.

He spreads out his arms and runs towards the other male. But the other male is prepared and pecks at *Anzu*'s head, taking a small chunk of skin off the top. Angry, *Anzu* jumps and kicks the other male. He can hear a crack, and the other male yelps in pain and falls, clutching his ribs.

Cocky, *Anzu* struts towards the female, who now looks at him with interest. But he stands too close to the other male, who, with one last burst of energy, thrusts himself onto *Anzu*'s foot and latches on with his beak.

Anzu struggles and pulls himself away with all his might. But the other male has surprising strength and holds his grip, causing *Anzu*'s tendon to be ripped away from his toe bone.

Anzu screeches in pain and limps away, no longer caring about the female. He gets as far away as he can before collapsing and tending to his wound.

Facts

- *Anzu wyliei* was an oviraptorosaur that lived in the Late Cretaceous in what is now North and South Dakota, United States.
- *Anzu* was bird-like, with a long tail, and had a sliding jaw joint that may have been used to eat plants and meat. Two of the three *Anzu* specimens discovered had injuries, one with a broken and healed rib and the other with an arthritic toe bone.
- According to Dr. Hans-Dieter Sues, co-author of the *Anzu* study, and his team, though climate change may have contributed to dinosaurs going extinct, *Anzu* proves that dinosaurs were still evolving and were diverse even at the end. This helps prove it was the asteroid that killed dinosaurs.
- The genus name *Anzu* refers to an ancient Mesopotamian feathered demon.
- The species name *wyliei* is in honor of Wylie J. Tuttle, a dinosaur enthusiast and the grandson of Mr. and Mrs. Foster, who have contributed to the Carnegie Museum of Natural History.

 Find out more in the I Know Dino *podcast, episode 17, "Anzu."*

Aquilops americanus: "American eagle face"

Aquilops americanus, courtesy of Brian Engh via Wikimedia Commons

From high overhead, no one can see the tiny dinosaur perusing the plants on the ground. Weighing only 3.5 lbs (1.6 kg) and measuring 24 in (0.6 m) long, *Aquilops americanus*—one of the smallest dinosaurs—snips off plants with his hook-like beak.

But none of the ferns or saplings nearby are of interest. *Aquilops* doesn't mind foraging. He has just spent the last few months with his herd, walking across the last piece of the Bering

Strait toward what will be known as North America, and his new home. It took multiple generations for his herd to make it to North America from Asia, and *Aquilops* hopes it was worthwhile.

The journey had been long and daunting, and not everyone made it. But *Aquilops* never gave up hope, and the thought of new, tasty food keeps him going. So he doesn't mind walking a little further in search for vegetation.

Aquilops walks on two legs, his long tail helping to keep his balance. On two legs, he can move faster and, although *Aquilops* hasn't quite found the perfect meal yet, he is getting hungry.

Deciding to change course, *Aquilops* bends down, using the prong on his rostral bone to dig for food. At first, nothing good comes up. Then *Aquilops*' prong hits a root. Curious, *Aquilops* cuts off a piece and tastes it.

The root has a sweet flavor and hits the spot. *Aquilops* digs to find more, grunting with pleasure.

Soon other *Aquilops* join the little dinosaur. But *Aquilops* is not willing to share with his herd. He stops digging and moves to cover the spot in the ground where he found the tasty root. He grunts, this time as a warning.

Most of the others back away, not willing to fight over an unknown plant. But one stays behind. She shuffles her feet, ready to attack.

Aquilops gets angry. He found the food first; he should not have to share. He lowers his head, preparing to strike.

After a few moments, the two dinosaurs run at each other. They hit one another with their prongs.

Aquilops feels the sting of the first blow, but that only fuels his anger. He moves backwards a couple of steps, only to run forward again, this time with greater momentum.

The female *Aquilops* is ready and braces herself for the impact. But *Aquilops* has much more force than he anticipated and, this time, part of the female's beak breaks. The pain is so intense that she cries out and quickly shuffles away.

Proud, *Aquilops* returns triumphantly to his meal. He digs into the roots without any hesitation, savoring every bite. The months of walking and struggling for this meal were worth it. This new land will give *Aquilops* a lot of opportunities, and he looks forward to digging up other new plants.

Though *Aquilops* is a juvenile, he will not grow much bigger. But he will lay the groundwork for bigger descendants. About 40 million years into the future, *Triceratops*—one of the most famous ceratopsians—will walk through the same area. Unlike *Aquilops*, *Triceratops* will have horns and a neck frill. And it will be 4,000 times bigger.

Facts

- *Aquilops americanus* was a ceratopsian that lived in the Early Cretaceous in what is now southern Montana, United States.
- Only the skull of *Aquilops* has been found. But the team that found *Aquilops* determined how the rest of its body looked based on the bodies of close relatives.
- *Aquilops* or its ancestors came from Asia, probably crossing the Bering Strait. It is more closely related to Asian dinosaurs than North American ones.
- *Aquilops* had a hook-like beak and a prong on its rostral bone, which forms its upper, parrot-like beak, and may have been used for fighting or digging.
- The name *Aquilops americanus* means "American eagle face"; the name *Aquilops* comes from its hook-like beak.

 Find out more in the I Know Dino *podcast, episode 13, "Aquilops."*

Arkansaurus fridayi: "Arkansas lizard"

Arkansaurus fridayi is always on the move. This ornithopod is about 7 ft (2.1 m) tall, and he feels most comfortable when running. He only likes to stop to eat and sleep. *Arkansaurus* is not picky; he'll eat whatever is available: leaves, eggs, insects, and even small animals. Sometimes he uses the three fingers on his hands to gather his food.

When he's not eating, *Arkansaurus* is running and exploring. Today, he's found himself in an unusually open area. It's a good place to stretch his legs but not necessarily the best place to hide from potential predators.

Arksansaurus pauses for a moment to take in his surroundings. He has large eyes and good vision. The plains are wide and inviting. Still, *Arkansaurus* must make sure it's safe before starting his run.

The ground begins to shake. Confused,

Arksansaurus looks around to try and find the source of the disturbance. A herd of sauropods appears on the horizon. *Arkansaurus* can't make out any specific details other than the facts that they're large and there are many of them. They are slow moving, taking careful steps to avoid accidentally tripping.

Though his plains are no longer completely open, *Arkansaurus* does not mind. The herd of sauropods can help alert him to any danger. Plus, he has an idea of how to have some fun.

Arkansaurus leans forward and heads toward the herd, quickly gaining speed. The sauropods barely notice him, at first. Once he gets closer, they start to make sounds to show their alarm. *Arkansaurus* is too small to be a threat, but he could easily get underfoot and cause an accident.

Arkansaurus accepts the challenge. He darts between the sauropods, zigging and zagging to avoid being trampled. The juvenile sauropods are a little startled, but soon they ignore him. Some of the adults, however, are displeased. A few of them stamp their feet as a warning to *Arkansaurus*. They're so heavy that they nearly throw the ornithopod off balance.

He shakes it off and continues running. It doesn't

take long before he's through the herd. *Arkansaurus* takes a break and looks back at the sauropods. They continue moving in the same direction as if nothing happened.

Arkansaurus spots something traveling with the sauropods: a small animal, running between their legs. All this running for fun has given *Arkansaurus* an appetite. He decides to race back toward the sauropods and grab a snack.

He catches up quickly. The sauropods make threatening noises again, and *Arkansaurus* ignores them. All his focus is on his prey. The small animal notices him and sticks even closer to the sauropods' feet.

It becomes an exciting game of chase. *Arkansaurus* stays low to the ground and stretches his arms out, ready to snatch his soon-to-be food. But, in his eagerness, he miscalculates his steps and smacks against the leg of a sauropod. The sauropod had stopped moving and was unfazed, but *Arkansaurus* bounces off the sauropod's leg and falls to the ground.

All the sauropods around him keep moving. *Arkansaurus* has to quickly get up to avoid getting crushed, but he has lost sight of his prey. Annoyed, *Arkansaurus* runs away from the herd. He needs a break.

Facts

- *Arkansaurus fridayi* was an ornithomimosaur that lived in the Early Cretaceous in what is now Arkansas, United States.
- The description of *Arkansaurus* is based on a "nearly complete right foot."
- *Arkansaurus* is the official state dinosaur of Arkansas.
- The genus name *Arkansaurus* means "Arkansas lizard."
- The species name *fridayi* is in honor of Joe Friday, who discovered the fossils in 1972.

 Find out more in the I Know Dino *podcast, episode 174, "Agustinia."*

Borealopelta markmitchelli: "Northern shield"

Borealopelta markmitchelli by Garret Kruger

It happens so quickly. First the sound of a low rumble, which grows in pitch to a growl, and then a loud, thunderous clap. The ground shakes with it, moving so much that *Borealopelta markmitchelli* nearly loses his balance.

He manages to keep his footing—a relief because he's most vulnerable on his back. Though he's large, about 18 ft (5.5 m) long, weighs about 2,500 lb (1,134 kg), and has body armor, he's still a potential predator target.

If he's on his back, the pair of long spikes on his shoulders and the heavy, sharp scales that cover his back are useless. Not to mention that he loses his camouflage: a reddish-brown coloration in the form of countershading, so that his back is darker and his belly is lighter in color to better blend in.

Borealopelta has been fortunate in life so far. His camouflage has served him well, and he's managed to avoid theropods and live enough years that his face has wizened with age. Scales cover his face and shield his eyes.

Borealopelta looks around. His surroundings haven't changed much after the shaking. He's in a flat area with short shrubs and a view of a nearby large body of water. Everything looks peaceful. He decides not to worry about the last few seconds and instead focuses on finding something to eat.

Another *Borealopelta* pads along in his direction. He's another male but smaller and younger than *Borealopelta*. *Borealopelta* huffs, wishing to be alone. The other male snorts in response and turns away. *Borealopelta* is pleased.

Some time passes, and *Borealopelta* eats, content. He takes his time, savoring each bite of shrubbery, occasionally looking around in case any unwanted visitors come by. The world is quiet, more so than usual.

Out of the corner of his eye, *Borealopelta* notices an odd movement. He turns his head and sees water rising above the land. He pauses, unsure of what to do. *Borealopelta* has never seen anything like it before.

The only thing he can think to do is stand his ground. *Borealopelta* digs his feet into the dirt and braces for impact.

Soon the water reaches him, and *Borealopelta* is surprised by its strength. Normally the water seems harmless, something to be splashed in and not taken seriously. This time, the water seems to be coming for him.

Borealopelta closes his eyes and tries to stay still. But he's no match for the tsunami. The water keeps coming, and *Borealopelta* loses his footing. He's swept away, no longer knowing which way is up and which way is down. All he knows is that he's moving fast.

The water rushes into his snout and fills his nose and mouth. He starts gasping for air. Realizing he's upside down, he flails his limbs, trying to get right side up again.

But it's no use. *Borealopelta* is not a good swimmer, and the flailing only confuses him more. He no longer sees the sky.

Facts

- *Borealopelta markmitchelli* was a nodosaurid ankylosaur that lived in the Early Cretaceous in what is now Alberta, Canada.
- The *Borealopelta* skeleton was preserved in 3D, with scaly skin, meaning that it looked almost the way it would have looked when it was alive. This is because the body washed out to sea, bloating and floating before bursting and sinking in the seabed where it was preserved.
- *Borealopelta* probably had a reddish-brown color, with a darker shading on its back and a lighter shading on its belly. This is called "countershading" and would have helped camouflage *Borealopelta* from predators.
- The genus name *Borealopelta* means "northern shield," which refers to being found in the north and having armor.
- The species name *markmitchelli* is in honor of Mark Mitchell, who spent more than 7,000 hours and 5.5 years preparing the specimen. He said it took a long time because the fossilized bone was so soft yet the rock it was preserved in was so hard.

Find out more in the I Know Dino *podcast, episode 130, "Puertasaurus," episode 142, "Alxasaurus," and episode 149, "Rebbachisaurus," with an interview featuring Dr. Caleb Brown, one of the co-authors who described Borealopelta.*

Dakotaraptor steini: "Plunderer of Dakota"

Dakotaraptor steini courtesy of Emily Willoughby via Wikimedia Commons

The air is warm and the ground is moist, almost spongy. *Dakotaraptor steini* takes slow, deliberate steps, keeping the sickle-like claws on her second toes off the ground. They are large at 9.5 in (24 cm) long—big enough to slash and kill a decent-sized meal.

Dakotaraptor is scouting the area for potential prey. At 18 ft (5.5 m) long, with long legs that allow her to reach speeds of 30-40 mph (50-65 kph), she doesn't have to worry about being attacked.

Still, she needs to be cautious. She has traveled only a short distance, down from her upland territory, but she is now in *Tyrannosaurus rex*'s domain.

Then she spots one, standing in front of a nearby ash tree. *Dakotaraptor* pauses for a moment, considering her options. The *T. rex* is larger but not yet fully grown. She may have a chance at intimidating it.

The tyrannosaur turns and sees her, and *Dakotaraptor* acts quickly. She opens her jaws, revealing a mouth full of sharp teeth, and spreads her wings, which extend 3 ft (0.9 m) from her body. Though she's too large to fly, her wings are big and bright.

The *T. rex* growls and moves closer to *Dakotaraptor*. *Dakotaraptor* doesn't back down. She takes a few swift steps and flexes her sickle claws, preparing for a fight.

Then she hears a loud snap. To her left is an *Ornithomimus*, a dinosaur with wispy feathers and long, juicy-looking legs. *Ornithomimus* blinks, and then runs away from both predators. *Dakotaraptor* forgets all about the *T. rex* and chases after the *Ornithomimus*.

Ornithomimus is fast, much faster than a *T. rex*, but *Dakotaraptor* has no trouble keeping up. Soon she gets so close that she can lean forward and almost touch *Ornithomimus* with her snout.

She continues her chase, enjoying the feeling of stretching her legs. From the corner of her eye, she notices another body catching up to them. She can smell the other *Dakotaraptor*, and her jaws drool with anticipation of her upcoming meal.

The two *Dakotaraptor* corner the *Ornithomimus* near a large body of water. The *Ornithomimus* tries to switch directions and outrun them, but *Dakotaraptor* anticipates the move. She changes directions just before *Ornithomimus*.

She jumps onto *Ornithomimus* and holds it down with her sickle-like claws. At first her prey struggles, but, the more it moves, the deeper her claws sink into its flesh. *Dakotaraptor* uses her wings to keep her balance. Her fellow *Dakotaraptor* joins in the fray. He beats his wings for balance as well, and *Dakotaraptor* admires their iridescence.

Ornithomimus stops moving, and both *Dakotaraptor* rip into their well-deserved lunch. They take turns stripping off chunks of meat, blood dribbling down the sides of their mouths.

Dakotaraptor takes a moment to look at her partner as she swallows a piece. She notes his large, strong wings again, with approval. Then she bends down to take another satisfying bite, happy to be filling her stomach.

Together they make a nice pair.

Facts

- *Dakotaraptor steini* was a dromaeosaur that lived in the Late Cretaceous in what is now South Dakota, United States.
- *Dakotaraptor* is a cousin of *Velociraptor*. Most dromaeosaurs have been found in Asia, and most were much smaller than *Dakotaraptor*.
- The largest dromaeosaur found so far is *Utahraptor*, which was 22 ft (6.7 m) long and weighed 1,100 lb (500kg) though *Dakotaraptor* would have been faster than *Utahraptor*. Also, *Dakotaraptor* is the first giant dromaeosaur from the Hell Creek Formation, and the most recent one in the worldwide fossil record.
- In addition to intimidation, display, and possibly hunting, *Dakotaraptor* may have used its feathers for brooding.
- The species name *steini* is in honor of the paleontologist Walter W. Stein.

Find out more in the I Know Dino *podcast, episode 51, "Alamosaurus."*

Daspletosaurus horneri: "Frightful lizard"

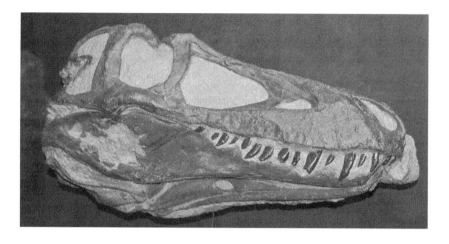

Daspletosaurus horneri courtesy of Tim Evanson via Wikimedia Commons

Daspletosaurus horneri grunts. She feels cool, and she's worried that her nest is too cold for her eggs. The nest is by a large river, so she can easily quench her thirst when necessary and find food. But the water is not the warmest, and neither is the ground near it.

She bends down and nuzzles the nest with her snout. At about 30 ft (9 m) long, and 7.2 ft (2.2 m) tall, she is quite large, especially compared to the eggs in her nest. She also has a massive skull and large, sharp teeth.

Fortunately, her snout is covered in a scaly protective layer, which is very sensitive to temperature and touch. *Daspletosaurus* takes advantage of her sensitivity to test the nest site. She's pleased—it has more heat than expected.

Still, she worries. This is her first year as a mother, and she wants the best for her eggs. Very slowly, and with great care, *Daspletosaurus* picks up one of the eggs with her teeth. Again, her snout aids her, ensuring that she is not putting too much pressure on the egg. She lifts the egg just above the ground and moves it to a slightly warmer part of the nest.

She lets go of the egg and lifts her head to study her handiwork. Then she hears a soft snort behind her—her chosen mate.

He takes a few steps toward her, so that his face is next to hers. He tries to rub his snout against her snout, as a way to court her.

Daspletosaurus jerks her head away to rebuff his advances. She is too busy taking care of her current eggs.

But the male *Daspletosaurus* doesn't take the hint. He takes a step forward, straining his neck, so that his face is once again next to her face. Annoyed, *Daspletosaurus* gives a warning growl.

She pushes his head away with her skull, but his head snaps right back. Out of patience, *Daspletosaurus* bites his face, not using her full strength but just enough for him to get the message. He yelps in pain and takes a few steps back, then turns and heads toward the water.

Daspletosaurus returns her attention to the nest. She bends down, opens her mouth, and picks up another egg with her teeth, careful not to crack it. She moves the egg over ever so slightly, so it sits in the same warm spot next to the first egg.

The eggs look cozy, nestled together. *Daspletosaurus* grunts, satisfied.

Facts

- *Daspletosaurus horneri* was a tyrannosaurid that lived in the Cretaceous in what is now Montana, United States.
- There are two valid species of *Daspletosaurus*: *Daspletosaurus horneri* and *Daspletosaurus torosus*. *Daspletosaurus torosus* was first named in 1970, and *Daspletosaurus horneri* was named in 2017.
- The scaly texture of the facial bones of *Daspletosaurus horneri* may have meant that there were more nerves and blood vessels, making their mouths more sensitive.
- The genus name *Daspletosaurus* means "frightful lizard."
- The species name *horneri* is in honor of paleontologist Jack Horner.

 Find out more in the I Know Dino *podcast, episode 124, "Majungasaurus."*

Dynamoterror dynastes: "Powerful terror ruler"

The air is hot and sticky. *Dynamoterror dynastes* treads lightly through the greenery, trying not to disturb any potential prey. At about 30 ft (9 m) long, with a mouth full of sharp teeth, this tyrannosaurid usually doesn't have a hard time finding meals.

However, he finds it hard to hunt on humid days like this, when all the vegetation seems to spring to life and stick together and all the tasty animals blend in with their surroundings. Plus, the heat makes *Dynamoterror* impatient.

He hasn't eaten in a few days, which doesn't help. *Dynamoterror*'s stomach growls. He pauses, annoyed. Any unusual sounds could tip off his lunch. Despite his hunger, *Dynamoterror* knows that he needs to stay calm and be on alert.

Dynamoterror continues to take careful steps,

but he makes the mistake of keeping his head level with his body instead of looking down, and he nearly trips.

His toe hits something sharp, and *Dynamoterror* lets out an unwanted yelp. He looks down to see what caused the pain and at first sees nothing but green and brown, like all the rest of the vegetation.

Then he notices movement from the backside of *Invictarx zephyri*, a nodosaurid covered in a nearly impenetrable shield of osteoderms. Not the best prey for a very hungry predator.

His cover blown, *Dynamoterror* opens his jaws wide to show his menacing teeth. *Invictarx* doesn't miss a beat and plants its four legs firmly in the ground, taking a defensive stance.

Invictarx opens its mouth and lets out a hissing warning sound. *Dynamoterror* pauses for a moment to consider his options.

Dynamoterror knows that his best chance is to get *Invictarx* on its back. It's a risky move. Though the osteoderms that make up *Invictarx*'s shield are relatively smooth, they are still thick and have spikes. *Dynamoterror* doesn't want to get injured or else he may starve. If he's unable to hunt, he cannot catch even small, more vulnerable prey. Time is also not on his side. The longer that *Dynamoterror* waits between meals, the weaker he gets.

On the other hand, *Invictarx* would make a nice, hearty meal, and *Dynamoterror* can't back away now. *Invictarx* is standing directly in his path, and *Dynamoterror* is getting desperate.

Dynamoterror takes a step toward *Invictarx* and opens his mouth even wider. He lets out a low growl. *Invictarx* is unfazed and keeps its stance.

Dynamoterror growls again. This time, the growl comes from his stomach. He lunges at *Invictarx* and tries to snap at its neck. *Invictarx* takes a step to the side. *Dynamoterror* misses, but he can't stop.

The only chance that *Dynamoterror* has is to flip *Invictarx* onto its back. *Dynamoterror* lowers his head to try and get under his prey's belly.

Invictarx starts to drop to the ground. *Dynamoterror* panics. He doesn't want his head crushed. He moves as quickly as he can away from *Invictarx*. It all happens so fast that *Dynamoterror* doesn't see the sharp rock next to him. He hits his head hard, and blood dribbles down his face.

Dynamoterror knows that this is a fight he is not going to win. Angry, he stomps off in search of an easier meal.

Facts

- *Dynamoterror dynastes* was a tyrannosaurid that lived in the Late Cretaceous in what is now New Mexico, United States.
- *Dynamoterror* is one of the oldest known tyrannosaurids.
- *Dynamoterror* and *Invictarx* are the only named dinosaurs from the Menefee Formation, and they help show the diversity of dinosaurs.
- The genus name *Dynamoterror* means "powerful terror."
- The species name *dynastes* means "ruler."

 Find out more in the I Know Dino *podcast, episode 204, "Coelophysis."*

Galeamopus pabsti: "Want helmet"

Galeamopus pabsti, courtesy of ArthurWeasley via Wikimedia Commons

Everything is quiet and peaceful. A low, rumbling sound breaks the serenity. It's *Galeamopus pabsti*'s stomach, growling from hunger. He uses his peg-like teeth to grab leaves, trying to swallow as quickly as possible to fill himself up.

Galeamopus has short spines made of keratin, which cover the length of his body. And though *Galeamopus* is robust with thick, sturdy legs, he's not yet fully grown. He has reached maturity, but he could still get larger. When he's done, he could be as long as 89 ft (27 m). But to do that, he's going to need a lot more food.

Galeamopus is a diplodocid, so he has a long tail. His tail is so long that it's actually more than half the total length of his body. The tail gives him comfort because he can use it to gain the attention of other *Galeamopus* and protect himself from predators.

Though he's not yet as large as he could be, *Galeamopus* feels pretty confident about being able to eat without any interruptions or threats. Plus, there are other diplodocids around. At least one of them could warn the others if necessary.

He continues to fit as many leaves as possible into his mouth at one time. A couple fall out of his mouth and flutter to the ground. His hunger pangs are starting to subside. But *Galeamopus* knows that he needs to keep feeding, so he can be full and continue growing.

Galeamopus swallows and pauses for a moment. Something feels wrong. From the corner of his eye, he sees movement. He can't tell what is moving, but his gut feeling is that it's some sort of theropod: a predator.

Galeamopus stands still for a second. He

knows what he needs to do, but he needs to wait for the right moment. He doesn't want to let the predator know that he's aware of its presence.

Then he hears the crackle of leaves. The predator is on the move. *Galeamopus* turns his body so his tail is facing the threat.

He wastes no time and moves his whip-like tail so fast that it breaks the sound barrier. There is a loud boom, and *Galeamopus* notices the predator taking a few steps back. His adrenaline high, *Galeamopus* can't tell for certain what type of theropod is attacking him. But he knows one crack of his tail is not enough.

Galeamopus whips his tail again, but his aim is off. The theropod has moved quickly to the side, to avoid his tail. The carnivore is too close, and all *Galeamopus* can see is its sharp teeth.

Galeamopus takes a step to the side, careful not to lose his balance, and whips his tail again. The loud crashing sound seems to intimidate the theropod. It flinches.

Galeamopus starts to feel confident again. He waits to see what the theropod will do next. He's so focused on the theropod in front of him that he doesn't notice the second theropod until it's too late.

Facts

- *Galeamopus pabsti* was a diplodocid that lived in the Jurassic in what is now Wyoming, United States.
- There are two valid species of *Galeamopus*: *Galeamopus pabsti* and *Galeamopus hayi*.
- For over 100 years, *Galeamopus hayi* was thought to be *Diplodocus hayi*. In 2015, Emanuel Tschopp, Octávio Mateus, and Roger Benson renamed it as a separate genus. Tschopp and Mateus were also the ones to name *Galeamopus pabsti*.
- The genus name *Galeamopus* means "need helmet" ("galeam" means "helmet" and "opus" means "need"). This combination of words is meant to be the German name Wilhelm (meaning "want helmet"), in honor of William Utterback and William Holland, who discovered and described *Galeamopus* in the early 1900s (then known as *Diplodocus*).
- The species name *pabsti* is in honor of Ben Pabst, who led the excavation of *Galeamopus pabsti* in 1995 and prepared it for mounting.

Find out more in the I Know Dino *podcast, episode 129, "Edmontosaurus."*

Nanuqsaurus hoglundi: "Polar bear lizard"

Nanuqsaurus hoglundi, courtesy of Tomopteryx (Tom Parker) via Wikimedia Commons

Among the tall conifer trees and flowering plants along the coast, a top predator looks for her dinner. The sun has started to set.

Nanuqsaurus hoglundi is not that large: only 20 ft (6 m) long and weighing 1,000 lb (454 kg). But she is still the top predator in the Arctic subcontinent Larimidia where she lives—partly because of her powerful bite.

The days are getting shorter, which means winter is coming. And *Nanuqsaurus* knows that she must find easy meals while she still can.

Life in the Arctic is difficult, though not because of the weather. Temperatures dip but never get so cold that *Nanuqsaurus* cannot walk around. The fuzz that covers her body also helps keep her warm.

But, in the winter season, the nights get longer and longer, sometimes lasting a full 24 hours. In addition to being hard to see, *Nanuqsaurus* knows that the prey she usually hunts will either migrate elsewhere or hide away and sleep for the next few months.

Nanuqsaurus sniffs around for signs of prey. She has a long nasal cavity and a strong sense of smell, which is especially useful in the dark. After a few moments, she gets a whiff of a herd of hadrosaurs not too far away.

She salivates at the thought. *Nanuqsaurus* quickly catches up to the herd. They are starting to head south. In big groups they are dangerous, but alone they are weak and not that bright.

Nanuqsaurus knows that she must separate one from the herd—one that is frail or small. She decides that the best way to do this is to scare them by making her presence known. The carnivore roars as loudly as she can to attract attention. It works.

Scared and confused, the hadrosaurs start to

run but in different directions. *Nanuqsaurus* takes her time and watches, looking for her best opportunity. Then she spots a juvenile hadrosaur. The prey brays, unhappy and afraid. *Nanuqsaurus* springs into action.

She starts running for the herbivore, jaws open and ready to bite, flashing her killer whale-like teeth.

The hadrosaur sees the carnivore coming, kicks into high gear, and runs away. It heads towards where the majority of the herd is running, but it cannot catch up in time.

Nanuqsaurus pounces, and bites down hard into the hadrosaur. It whimpers, as *Nanuqsaurus'* teeth tear into its flesh. Eventually the hadrosaur bleeds out and stops making sounds.

In a few short weeks, it will not be this easy to find food, so *Nanuqsaurus* knows that she must enjoy it while it lasts. Life in the North is not easy and, though *Nanuqsaurus* is fairly small—especially compared to her cousins *T. rex* and *Tarbosaurus*—and has adapted to her habitat, the long months before summer are difficult to survive.

It will take a lot of skill to sniff out food sources and successfully hunt them.

For now, *Nanuqsaurus* enjoys the warmth of the blood and relishes every morsel. She uses her twiggy arms to help her balance as she digs in.

Facts

- *Nanuqsaurus hoglundi* was a tyrannosaur that lived in the Cretaceous in what is now Alaska, United States.
- *Nanuqsaurus* lived in the Arctic, 70 million years ago, but enjoyed weather that was similar to modern-day Seattle.
- The Arctic in *Nanuqsaurus*' lifetime was warm, with lots of tall trees and flowering plants, though it did have extra-long days in the summer and sometimes 24 hours of darkness in the winter.
- *Nanuqsaurus* had a great sense of smell, which would have been useful in winter when it was dark.
- The genus name *Nanuqsaurus* means "polar bear lizard."

 Find out more in the I Know Dino *podcast, episode 11, "Nanuqsaurus."*

Probrachylophosaurus bergi: "Before *Brachylophosaurus* (short-crested lizard)" a.k.a. Superduck

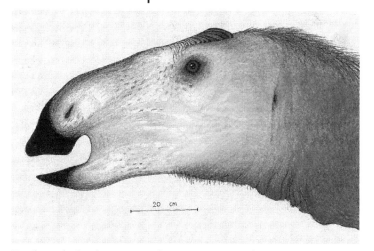

Probrachylophosaurus bergi courtesy of Danny Cicchetti via Wikimedia Commons

The world is green. Lush vegetation in all varieties surround *Probrachylophosaurus bergi*–food as far as the eye can see. *Probrachylophosaurus* is happy. His herd has chosen today's lunch spot well.

With his hundreds of teeth, packed tightly in the back of his mouth, *Probrachylophosaurus* grinds down vegetation in a slow, methodical manner: Bend down and open mouth. Bite down on plant. Chew, chew, chew. Swallow and repeat.

Surrounded by his herd, *Probrachylophosaurus* feels safe. All he has to do is eat.

He and his fellow *Probrachylophosaurus* spend hours on all fours, using their thick, stiff tails to help counterbalance. Occasionally one looks up from his meal to check for any tyrannosaurs or other threats. Since they are in a big group, none of them are too concerned. At least one of them will spot any stalking predators and warn the rest.

As adults, they all have small, triangular nasal crests that taper into a "U" shape. *Probrachylophosaurus* is 14 years old and well into adulthood. He is 30 ft (9 m) long and weighs over 5 tons. But even though he's an adult, he's not as large as his elders.

Probrachylophosaurus grabs another mouthful of food and lifts his head to chew. As he munches, he looks around him. The sun is high in the sky, but there are enough trees nearby to give *Probrachylophosaurus* some shade.

Just beyond the trees, *Probrachylophosaurus* sees

a figure. It is similar in shape to *Probrachylophosaurus* and also walking on all fours. *Probrachylophosaurus* stiffens and hastily swallows. The others take notice, and they all lift their heads and stop eating.

Probrachylophosaurus squints in the sun. He is not yet sure if this figure is a threat or a friend. It doesn't act like a carnivore, but *Probrachylophosaurus* doesn't want to take any chances.

Out of instinct, *Probrachylophosaurus* takes a step closer to another in his herd. The others also shuffle closer together. As a group, they stand a better chance to help each other fend off predators.

The figure continues to take slow steps towards *Probrachylophosaurus*. In preparation, *Probrachylophosaurus* shifts his weight and stands on his two back legs. On two feet, he has the option to fight or to run.

The figure finally steps into the shade, and *Probrachylophosaurus* can see its broad, triangular nasal crest. Another *Probrachylophosaurus*. *Probrachylophosaurus* relaxes and moves back to all fours. The others in his herd also let their guards down and welcome the newcomer—a female.

She greets them with a snort and finds a spot next to *Probrachylophosaurus*. Once she surveys her food options, she bends down to bite off her first mouthful.

The female lifts her head and turns to face *Probrachylophosaurus* as she chews. *Probrachylophosaurus* nods his head in acceptance. Satisfied, he chomps down on a large bunch of leaves and turns back to face the female.

They watch each other eat, content. The only sounds they hear are the crunching of the leaves they feast on.

Facts

- *Probrachylophosaurus bergi* was a hadrosaur that lived in the Late Cretaceous in what is now Montana, United States.
- The first *Probrachylophosaurus* bones were excavated in 1981 and 1994 by Mark Goodwin and a University of California Museum of Paleontology (UCMP) crew. More fossils were found in 2007 and 2008, though *Probrachylophosaurus* was not formally described until 2015.
- *Probrachylophosaurus* shows the evolution of head crests on hadrosaurs (duck-billed dinosaurs). *Probrachylophosaurus*' ancestor *Acristavus* did not have a crest, and its descendent *Brachylophosaurus* had a larger crest.
- *Probrachylophosaurus* got its nickname "Superduck" because it was a large hadrosaur, though it's not the largest one found.
- The species name *bergi* is in honor of Sam Berge, who supported paleontologic research for many years and co-owned the land *Probrachylophosaurus* was found on.

Find out more in the I Know Dino *podcast, episode 51, "Alamosaurus."*

Rativates evadens: "Ratite foreteller"

Rativates evadens, courtesy of Anniel via Wikimedia Commons

Rativates evadens is bent over, picking at small insects with his toothless beak. A twig snaps. *Rativates* immediately jerks his head up. At 5 ft (1.5 m) tall, 11 ft (3.3 m) long, and weighing 200 lb (90 kg), he's not that big compared to other dinosaurs in the area, and he doesn't want to take any chances.

He hears another twig snap and doesn't bother to look at what caused the noise. *Rativates* takes off and runs as fast as he can in the opposite direction. Behind him, he hears pounding footsteps, the familiar sound of a *Gorgosaurus* giving chase.

Rativates keeps running. *Gorgosaurus* is large, with a mouth full of sharp teeth, but *Rativates* is confident he can outrun the predator. It's a windy day, and *Rativates* is moving against the wind, but he persists. He moves so fast that he can feel the air ruffling the downy coat of feathers that cover his body.

After a few minutes, *Rativates* can no longer hear the *Gorgosaurus*, but *Rativates* doesn't pause to check if the carnivore is still behind him. He keeps up his fast pace until he reaches a small group of *Struthiomimus*.

Struthiomimus looks similar to *Rativates* but is about twice as big. *Rativates* knows they won't bother him if he doesn't bother them, so he gives them a wide berth. He stops just outside their circle and waits.

There are three of them, and they are all busy pecking at a small carcass. *Rativates* stomps loudly to get their attention—he wants to avoid startling them. They either don't notice or don't care, and they keep eating.

Rativates' stomach starts to growl. He cocks his head and sees a young tree nearby. The leaves look tender, and *Rativates* bites into a mouthful. Then he sees something small crawling on one of the branches. *Rativates* grabs at it in delight and swallows it whole.

Still hungry, *Rativates* walks carefully around the group of *Struthiomimus* in search of more food. They shift positions but otherwise don't seem to notice *Rativates*.

Once *Rativates* is out of their range, he becomes more alert. From the corner of his eye, he sees movement. A small mammal scurries away from him. It tries to find cover, but there's too much open space between it and *Rativates*.

Rativates runs toward the small animal, quickly catching up. They play a game of chase, the mammal zigzagging and trying to dodge *Rativates*. But *Rativates* is much larger, and fast, so the game doesn't last long.

Rativates pounces on the creature and traps it with his feet. The animal struggles but can't escape. *Rativates* delivers the final blow with his beak. He stabs it in the neck and pecks at it. The meat is warm. A welcome meal.

Every once in a while, *Rativates* looks up from his food to make sure he's alone and safe. He sees the group of *Struthiomimus* from before, heading in his direction. *Rativates* continues to eat, keeping his head down so as not to attract attention. They either don't notice or don't care, and they walk right past him.

Facts

- *Rativates evadens* was an ornithomimid that lived in the Late Cretaceous in what is now Alberta, Canada.
- *Rativates* was originally found in 1934 and was thought to be *Struthiomimus atlas*. It was found in Dinosaur Provincial Park, where *Struthiomimus* has been found.
- The *Rativates* specimen found was about half the size of *Struthiomimus*, and it had dense (not spongy) bone, which is the sign of being an adult. It also had a different skull, tail, pelvis, and feet, including foot claws. *Rativates* was about the same size as a modern ostrich.
- The genus name *Rativates* comes from the word "rati" (from ratite birds, including ostriches) and "vates," which means "foreteller." It "alludes to the paradox of an ostrich mimic dinosaur existing before ostriches," according to the Cleveland Museum of Natural History.
- The species name *evadens* comes from the Latin word "evadere," which means "evade."

 Find out more in the I Know Dino *podcast, episode 97, "Argentinosaurus."*

Regaliceratops peterhewsi: "Royal horn face" a.k.a. Hellboy

Regaliceratops peterhewsi courtesy of Arcovenator via Wikimedia Commons

The sun has only been up for a couple hours, but already *Regaliceratops peterhewsi* can barely stand the heat. On a normal day, *Regaliceratops* has a short temper. But today, with the heat, he is ready to snap.

He looks up, hoping to see some clouds in the sky so he can find a shady spot to stand in. There are a few conifers in the distance, but *Regaliceratops* can't tell if they are large enough to provide him any comfort.

He snorts. The small horns over his eyes, large nose horn, and elaborate, bright orange-and-red frills on top of his head draw a lot of attention. And the frills look almost like a crown. His small eyes, set high on his face, coupled with his large, stout beak give him an almost haughty look.

At 16.4 ft (5 m) long and weighing 1.5 tons, *Regaliceratops* is big enough to not mind the extra attention. Today, he actually craves the attention. It would be nice to challenge another male *Regaliceratops* to a fight.

But there are no other *Regaliceratops* in sight. They are all either hiding in the few cool spots under tree cover or they are doing what *Regaliceratops* is doing: pacing in anger in a remote area and waiting for an opportunity to defend his territory.

Regaliceratops makes his way to a small pond. Perhaps a sip of water will calm him down. Or, better yet, he'll run into another *Regaliceratops*.

At the edge of the pond, *Regaliceratops* bends his head and slurps at the liquid. Even the water is warm today. *Regaliceratops* spits some out, dissatisfied. When he looks up, he makes eye contact with another male *Regaliceratops*.

His heart rate increases. The other male

is about the same size, maybe a little smaller. Perfect.

Regaliceratops snorts again and stomps the ground, indicating he is ready to fight. The other male takes a step back, unsure.

Regaliceratops does not wait. He charges at the other male, splashing water as he runs. He lowers his head and rams his large nasal horn as hard as he can against his opponent's side.

The smaller male turns just in time, avoiding the horn from spearing him. Instead, the side of *Regaliceratops'* horn crashes into the other male's tough hide, causing *Regaliceratops* to stumble. He shakes his head and prepares to charge again.

This time the smaller male also charges, and the two ceratopsids lock horns. *Regaliceratops* pushes with all his might, but the other horned dinosaur pushes back. *Regaliceratops* stomps in frustration, but the shift in weight causes him to lose his footing in the shallow water.

The smaller ceratopsid wastes no time and pushes harder, causing *Regaliceratops* to fall. Fortunately for *Regaliceratops*, his opponent has no wish to pursue the fight. The other male turns around and quickly walks away from the pond.

His ego bruised, *Regaliceratops* gets up and lets the water drip off his body. He looks around and sees no one else from his herd. But, just in case, he bends down and takes a small sip of water, pretending that was what he meant to do all along.

Facts

- *Regaliceratops peterhewsi* was a ceratopsid that lived in the Late Cretaceous in what is now Alberta, Canada.
- *Regaliceratops* is a chasmosaurine, a subfamily of ceratopsids (horned dinosaurs). The other subfamily is centrosaurine. *Regaliceratops'* elaborate frills make the dinosaur so special because it is an example of evolutionary convergence (i.e., despite being a chasmosaurine, it evolved similar traits to centrosaurines, such as the long nose horn and small horns over its eyes). It also lived after centrosaurines went extinct.
- Because of *Regaliceratops*, scientists think we will eventually find other, stranger-looking ceratopsids.
- The genus name *Regaliceratops* means "Royal horn face," but the dinosaur is also known by its nickname "Hellboy." The name "Hellboy" comes partially from the comic book character Hellboy and partially from the fact that the fossils were so hard to collect. According to the paleontologists who excavated "Hellboy," the bones were in hard rock, on steep cliffs, and near a protected fish dwelling.

- The species name *peterhewsi* is in honor of the geologist Peter Hews, who discovered *Regaliceratops* in 2005.

 Find out more in the I Know Dino *podcast, episode 28, "Hypsilophodon."*

Spiclypeus shipporum: "Spiked shield"

Spiclypeus shipporum courtesy of Nobu Tamura via Wikimedia Commons

It hurts to walk. At 20 ft (6 m) long and weighing 4 tons, *Spiclypeus shipporum* limps, one step at a time. Her forelimb is infected and has been for weeks now. The leg is swollen and stiff, and each movement brings fresh pain.

But *Spiclypeus* knows she must keep going. She's near a known theropod watering hole, and her limp makes her an easy target. She has a menacing-looking, hooked upper beak; a large, intimidating frill with bony spikes; and horns over her eyes. It wouldn't take long for a predator to figure out her weakness and attack her.

Spiclypeus marches on, at a slow and steady pace. The effort wears on her, and she soon becomes thirsty. The ground is spongy, and she realizes she's right next to the watering hole. *Spiclypeus* pauses for a moment and listens. Nothing. She waits another moment and sniffs. She's safe, for now.

She trudges onto the beaten path that most dinosaurs follow to reach the water. She tries to pick up her pace and winces from the pain. But she doesn't dare stay longer than she has to, so she drags her foot and tries to ignore it.

The water is shallow and cool, and *Spiclypeus* wades in, just far enough to submerge her infected leg. She immediately feels relief—mud at the bottom of the hole covers her toes. So soothing. The risk was worth it. After another look around to make sure there are no nearby predators, *Spiclypeus* lowers her head and takes a few sips. Her thirst takes over, and she starts to slurp up the water as fast as she can.

It takes her too long to realize her mistake. A large theropod jumps onto her back—it happens so fast *Spiclypeus* doesn't even see what kind it is—and digs a sharp claw into her. *Spiclypeus* lets out a cry and shifts her weight to try and throw off the predator. Her infected leg protests, and she slips and falls into the water.

The two of them thrash in the watering hole, *Spiclypeus* trying to angle herself so she can either use her horns or her tail against her attacker. The theropod tries to climb onto her back again.

They both struggle for a while, but *Spiclypeus* knows she has lost. Her leg is in agony, and she can't stand on it for much longer. In one final attempt at survival, she uses the last of her strength to rear up. The theropod falls into the water, and *Spiclypeus* seizes the opportunity. She wades as fast as she can out of the water, to the shore, but she's too slow.

The theropod recovers and catches up to *Spiclypeus*. *Spiclypeus* tries to hit the predator with her horns. The theropod changes direction in time. *Spiclypeus'* leg gives out, and she stumbles. She can't put any more weight on it. She braces herself as the theropod sinks its teeth into her neck.

Facts

- *Spiclypeus shipporum* was a chasmosaurine ceratopsian that lived in the late Cretaceous in what is now Montana, United States.
- *Spiclypeus* had big brow horns that probably curved out toward the side of its head, and an ornamental frill with epiossifications around the edge and four taller points around the top.
- The *Spiclypeus* specimen found was at least 10 years old when it died, and it may have been scavenged or hunted, based on tooth marks. It also had osteomyelitis, a type of infection, and arthritis.
- The genus name *Spiclypeus* means "spiked shield." The holotype was nicknamed "Judith" after the Judith River Formation, where it was found.
- The species name *shipporum* is in honor of Dr. Bill and Linda Shipp, who first owned the holotype.

 Find out more in the I Know Dino *podcast, episode 79, "Abelisaurus."*

Tototlmimus packardensis: "Bird mimic of the Packard Shale"

Another hot day. To cool off, *Tototlmimus packardensis* steps into a pool of water.

Her long legs keep her body dry, and she still gets to enjoy the coolness of the water on her feet. She walks on her toes, extending the length of her already elongated legs.

Other *Tototlmimus* mill around her. One steps into the water with *Tototlmimus*, but she ignores him. Now, with some relief from the heat, she focuses on finding food. Nothing nearby looks appetizing, and *Tototlmimus* resigns herself to the fact that she will have to leave the comfort of the water to satisfy her growling stomach.

She decides to wait a few more moments.

From the corner of her eye, she sees the male *Tototlmimus* stiffen. Then, with almost no warning, he sprints out of the water, splashing her as he passes. Out of instinct, *Tototlmimus* follows. She forgets all about why she is in the water and uses all her energy to get out and as far away from it as possible.

Her legs kick up water, and behind her she hears a growl: a predator. She doesn't know who the predator is, and she doesn't care.

Her body is built for running, and by keeping on her toes she can move even faster. Others in the group join her and the male *Tototlmimus* in running.

The key to survival is to not be the last in the group. *Tototlmimus* is glad she had a head start.

She keeps running, checking around her every few seconds to make sure she's still ahead. When she does, her long neck shifts to follow her small head. Her arms are covered in feathers, and she keeps them tucked into her sides.

Behind there are too many *Tototlmimus* for her to see the predator. She doesn't mind.

Ahead of her are some trees, but *Tototlmimus* does not want to take any chances. She reaches the trees and keeps going as fast as she can. In this cover, she takes the lead, ahead of the male

Tototlmimus. The others are not far behind.

Without knowing anything about the predator, *Tototlmimus* has no idea how long the pursuit will last. She almost wishes it would take one of her group down, so it would be satisfied and she would be safe.

She shifts her head to take another look. The male *Tototlmimus* is a few feet behind her. *Tototlmimus* glances for a little too long and trips on the root of a tree.

Her body lands hard on the ground, and the male *Tototlmimus* hops over her, not bothering to look back.

In a panic, *Tototlmimus* rolls around and gets back on her feet, ignoring the pain in her toe where she hit the root. As she is about to start running again, she makes eye contact with the predator just as it catches up to a juvenile in her group. It slashes at the juvenile, causing it to fall.

Tototlmimus can see the hunger in its eyes. She doesn't wait to see what happens next. She takes off running and doesn't look back.

Facts

- *Tototlmimus packardensis* was an ornithomimid that lived in the Late Cretaceous in what is now Mexico.
- Paleontologists only know of one species of *Tototlmimus*, based on the partial skeleton without a skull. They discovered parts of its feet and hands and found it different enough to be its own genus.
- *Tototlmimus* is about the same size as *Gallimimus*, another ornithomimid.
- The genus name "Tototl" means "bird" in Nahuatl.
- The species name *packardensis* is in honor of the formation where it was found.

Find out more in the I Know Dino *podcast, episode 52, "Lythronax."*

Yehuecauhceratops mudei: "Ancient horned face"

Yehuecauhceratops mudei tilts her head back and up, and lets out a short bellow. She's feeling satisfied. Her herd has found an ideal spot for grazing, with lots of plants close to the ground, and some trees to provide shade on this hot day.

She and her herd are centrosaurines, which means that they are herbivores and stand on all fours. They also have frills and horns on their heads. Like the others in her herd, *Yehuecauhceratops* has a parrot-like beak, tall and relatively short. She and her herd are also small for centrosaurines—only about 10 ft (3 m) long.

To stay safe, she keeps close to the other *Yehuecauhceratops*. Most of them are adults, and they try not to have contact with any other animals. Other ceratopsians live in the area. Some are centrosaurines, like *Yehuecauhceratops*, with shorter brow horns and frills, and spines coming out of their frills. Others are chasmosaurines, with large brow horns and long frills.

All of these other dinosaurs are larger than *Yehuecauhceratops*. But each group has their own territory, so there is rarely any conflict.

The *Yehuecauhceratops* herd has the smallest territory. *Yehuecauhceratops* doesn't mind because they are a small group. There is plenty of vegetation for them to feed on.

Yehuecauhceratops bends down and snips off some leaves with her beak. She enjoys these quiet days, where all she has to do is eat. While she chews, she looks around. The others in her herd seem to be enjoying themselves too.

Then she notices a larger dinosaur heading their way. It's a chasmosaurine, a large male. *Yehuecauhceratops* snorts to signal her herd. They all stop eating and look up at the intruder.

The chasmosaurine stomps his foot and lifts his head to fully display his large frill. *Yehuecauhceratops* knows what this means. Their lunch spot was too good.

Yehuecauhceratops' frill flushes in anger. But the rest of her herd doesn't want to fight. They turn their backs to the chasmosaurine and start to walk away. *Yehuecauhceratops* lets out another bellow, this time one of frustration. But her herd ignores her.

The chasmosaurine takes an aggressive step towards *Yehuecauhceratops*. She can see more chasmosaurines coming. *Yehuecauhceratops* lets out another quick bellow in protest, and then turns and follows her herd. She's too small and knows that she could not win this fight alone.

The *Yehuecauhceratops* herd moves to a nearby watering hole. The water is far enough away to show the chasmosaurines that they have given up their feeding spot.

Yehuecauhceratops decides to forget the incident and dips her beak in the water. She's lost her shade from the trees, but at least the water is cool. It's also pretty shallow. She dips her beak again, this time deeper so the water covers most of her face.

She lifts her head and has an idea. *Yehuecauhceratops* takes a couple of tentative steps into the water. Once she has her footing, she gets braver. She wades through the water at a quicker pace, splashing some of her herd. They look at her but allow her to keep splashing.

Facts

- *Yehuecauhceratops mudei* was a centrosaurine ceratopsid that lived in the Cretaceous in what is now Coahuila, Mexico.
- *Yehuecauhceratops* lived among two other types of ceratopsians that were bigger. They may have filled different niches in their habitat.
- *Yehuecauhceratops* is currently the southernmost named centrosaurine.
- The genus name *Yehuecauhceratops* is Nauhuatl for "ancient horned face."
- The species name *mudei* is in honor of the Museo del Desierto at Saltillo, Coahuila, Mexico.

Find out more in the I Know Dino *podcast, episode 115, "Rajasaurus."*

Zuul crurivastator: "Destroyer of shins"

Zuul crurivastator, courtesy of FunkMonk, via Wikimedia Commons

Zuul crurivastator is a confident ankylosaur. And why wouldn't he be? He is the largest *Zuul* around, measuring 20 ft (6 m) long and weighing 2.5 tonnes. His body is wide and flat and covered in bony armor. In fact, he has several rows of large, sharp, bony spikes all along his body.

His snout is short and round and has horns, including

a couple of prominent ones behind his eyes. And he has a long tail with sharp, pointed spikes along the sides and a large club at the end. The tail has five pairs of osteoderms, or bony structures, along the sides of the handle, near the end of the tail. Three of the pairs are covered in keratin sheaths, and two of the pairs—the larger ones—are positioned on each side of his tail.

In addition to all of his armor, *Zuul* is also coated in ornamentation: scaly armor all over his face, which matches the rest of his body.

Zuul is a four-legged, walking tank, meant to be looked at but not trifled with. His tail alone can crush bone.

He walks slowly and with purpose. Every animal in the vicinity should know that this is his territory, and they should not come near him.

Then *Zuul* sees another *Zuul*. It's a male but a little smaller. *Zuul* flares his large nostrils and heads towards the other male. He barks a warning and lifts his tail.

The other male barks back and lifts his tail. Angry, *Zuul* turns his body so he can whack the other *Zuul* with his tail. The other male also turns his body, and the two end up circling each other, waiting for the best moment to strike.

Their circles get wider and wider until they end up parallel to each other. *Zuul* tries his best to intimidate the other male—first by stomping as hard as he can, and then by hitting his tail against nearby trees, breaking some of the thinner branches.

Zuul is so focused on the other male that he doesn't realize they're no longer in his territory—until he hears the wail of an animal in pain. He snaps out of his territorial mode and looks around. A large theropod is biting into a *Spiclypeus*. They're fighting in some shallow water, but the *Spiclypeus* looks like she has an injured leg and can no longer defend herself.

Zuul makes a low, rumbling sound to alert the other *Zuul* to danger. They both get into a defensive stance, just in time for the theropod to notice them.

The theropod growls and bares its teeth. *Zuul* turns himself to the side, so he can strike with his tail if necessary. Even though he's heavily armored, he doesn't want to risk turning his back on the predator. He knows that he can't leave this spot until the threat goes away.

The theropod looks at *Zuul* and the other male *Zuul*. It knows it's outmatched. It gives one last growl, and then moves away from the bleeding *Spiclypeus*.

Zuul makes eye contact with the other male and nods. For now, territory doesn't matter. They both turn and walk in opposite directions.

Facts

- *Zuul crurivastator* was an ankylosaurid that lived in the Late Cretaceous in what is now Montana, United States.
- *Zuul*'s skeleton, with a complete skull and tail, is the most complete ankylosaur found in North America. Osteoderms, keratin, and skin remains were also found with *Zuul*.
- *Zuul* was originally thought to be a new species of *Euoplocephalus*. When *Zuul*'s skeleton was first found, it was nicknamed "Sherman."
- The genus name *Zuul* refers to the character Zuul from the 1984 movie *Ghostbusters*. In the movie, Zuul is the gatekeeper of Gozer.
- The species name *crurivastator* means "destroyer of shins" and refers to *Zuul*'s tail club, which may have been used to fight predators or other ankylosaurs (when trying to attract mates or claim territory).

Find out more in the I Know Dino *podcast, episode 130, "Puertasaurus," episode 137, "Olorotitan," with an interview with Dr. Victoria Arbour, one of the co-authors who described Zuul, and episode 241, "Tsintaosaurus," with an interview with Dr. David Evans, the other co-author who described Zuul.*

More Dinosaurs From North America

Acantholipan gonazalezi

- *Acantholipan gonazalezi* was a nodosaur that lived in the Late Cretaceous in what is now Coahuila, Mexico.
- *Acantholipan* was the first named ankylosaur from Mexico.
- The specimen found was of a juvenile and was about 11 ft (3.5 m) long.
- The genus name *Acantholipan* comes from the Greek word akanthos, which means "spine," and "Lipan," after a local Apache tribe.
- The species name *gonazalezi* is in honor of the Mexican paleontologist Arturo Homero González-González.

Find out more in the I Know Dino *podcast, episode 187, "Indoraptor."*

Agujaceratops mavericus

- *Agujaceratops mavericus* was a ceratopsid that lived in the Cretaceous in what is now Texas, United States.
- *Agujaceratops mavericus* is the second species in the genus. The first named species is *Agujaceratops mariscalensis*.
- *Agujaceratops* was originally classified as *Chasmosaurus*, when it was first described in 1989 (based on fossils found in 1938). But then, in 2006, Spencer G. Lucas, Robert M. Sullivan, and Adrian Hunt analyzed a partial skull and found enough differences between *Agujaceratops* and *Chasmosaurus* to rename it.
- *Agujaceratops* had a short frill and is similar to *Pentaceratops* and *Chasmosaurus*. *Agujaceratops* may have lived in a swampy area, along with *Chasmosaurus, Edmontonia, Euoplocephalus, Angulomastacator, Saurornitholestes, Richardoestesia,* and *Deinosuchus*.
- The genus name *Agujaceratops* means "horned face from Aguja." The species name *mavericus* means "maverick."

Akainacephalus johnsoni

- *Akainacephalus johnsoni* was an ankylosaurid that lived in the Late Cretaceous in what is now Utah, United States.
- *Akainacephalus* had a very spiky, ornamented skull, many osteoderms on its wide body, and a tail club.
- *Akainacephalus* is most closely related to *Nodocephalosaurus kirtlandensis* (found in New Mexico) and Asian ankylosaurs such as *Minotaurasaurus* and *Tarchia*.
- The genus name *Akainacephalus* means "spiky head."
- The species name *johnsoni* refers to Randy Johnson, a volunteer who prepared the specimen at the fossil preparation lab in the Natural History Museum of Utah.

Find out more in the I Know Dino *podcast, episode 191, "Koreaceratops."*

Albertavenator curriei

- *Albertavenator curriei* was a troodontid theropod that lived in the Cretaceous in what is now Alberta, Canada.
- Only one bone has been found of a "partial frontal" (the bone above the left eye in the middle of the top of the head).
- The bone was found in 1993 and originally thought to belong to *Troodon*. However, a re-examination found it to be more robust and shorter than *Troodon*, which is how it became classified as its own genus.
- The genus name *Albertavenator* refers to Alberta where the fossils were found.
- The species name *curriei* is in honor of the paleontologist Phil Currie.

 Find out more in the I Know Dino *podcast, episode 139, "Bahariasaurus."*

Alcovasaurus longispinus

- *Alcovasaurus longispinus* was a stegosaurid that lived in the Jurassic in what is now Wyoming, United States.
- Until 2016, *Alcovasaurus longispinus* was known as *Stegosaurus longispinus*. It's also been considered to be *Kentrosaurus longispinus*, and *Natronsaurus*, though that name was never considered to be valid.
- *Alcovasaurus* (then *Stegosaurus longispinus*) was discovered in 1908 and described in 1914 by Charles Whitney Gilmore. It had large tail spines, though it was unclear if the spines were for sexual dimorphism or display. Peter Galton and Kenneth Carpenter revised the genus to *Alcovasaurus* in 2016, based on five, unique derived traits.
- The type specimen of *Alcovasaurus* was damaged in the 1920s, when the water pipes at the University of Wisconsin museum, where it was housed, burst.
- The genus name *Alcovasaurus* means "Alcova lizard" and is named after the Alcova Quarry, where the fossils were found. The species name *longispinus* means "long spined."

 Find out more in the I Know Dino *podcast, episode 128, "Yutyrannus."*

Anodontosaurus inceptus

- *Anodontosaurus inceptus* was an ankylosaurid that lived in the Late Cretaceous in what is now Alberta, Canada.
- There are two species of *Anodontosaurus*: *lambei* and *inceptus*. *Anodontosaurus inceptus* is the second named species and *Anodontosaurus lambei* was named in 1928.
- *Anodontosaurus inceptus* lived a few million years after *Anodontosaurus lambei*.
- The genus name *Anodontosaurus* means "toothless lizard."
- The species name *inceptus* means "begin" in Latin.

Apatoraptor pennatus

- *Apatoraptor pennatus* was a caenagnathid that lived in the Cretaceous in what is now Alberta, Canada.
- The *Apatoraptor* holotype includes the lower jaws, sternum, gastralia, partial ilium, and partial hind limb.
- *Apatoraptor* had a long neck and quill knobs on its upper arm, which means it had wings.
- The genus name *Apatoraptor* means "deceptive plunderer."
- The species name *pennatus* means "feathered."

Find out more in the I Know Dino *podcast, episode 74, "Scipionyx."*

Boreonykus certekorum

- *Boreonykus certekorum* lived in the Cretaceous, in what is now Alberta, Canada, in the Wapiti Formation.
- Though many dinosaur fossils have been found in the Wapiti Formation, many of the bones do not provide enough detail to name the genus. As a result, only the hadrosaurid *Edmontosaurus regalis* and the ceratopsid *Pachyrhinosaurus lakustai* have been identified in the area.
- *Boreonykus* was a carnivorous dromaeosaurid, possibly within the subfamily Velociraptorinae.
- The discovery of *Boreonykus* shows that there are more Velociraptorinae dinosaurs than previously thought in North America (many members of the group are from Asia).
- The genus name *Boreonykus* means "northern claw." The species name *certekorum* is in honor of Certek Heating Solutions, a company that helped support the excavation of *Boreonykus*.

 Find out more in the I Know Dino *podcast, episode 70, "Mapusaurus."*

Crittenceratops krzyzanowskii

- *Crittenceratops krzyzanowskii* was a nasutoceratopsian that lived in the Late Cretaceous in what is now Arizona, United States.
- *Crittenceratops* had fancy frill ornamentation with large openings in the frill that were wider than they were tall.
- *Crittenceratops* was found farther south than other nasutoceratopsians, so scientists think this may show that nasutoceratopsians moved pretty freely, and Laramidia wasn't separated into distinct northern and southern regions.
- The genus name *Crittenceratops* means "Crittenden horned face." The dinosaur was found in the Crittenden Formation.
- The species name *krzyzanowskii* is in honor of the late Stan Krzyzanowski, who found *Crittenceratops*.

 Find out more in the I Know Dino *podcast, episode 210, "Yangchuanosaurus."*

Dryosaurus elderae

- *Dryosaurus elderae* was an ornithischian that lived in the Late Jurassic in what is now Utah, United States.
- There are two species of *Dryosaurus*: *altus* and *elderae*. *Dryosaurus elderae* is the second named species. *Dryosaurus altus* was named in 1894.
- *Dryosaurus elderae* had longer neck vertebrae and a longer, lower ilium (hip bone).
- The genus name *Dryosaurus* means "tree lizard."
- The species name *elderae* is in honor of Ann Schaffer Elder, who worked with Kenneth Carpenter at the Carnegie Quarry in Dinosaur National Monument. Carpenter named *Dryosaurus elderae*.

 Find out more in the I Know Dino *podcast, episode 199, "Bonitasaurus."*

Eotrachodon orientalis

- *Eotrachodon orientalis* was a basal hadrosaurid that lived in the Cretaceous in what is now Alabama, United States.
- *Eotrachodon* helps scientists better understand the early evolution of hadrosaurids because it's the most complete hadrosaurid from the eastern half of North America found so far.
- *Eotrachodon* had a slender, crestless nasal. The specimen found was between 13 to 17 ft (4 to 5 m) long but was probably still growing when it died.
- The genus name *Eotrachodon* means "dawn Trachodon" or "dawn rough tooth." It refers to *Eotrachodon* living earlier than the genus *Trachodon* (a now dubious genus).
- The species name *orientalis* means "eastern."

 Find out more in the I Know Dino *podcast, episode 62, "Fosterovenator."*

Foraminacephale brevis

- *Foraminacephale brevis* was a pachycephalosaurid that lived in the Cretaceous in what is now Alberta, Canada.
- *Foraminacephale* had many small pits at the top of the thick dome on its skull.
- *Foraminacephale brevis* was originally assigned to *Stegoceras* in 1918 by Lawrence Lambe. After, it was assigned to *Prenocephale*. Then, in 2011, Ryan Schott suggested it be *Foraminacephale brevis*. However, it was considered an invalid nomen ex dissertatione until Schott and David Evans formally renamed it *Foraminacephale brevis* in 2016.
- The genus name *Foraminacephale* means "foramina head." A foramina is an opening or a hole in a bone.
- The species name *brevis* means "short."

Galeamopus hayi

- *Galeamopus hayi* was a diplodocid that lived in the Jurassic, in what is now Colorado and Wyoming in the United States.
- *Galeamopus* was originally classified as *Diplodocus*, but, in 2015, paleontologists determined it was distinct enough to be its own genus.
- *Galeamopus* had a whip-like tail and could probably move it so fast that it would make loud, cracking sounds.
- *Galeamopus* had a fragile braincase.
- The genus name *Galeamopus* means "need helmet."

 Find out more in the I Know Dino *podcast, episode 129, "Edmontosaurus."*

Gastonia lorriemcwhinneyae

- *Gastonia lorriemcwhinneyae* was an ankylosaur that lived in the Cretaceous in what is now Utah, United States.
- *Gastonia lorriemcwhinneyae* is the second species of *Gastonia*.
- The first described species is *Gastonia burgei*, named in 1998.
- *Gastonia* had a sacral shield, a group of osteoderms over its hips, and shoulder spikes.
- The genus name *Gastonia* means "Gaston's lizard" in honor of the paleontologist Rob Gaston. The species name *lorriemcwhinneyae* is in honor of Lorrie McWhinney, who found the *Gastonia* bone bed in 1999.

Gryposaurus alsatei

- *Gryposaurus alsatei* was a hadrosaur that lived in the Cretaceous in what is now Texas, United States.
- *Gryposaurus alsatei* is a possible fourth species of *Gryposaurus*. Other *Gryposaurus* species include *G. notabilis*, *G. latidens*, and *G. monumentensis*.
- *Gryposaurus alsatei* was in saurolophinae, a hadrosaurid subfamily.
- *Gryposaurus alsatei* was a "flat-headed" saurolophine.
- The genus name *Gryposaurus* means "hooked-nosed lizard." The species name *alsatei* is an homage to Alsate, the legendary renegade last chief of the Chisos Apaches.

Find out more in the I Know Dino *podcast, episode 131, "Gryposaurus."*

Invictarx zephyri

- *Invictarx zephyri* was a nodosaurid that lived in the Late Cretaceous in what is now New Mexico, United States.
- *Invictarx* had relatively smooth osteoderms, which were probably part of the pelvic shield.
- *Invictarx* was found in the Allison Member of the Upper Cretaceous Menefee Formation and is the first identifiable dinosaur from that formation.
- The genus name *Invictarx* means "invincible or unconquerable fortress."
- The species name *zephyri* means "west wind" and refers to the windy conditions where the dinosaur fossils were found.

Find out more in the I Know Dino *podcast, episode 199, "Bonitasaurus."*

Latenivenatrix mcmasterae

- *Latenivenatrix mcmasterae* was a troodontid theropod that lived in the Cretaceous in what is now Alberta, Canada.
- *Latenivenatrix* fossils were "hiding" in museum collections for nearly a century before being officially described.
- Fragmentary bones from four individuals were found, and scientists estimate *Latenivenatrix* to be about 5.9 ft (1.8 m) tall and 11.5 ft (3.5 m) long, possibly making it the largest known troodontid.
- The genus name *Latenivenatrix* means "hiding female hunter" or "latent female hunter" in Latin.
- The species name *mcmasterae* is in honor of lead author Aaron J. van der Reest's late mother, whose maiden name was McMaster.

 Find out more in the I Know Dino *podcast, episode 144, "Buitreraptor."*

Lepidus praecisio

- *Lepidus praecisio* was a theropod that lived in the Triassic, in what is now Texas, United States.
- *Lepidus* bones were originally discovered in 1941, but it wasn't described until 2015. Only the ankle joint, femur, and the upper jaw have been found.
- Fossils from the Triassic period are much rarer than fossils from the Jurassic and Cretaceous. But, in the past 25 years, more fossils from the Triassic have been found, which allows scientists to better connect the dots with fragmentary fossils from the era.
- *Lepidus* helps to fill a gap about theropods that lived in the Triassic.
- The genus name *Lepidus* means "fascinating." The species name *praecisio* means "scrap."

Maraapunisaurus fragillimus

- *Maraapunisaurus fragillimus* was a rebbachisaurid that lived in the Late Jurassic in what is now Utah and Colorado, United States.
- *Maraapunisaurus* was originally named *Amphicoelias fragillimus* in 1878 because of similarities to *Amphicoelias altus*. However, after further study, it appears to be a more distant relative. This reclassification was done based on drawings alone since the holotype was lost or destroyed.
- *Maraapunisaurus* is estimated to be about 99 to 105 ft (30.3 to 32 m) long, which is much shorter than the original estimates when it was considered *Amphicoelias fragillimus*.
- The genus name *Maraapunisaurus* means "huge reptile."
- The species name *fragillimus* means "fragile," a name that foreshadowed its future demise.

Find out more in the I Know Dino *podcast, episode 210, "Yangchuanosaurus."*

Machairoceratops cronusi

- *Machairoceratops cronusi* was a ceratopsian that lived in the Cretaceous in what is now Utah, United States.
- *Machairoceratops* was about 20 to 25 ft (6 to 8 m) long and weighed about 1 to 2 tons.
- The discovery of *Machairoceratops* shows the diversity of ceratopsians, especially in the frill.
- The genus name *Machairoceratops* means "bent sword," and refers to the two horns on top of its frill that curve forward.
- The species name *cronusi* is in reference to the Greek god Cronus, who castrated his father Uranus with a sickle, and is depicted as carrying a curved weapon.

 Find out more in the I Know Dino *podcast, episode 80, "Ornitholestes."*

Mierasaurus bobyoungi

- *Mierasaurus bobyoungi* was a sauropod that lived in the Cretaceous in what is now Utah, United States.
- *Mierasaurus* is part of the Turiasauria clade, though most of the dinosaurs in that clade have been found in Europe.
- The first *Mierasaurus* bones were found by Gary Hunt in 2010 after a flash flood.
- The genus name *Mierasaurus* is in honor of Bernardo de Miera y Pacheco, a Spanish cartographer and "the first European scientist to enter what is now Utah."
- The species name *bobyoungi* "acknowledges the importance of the underappreciated research by Robert Young on the Early Cretaceous of Utah," according to the paper in *Scientific Reports*.

 Find out more in the I Know Dino *podcast, episode 157, "Amargasaurus."*

Platypelta coombsi

- *Platypelta coombsi* was an ankylosaur that lived in the Late Cretaceous in what is now Alberta, Canada.
- *Platypelta* was originally thought to be *Euoplocephalus*. Walter Coombs assigned the fossils to *Euoplocephalus* in 1971. (The fossils were originally found in 1914 by Barnum Brown.)
- *Platypelta* was about 20 ft (6 m) long.
- The genus name *Platypelta* means "wide plate," named for the dinosaur's wide osteoderms.
- The species name *coombsi* is in honor of Walter Coombs.

Find out more in the I Know Dino *podcast, episode 180, "Nipponosaurus."*

Saurornitholestes sullivani

- *Saurornitholestes sullivani* is a theropod that lived in the Cretaceous, in what is now New Mexico, United States.
- Scientists originally thought that *Saurornitholestes sullivani* was the same species as *Saurornitholestes langstoni* until they did a comparative analysis of the two species.
- *Saurornitholestes sullivani* has a large olfactory bulb in its brain, which means it had a better sense of smell than other dromaeosaurids.
- *Saurornitholestes sullivani* was small, about 6 ft (1.8 m) long and 3 ft (90 cm) tall, but it was fast. *Saurornitholestes sullivani* may have hunted in packs.
- The genus name *Saurornitholestes* refers to the group Saurornithoididae, a synonym for the group Troodontidae. The species name *sullivani* is in honor of Robert Sullivan, the paleontologist who discovered the partial skull in 1999.

Scolosaurus thronus

- *Scolosaurus thronus* was an ankylosaur that lived in the Late Cretaceous in what is now Alberta, Canada.
- There are two species of *Scolosaurus*: *cutleri* and *thronus*. *Scolosaurus thronus* is the second named species. *Scolosaurus cutleri* was named in 1928.
- *Scolosaurus thronus* is a descendant of *Scolosaurus cutleri*.
- The genus name *Scolosaurus* means "pointed spike lizard."
- The species name *thronus* means "throne."

 Find out more in the I Know Dino *podcast, episode 180, "Nipponosaurus."*

Ugrunaaluk kuukpikensis

- *Ugrunaaluk kuukpikensis* was a hadrosaur that lived in the Cretaceous, in what is now Alaska, United States, in the Prince Creek Formation.
- *Ugrunaaluk* fossils were first found in 1961 by Robert Liscomb when he was mapping for Shell Oil Co. He thought the bones were of mammals, and they were in storage for about 20 years before someone realized they were dinosaur bones. Over the course of 25 years, scientists examined 6,000 bones, which were at first thought to be *Edmontosaurus*. But it had different skull and mouth features, enough to make it its own genus.
- *Ugrunaaluk* was about 33 ft (10 m) long. Juvenile *Ugrunaaluk* were about 9 ft (2.7 m) long.
- In the Cretaceous, Alaska was much warmer and had a less harsh climate. Scientists think that *Ugrunaaluk* may have lived there all year, like musk oxen and caribou, instead of migrating south each year.
- The name *Ugrunaaluk kuukpikensis* means "ancient grazer" in Inupiaq, the language spoken by Alaska Inupiat Eskimos.

 Find out more in the I Know Dino *podcast, episode 44, "Pachyrhinosaurus."*

Wendiceratops pinhornensis

- *Wendiceratops pinhornensis* was a ceratopsian that lived in the Cretaceous, in what is now Alberta, Canada, in the Oldman Formation.
- *Wendiceratops* was about 20 ft (6 m) long and weighed over 1 ton.
- *Wendiceratops* had a parrot-like beak; a tall, conical nasal horn; and hook-like horns coming out of its wide frill.
- The genus name *Wendiceratops* means "Wendy's horn face," and refers to Wendy Sloboda, a fossil hunter who found the bone bed of *Wendiceratops* in 2010.
- The species name *pinhornensis* is in honor of the Pinhorn Provincial Grazing Reserve, where the bones were discovered.

 Find out more in the I Know Dino *podcast, episode 34, "Utahraptor."*

South America

Chilesaurus diegosuarezi: "Chile lizard" a.k.a. the platypus dinosaur

Chilesaurus diegosuarezi courtesy of Arcovenator via Wikimedia Commons

Water flows everywhere. The area is green and lush, with many rivers crisscrossing the land. *Chilesaurus diegosuarezi* licks his lips, happy to have so many choices.

Chilesaurus looks like a mishmash of dinosaurs: a theropod with a small head and a blunt, rounded skull; a slender neck; and stocky forelimbs, with two stumpy fingers and two claws. His arms and hands look a lot like his relative *Allosaurus*, but, unlike *Allosaurus*, *Chilesaurus* is a plant-eater.

He sets his broad, four-toed feet onto the ground, preparing to stay in one spot for a good long while. The first toes of each of his feet help to bear his weight, like many other herbivorous dinosaurs. At 9 ft (3 m) long, he is not too large, but he does have a wide gut—perfect for digesting his favorite tough plants. In front of him are bushes full of tasty, tender leaves.

Chilesaurus opens his mouth, revealing long, spatula-shaped teeth. With his horny beak, he snips at the fronds of plants. Because he is not a fast runner, *Chilesaurus* keeps an eye on his surroundings for any potential threats. No other predators are around, but *Chilesaurus* flexes his claws instinctively. If he needs to, he can use his strong arms and claws, the same way sauropodomorphs defend themselves.

Two *Chilesaurus* juveniles scamper around him. They are much smaller, about the size of a turkey. And they are loud. *Chilesaurus* glares at them, but they pay him no mind. They play-fight with one another and end up rolling around in the bushes, right next to *Chilesaurus*.

Annoyed, *Chilesaurus* takes a couple of steps to the side and returns his focus to his dinner of succulent vegetation.

The sun is starting to set, and *Chilesaurus* chews

faster. Although he has large, wide eyes, he needs to soon settle in for the night. With the darkness comes new dangers.

Chilesaurus' stomach grumbles. He has not eaten enough for the day, and now he must decide whether he should go to bed hungry yet safe or continue to eat and risk being vulnerable.

He decides to play it safe. The grumbling gets louder, and *Chilesaurus* stomps his feet, wishing he could eat more. He blames the juveniles for distracting him. They have gotten out of the bushes, and *Chilesaurus* nudges them with his beak as they rush by him.

The colors in the sky have changed from orange to pink to red to purple, and the moon is getting brighter. *Chilesaurus* follows the juveniles back to their shared resting area. They are not his, but they stumbled into each other a few weeks back and have been keeping each other company ever since.

On the way to meet the juveniles, *Chilesaurus* passes a huge diplodocid. He nods to the massive sauropod and gives it a wide berth. The diplodocid does not notice.

Back home, the juveniles are already snuggled together for the night. *Chilesaurus'* stomach growls again, but this time he ignores it and huddles up next to the young ones. Comfortable, he takes one last look at the moon before closing his eyes.

Facts

- *Chilesaurus diegosuarezi* was a theropod that lived in the Late Jurassic in what is now Chile.
- *Chilesaurus* was found in the Toqui Formation in Chile. Based on the fossils scientists have found in that area so far and from that time period, *Chilesaurus* is the most common dinosaur in southwest Patagonia when it lived 145 million years ago.
- *Chilesaurus* is an example of mosaic convergent evolution, which means that different parts of its body resemble different dinosaur groups. For example, *Chilesaurus* had teeth similar to primitive sauropods but arms like an *Allosaurus*. Because *Chilesaurus* is such an odd mix, it has been referred to as platypus-like.
- *Chilesaurus* is a theropod, but unlike most theropods, which are carnivorous, *Chilesaurus* switched to a plant-eating diet.
- The species *diegosuarezi* is in honor of Diego Suárez, the seven-year-old boy who found the first fossils in 2004 with his geologist parents.

 Find out more in the I Know Dino *podcast, episode 25, "Allosaurus."*

Dreadnoughtus schrani: "Fear nothing"

Thud.   Thud.   Thud.   Thud.

The trees shake as the 85 ft (26 m) long *Dreadnoughtus schrani*—one of the biggest dinosaurs to ever live—moves a few feet to a new grazing spot.

He lets his 65-ton frame settle in, the ground spongy and soft and sinking under the weight. At 30 ft (9 m) tall, and with a 37 ft (11 m) long neck, *Dreadnoughtus* can see for miles. He is happy with what he sees: enough vegetation to eat for many hours, possibly days. Not too far away is a lake, which *Dreadnoughtus* plans to visit later for a drink. From a short distance, the lake looks full and sparkling; the water is clear.

Dreadnoughtus is still a growing dinosaur, and he needs to eat at least half a ton of food every day to sustain himself. The juvenile strips the surrounding leaves with his cylindrical, 1 in

(3 cm) long teeth, swallowing his food whole.

The process delights *Dreadnoughtus*, who plans to spend the next four hours in this same spot. His stomach is like a bottomless pit, and he never feels quite full. But spending the day eating makes him happy.

Dreadnoughtus keeps his neck horizontal as he eats. The day is warm, but *Dreadnoughtus* has air sacs inside his tail to help keep him cool.

Below the trees, younger, smaller *Dreadnoughtus* run around, scrambling to eat as much food as possible while staying out of sight of predators. They are not yet big enough to defend themselves. But they are big enough to catch the larger *Dreadnoughtus*' eye.

Annoyed, the larger juvenile *Dreadnoughtus* flexes his claws on his back feet. He has staked out this area for himself and will not tolerate others eating his food. The claws are sharp and long. The smaller *Dreadnoughtus* take the warning seriously and move away.

Satisfied, *Dreadnoughtus* returns to stripping and swallowing leaves. The ground starts to shake. Confused, *Dreadnoughtus* looks down but cannot tell what is happening. Everything below is moving, and *Dreadnoughtus* can feel his body vibrating, but he knows he is standing still.

After a few seconds, the shaking stops.

When *Dreadnoughtus* looks back up, he sees the water from the nearby lake, now in the form of a large wave, rushing towards him.

Unsure of what to do, *Dreadnoughtus* decides to stand his ground. He plants his feet more firmly in the ground, digging his claws into the dirt and bracing for the water to hit.

The water rushes towards the dinosaur quickly, sweeping away smaller dinosaurs and crushing trees in its path.

But *Dreadnoughtus* is not afraid. He is large and confident that he can survive. But he is aggravated that he has to pause his eating for this inconvenience.

The water hits *Dreadnoughtus* with such a force that it nearly knocks over the dinosaur. The first impact reaches the base of his neck, but soon more water hits.

Dreadnoughtus feels cold but manages to keep his footing—for now. More and more water comes, each time higher than before. *Dreadnoughtus* raises his head as high as he can, but it's not enough. The water keeps coming.

Facts

- *Dreadnoughtus schrani* was a titanosaur that lived in the Late Cretaceous in what is now Argentina.
- Dr. Kenneth Lacovara and his team discovered 45 percent of a complete *Dreadnoughtus* skeleton during excavations in Argentina between 2005 and 2009.
- The dinosaur was so big that it probably had no predators.
- *Dreadnoughtus* had such a large stomach that its food would have stayed undigested for months.
- The genus name *Dreadnoughtus* means "fear nothing"; the species name *schrani* comes from Adam Schran, who helped fund the research.

Find out more in the I Know Dino *podcast, episode 9, "Dreadnoughtus."*

Gualicho shinyae:
"Evil spirit"

Gualicho shinyae, courtesy of Nobu Tamura via Wikimedia Commons

Gualicho shinyae is hot and sticky. She's been wandering all morning in search of a quick meal, but nothing is coming easily today.

She stands on top of a hill to take a look around. Below her is an adult *Argentinosaurus*, much too big for *Gualicho* to even attempt to attack. The titanosaur's tail alone could break all of *Gualicho*'s bones, if given the chance.

Next to the adult titanosaur is a juvenile *Argentinosaurus*. It's the right size but too close to the adult to be worth it. If *Gualicho* had help, it might be possible to drive the two apart and chase after the smaller sauropod, but that's not an option today.

At 25 ft (7.6 m) long, and weighing about 1 ton, *Gualicho* is a sizable carnivore, and *Argentinosaurus* isn't the only game around. *Gualicho* walks down the hill, away from the titanosaur pair, and continues her search for food.

Fortunately, she doesn't have to go far. She comes across a small group of ornithopods, who are busy chewing on some leaves. They all pause and grow stiff when *Gualicho* approaches them.

Gualicho hesitates a moment to assess. She has the advantage. Though she has weak forelimbs with only two digits—a thumb and forefinger—she doesn't need to rely on them. She has a strong bite force. But she does need to be able to catch one of the ornithopods.

Then she notices that one of the ornithopods is favoring its right leg as it stands. An injured ornithopod is much easier to catch. *Gualicho* and the ornithopod look at each other for a brief moment, and then all the ornithopods take off at once.

Gualicho locks her eyes on the injured one and runs at it, her mouth wide open, jaws ready to clamp on to her prey.

It doesn't take her long to catch up to the dinosaur. Its eyes widen as it realizes this is the end. *Gualicho* takes a bite out of its back as it runs from her, causing it to stumble and fall. She jumps on top of the body and rips open its neck with her teeth. The ornithopod becomes still and limp.

Satisfied, *Gualicho* begins to feast. But, after only two bites, she senses something is wrong. She lifts her head and sees a *Mapusaurus* making its way toward her.

Mapusaurus is larger than her, about 33 ft (10 m) long and weighing three times as much. *Gualicho* knows she needs to give up her meal. She takes one last large bite, and then backs away slowly, to show submission.

The *Mapusaurus* gains ground and barks at *Gualicho*. Taking the hint, she sprints back up the hill, far enough to not be a threat but close enough to keep an eye on *Mapusaurus*. It probably won't eat everything, and *Gualicho* may still be able to pick off chunks.

Pieces of meat are stuck between *Gualicho*'s teeth, and some blood covers her face. She gives out a low growl, unhappy to have to leave behind her kill.

Facts

- *Gualicho shinyae* was a theropod that lived in the Cretaceous in what is now Patagonia in South America.
- *Gualicho* has many features found in different types of theropods, such as small arms with only two fingers, similar to *T. rex*.
- The genus name *Gualicho* comes from the northern Tehuelche language and is the name of a goddess who owns animals, which was later reinterpreted to be a demonic entity.
- The genus name *Gualicho* was chosen because there were many issues excavating the skeleton, including an accident where the truck carrying the scientists flipped. Luckily no one was seriously injured.
- The species name *shinyae* is in honor of Ms. Akiko Shinya, Chief Fossil Preparator at the Field Museum of Natural History in Chicago, and the one who discovered Gualicho.

 Find out more in the I Know Dino *podcast, episode 87, "Iguanodon."*

Isaberrysaura mollensis: "Isabel Berry's dinosaur"

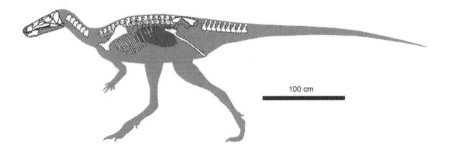

Isaberrysaura mollensis, courtesy of Leonardo Salgado, José I. Canudo, Alberto C. Garrido, Miguel Moreno–Azanza, Leandro C. A. Martínez, Rodolfo A. Coria, and José M. Gasca via Wikimedia Commons

Isaberrysaura mollensis is always on the move.

He runs on two legs, and he has a long tail that helps him keep balance. And he's a decent size at 16-20 ft (5-6 m) long, so he's not the easiest target for predators. But *Isaberrysaura* does not want to take any chances. Whenever possible, he feels the need to run.

The problem with running so much is that it makes *Isaberrysaura* work up an appetite. And although he has tried in the past, eating while running has never worked out well. Either he's running so fast that the food flies out of his mouth before he has a chance to swallow, or he nearly chokes. So instead, *Isaberrysaura* has figured out a way to spend as little time eating as possible.

He spots a couple of tasty-looking cycads and stops running abruptly. *Isaberrysaura* makes his way to the plant and plucks as many seeds as possible with his beak. Though he has teeth, he does not bother to chew. Chewing takes too long, and *Isaberrysaura* never knows when he might need to start sprinting for his life.

The cycad seeds *Isaberrysaura* swallows have toxic chemicals. But, fortunately for *Isaberrysaura*, he has fancy gut flora that helps him digest. Not that he's thinking about any of that. He's busy trying to swallow seeds so he can start running again.

Isaberrysaura bends down and picks up a few more seeds with his mouth. He notices a quick movement. Startled, he jumps up but soon realizes that there is no threat to him. A lizard peeks its head out from behind one of the cycads.

Isaberrysaura looks at the lizard, tempted. Lizards are much more filling than seeds, even though they do require chewing. He makes a decision and lunges at the lizard.

But the lizard is quick, even for an animal as quick as *Isaberrysaura*. The lizard runs behind the second cycad.

Isaberrysaura reaches for the lizard again, and again the lizard is too quick. It moves back to the first cycad. *Isaberrysaura* waits for a moment, to lull the lizard into a false sense of security. The lizard stays completely still, never taking its eyes off *Isaberrysaura*. Finally, *Isaberrysaura* makes his move, but again the lizard is too fast.

This game goes on for a while, but each time the lizard gets away. Finally, the lizard runs away from the cycads, and *Isaberrysaura* is too frustrated to go after it.

He resigns himself to eating more seeds. As he is about to pluck another seed from the cycad, he hears the snap of a twig. *Isaberrysaura* senses danger, and his instincts kick in.

Isaberrysaura springs up, sees the teeth of a theropod, and takes off running in the opposite direction. He doesn't stop, and he doesn't even look back to see if the theropod is chasing him. If only he hadn't stayed in one spot for so long while trying to catch that lizard.

Facts

- *Isaberrysaura mollensis* was an ornithischian, with some stegosaur traits, that lived in the Jurassic in what is now Patagonia, Argentina.
- *Isaberrysaura* is believed to be a close relative to *Kulindadromeus*.
- *Isaberrysaura* may have been an omnivore, based on its teeth.
- The genus name *Isaberrysaura* is in honor of Isabel Valdivia Berry, who found the dinosaur.
- The species name *mollensis* comes from the Los Molles Formation where it was found.

Find out more in the I Know Dino *podcast, episode 118, "Suchomimus."*

Lavocatisaurus agrioensis: "Lavocat lizard"

Lavocatisaurus agrioensis, courtesy of Jcarballido via Wikimedia Commons

Lavocatisaurus agrioensis is bored. He's only a juvenile. He hasn't yet figured out his world, which, dry and mostly barren, can be dull at times.

Fortunately for *Lavocatisaurus*, he has his sister and mother with him. His mother is big and strong, about 39 ft (12 m) long, while *Lavocatisaurus* and his sibling are only about 19 ft (6 m) long.

They spend all their time together, mostly walking. *Lavocatisaurus* is always walking somewhere to find water and food. Every day, they plod along, and *Lavocatisaurus* senses that they still have a long way to go.

The ground beneath them is dusty and full of cracks. *Lavocatisaurus* and his family take slow, careful steps to avoid tripping over rocks or stubbing their toes.

Lavocatisaurus spots something exciting: water. It's not much. It's only a small lake, and there are no other animals in sight. Perfectly safe to play in.

Lavocatisaurus follows his mother and sister to the lake. He watches his mother bend her knees and lean her neck forward into the water. She slurps quickly. His sister follows suit. *Lavocatisaurus* does the same but only takes a few quick sips. This may be his only chance all day.

While his mother is busy drinking, *Lavocatisaurus* sidles next to his sister, and then lightly nudges her side with his head. She bristles and takes a step away from him.

Undeterred, *Lavocatisaurus* plants his feet firmly in the mud and rubs the side of his head against his sister's front leg. Then he pushes, forcing her to shuffle to the side to avoid falling.

She looks at him, and then heads his way to retaliate. With glee, *Lavocatisaurus* runs into the water, splashing both his mother and sister.

His mother opens her mouth and lets out a low bellow as a warning. She shows some of her teeth. The upper teeth are longer and wider than the bottom teeth. *Lavocatisaurus* moves further into the water, away from his mother. His sister follows him.

The lake is deeper than it looks, and soon both juvenile *Lavocatisaurus* are nearly covered up to their shoulders. Not that *Lavocatisaurus* minds. He welcomes the coolness.

His sister catches up to him and kicks up her front legs, sending water into *Lavocatisaurus'* face. He splashes back. For the next few minutes, the two half walk, half paddle in the water, chasing each other and splashing. It's the most excitement *Lavocatisaurus* has had in days, and he relishes every second of it.

Finally, *Lavocatisaurus'* mother gets tired of their antics. She takes one last sip of water, bellows again, and turns around.

Lavocatisaurus and his sister stop, and then paddle back to the shore. When their mother calls like that, they know she means business. She's already started to walk away toward the dust.

Lavocatisaurus takes his first steps back on land. He shakes his whole body in an attempt to dry off. Not that it matters. The sun will soon take care of it.

Facts

- *Lavocatisaurus agrioensis* was a rebbachisaurid sauropod that lived in the Early Cretaceous in what is now Argentina.
- Scientists found most of the skull, which is the first rebbachisaurid skull from South America.
- *Lavocatisaurus* had longer, wider upper teeth than bottom teeth.
- The genus name *Lavocatisaurus* is in honor of René Lavocat, who named *Rebbachisaurus*.
- The species name *agrioensis* refers to the locality of Agrio del Medio, where the dinosaur was found.

 Find out more in the I Know Dino *podcast, episode 208, "Crichtonpelta."*

Murusraptor barrosaensis: "Wall thief"

Murusraptor barrosaensis courtesy of Nobu Tamura via Wikimedia Commons

Something sweet fills the air. Sweet...and pungent. Intrigued, *Murusraptor barrosaensis* follows the scent until he spots her, an irresistible *Murusraptor*. *Murusraptor* is not yet fully grown, but at 21 ft (6.5 m) long, he's far from a baby. He decides to try his luck and approaches the female with the tantalizing smell.

He puffs out his chest and walks in front of her, trying to appear as large as possible. He even strains his neck to make his snout look longer. She's not impressed and turns away.

Murusraptor tries again. This time when he walks by, he opens his mouth wide and lets out a loud roar for good measure.

She doesn't acknowledge him, but she doesn't turn away either.

Murusraptor walks in a wide circle around her, contemplating what to do next. Before he has a chance to make another move, a larger male appears.

Murusraptor takes a defensive stance and waits for the larger male to take action. The larger male looks over *Murusraptor*, and then growls, daring *Murusraptor* to come closer.

Murusraptor hesitates for a moment. Then the wind shifts, and he gets a full whiff of the female. He stops thinking and runs at the other male as fast as he can. With his hollow bones, he is surprisingly lightweight for his size and can move quickly.

But the other male is prepared and greets *Murusraptor* with his jaws open wide. *Murusraptor* sees the mouth full of teeth and hesitates at just the wrong second. He loses some of his momentum and nearly stumbles into the other male. Seizing the opportunity, the other male bites down into *Murusraptor*'s head.

Murusraptor is fast enough to dart away before the jaws pierce him too deeply, but the injury leaves him woozy. He takes a few unsteady steps.

The other male charges at *Murusraptor*, butting his head into *Murusraptor*'s ribs, breaking a few. *Murusraptor* howls in pain. From the corner of his eye, he can see that the female has lost interest and is walking away.

Murusraptor thrashes at the other male with his large claws. Now it's about survival. He manages to leave some marks but nothing too serious. Mostly he just angers the other male, who opens his mouth again for another attack.

Murusraptor ducks just as the other male snaps at him, causing his opponent to lose balance. *Murusraptor* takes advantage of his opponent's mistake and starts to run as fast as he can. His head aches, but he can't worry about that now—not until he is safe.

He runs for a while until his head starts to hurt so much that his steps become wobbly. He stops. No one is behind him, so the other male must have lost interest as soon as he realized the female was gone.

Murusraptor shakes his head in an attempt to lessen the pain, but it only gets worse.

In between a few trees is a small clearing. *Murusraptor* decides to rest there. He falls onto the ground and lies on his right side, panting from all the energy he just spent.

Facts

- *Murusraptor barrosaensis* was a megaraptorid that lived in the Late Cretaceous in what is now Argentina.
- *Murusraptor* looked a lot like *Allosaurus*, but it is more derived and a little smaller.
- *Murusraptor* was originally found in 2000, but it took a few years to excavate the specimen because it was in the base of a nearly vertical cliff.
- The genus name *Murusraptor* means "wall thief." The word "murus" refers to the fact that the dinosaur was found in the wall of a canyon.
- The species name *barrosaensis* is in honor of Sierra Barrosa, where the fossils were collected.

 Find out more in the I Know Dino *podcast, episode 88, "Baryonyx."*

Notocolossus gonzalezparejasi: "Southern colossus"

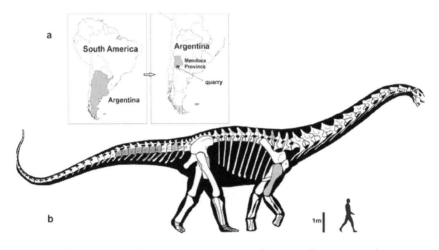

Notocolossus gonzalezparejasi, courtesy of Bernardo J. González Riga, Matthew C. Lamanna, Leonardo D. Ortiz David, Jorge O. Calvo, and Juan P. Coria via Wikimedia Commons

Thud. Silence. Thud.

Notocolossus gonzalezparejasi and her friend walk along the river. The second *Notocolossus* limps from an earlier injury, and *Notocolossus* is taking her to somewhere bountiful where she knows they can eat in peace.

From the corner of her eye, *Notocolossus* can see

the leaves around her jiggle whenever they take a step.

There are other titanosaurs around: *Mendozasaurus*, with their long necks and osteoderm armor, and *Quetecsaurus*, with their subtle neural spines.

Together, the titanosaurs can make the ground shake, just by walking.

Notocolossus walks at a leisurely pace, each step slow but covering a great distance. She weighs 44 tons, but her tree trunk-like ankles and feet, with small toes, support her giant figure.

She hears a low growl, but the sound is coming from far enough away that *Notocolossus* doesn't pay too much attention to it. Her friend, however, is more cautious, and stops walking.

Notocolossus looks down, which is not easy with such a long neck, and sees the creature making the noise: a subadult megaraptoran. It opens its jaws wide and flashes its teeth, but *Notocolossus* knows it poses no real threat. At 82 ft (25 m) long, *Notocolossus* is much bigger, plus she has a long, dangerous tail.

She snorts in the megaraptoran's general direction and starts to walk again, urging her friend to do the same. The day is warm, but clouds cover the sky, providing some welcome shade. *Notocolossus* and her friend continue alongside a river, whose babbling sound is soothing. They're almost to *Notocolossus'* favorite spot for grazing. Her stomach rumbles in anticipation.

When she finally gets to her favorite trees, *Notocolossus* immediately grabs a mouthful of leaves. She's too hungry to wait for her friend to catch up. She swallows and takes another, and then another. After a while, she realizes her friend still hasn't made it to their lunch spot.

She hears the cries of distress. *Notocolossus* turns around and sees her friend in the defensive position against the megaraptoran. But now there are three of them.

Notocolossus moves toward the group, angry at being interrupted from eating. She reaches the megaraptorans and lets out a booming warning sound. She towers over them.

The megaraptorans, knowing they cannot successfully fight two titanosaurs, back away slowly.

Notocolossus stops, satisfied. Her friend relaxes her position too. But then the first megaraptoran runs toward *Notocolossus'* friend and lunges at her. She manages to rear up in time, so the carnivore loses its balance, and its teeth barely graze her.

She also loses her balance and falls heavily onto her injured leg. *Notocolossus* steps in front of her friend, aiming her tail at the megaraptoran, daring it to attack again.

The megaraptoran snarls but finally admits defeat. It slinks back to the other two megaraptorans, and they walk away.

Notocolossus watches them until she can no longer see them, and then turns back to her friend. She nudges her friend with her head, and they head back to the trees.

Facts

- *Notocolossus gonzalezparejasi* was a titanosaur that lived in the Cretaceous in what is now Argentina.
- *Notocolossus* was one of the largest known dinosaurs, based on its humerus, which is 5 ft 9 in (1.76 m) long. This is the longest of any known titanosaur upper-arm bone. One hind foot has been found and is complete and articulated, which will help scientists understand how such large, heavy animals walked around.
- *Notocolossus* is a sister taxon of *Dreadnoughtus*, another titanosaur. *Dreadnoughtus* had a 5 ft 3 in (1.6 m) long humerus, which is about 10% shorter than *Notocolossus*.
- The genus name *Notocolossus* means "southern colossus."
- The species name *gonzalezparejasi* is in honor of Dr. Jorge González Parejas, who has worked with and given legal guidance for dinosaur fossils for almost 20 years in the Mendoza Province, Argentina, where *Notocolossus* was found.

 Find out more in the I Know Dino *podcast, episode 62, "Fosterovenator."*

Sarmientosaurus musacchioi: "Sarmiento lizard"

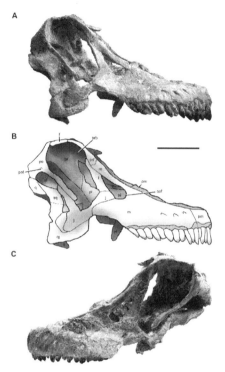

Sarmientosaurus musacchioi, courtesy of Rubén D. F. Martínez, Matthew C. Lamanna, Fernando E. Novas, Ryan C. Ridgely, Gabriel A. Casal, Javier E. Martínez, Javier R. Vita, and Lawrence M. Witmer via Wikimedia Commons

Sarmientosaurus musacchioi's bones ache. She's getting on in years and doesn't like to move more than she has to. At 39 ft (12 m) long and weighing 10 tons, she doesn't have to move much.

She's big enough to not have to worry about predators. Plus, she has large eyes and keen vision.

It's a hot day, and there's not much shade, but *Sarmientosaurus* tries to ignore her discomfort. Instead, she focuses on the task at hand. She's found a large area, full of bushes, ready to eat. It took her half a day to get to the bushes, but she had no choice. She had devoured everything edible in her last spot, and she needs to eat more.

Sarmientosaurus lowers her head and keeps it down. Her snout faces downward. She has a multitude of neck bones and a neck tendon, which makes it easier for her to eat low-growing vegetation.

She keeps her feet planted firmly on the ground and starts grazing. Her long neck moves around like the wand of a vacuum cleaner, her head taking in all the low-growing plants around her.

Sarmientosaurus eats in a mechanical way. Chew. Swallow. Chew. Swallow. She doesn't even think about what she's doing. The hours while away, and the vegetation around her disappears. Then she hears something. A low sound, at a frequency few but her can hear. It's the call of another *Sarmientosaurus*.

Sarmientosaurus responds, hoping to keep the other titanosaur at bay. There is only enough food for one of them—and besides, she found this spot first.

But the other *Sarmientosaurus* doesn't seem to care, and he trudges slowly up to her. She snorts in his direction to show her displeasure. The other *Sarmientosaurus* ignores her and starts to graze.

Annoyed, *Sarmientosaurus* stomps her foot. The other *Sarmientosaurus* lifts his head up, just high enough to meet *Sarmientosaurus*' eye, and then returns to eating.

Sarmientosaurus decides to give him a nudge. She pushes against his side, just hard enough to make him lean to the side. He snorts in response but continues to eat.

Sarmientosaurus looks at the vegetation below them. Not much is left, but she feels miffed that she won't be the one to polish off the food. She decides to take a stand in another way.

She lowers her head and grabs at the leaves as fast as she can, stuffing more into her mouth than can fit. She swallows in a hurry and does it again. If she can't make the other titanosaur leave, at least she can make sure he doesn't get much to eat.

He notices and does the same. Grab. Swallow. Grab. Swallow. Soon the two titanosaurs find themselves in an eating contest.

Sarmientosaurus sucks up her food as fast as she can. There's only one bush left, and she refuses to let the other *Sarmientosaurus* win. But he's just as stubborn, and they both reach for the last few leaves at the same time.

Sarmientosaurus leans into him and tries to push him away. He leans back and pushes against her face. But they're both leaning too much on each other, and they lose their balance. *Sarmientosaurus* manages to regain her balance before falling but not before the other *Sarmientosaurus* eats the last bite of food.

Facts

- *Sarmientosaurus musacchioi* was a titanosaur that lived in the Cretaceous in what is now Argentina.
- A nearly complete skull was found, which is very rare for a titanosaur. It had a downward-facing snout and a different structure from other titanosaurs. Scientists CT scanned the skull and found that *Sarmientosaurus* could probably hear lower frequencies than other titanosaurs and had better vision.
- *Sarmientosaurus* lived 100-90 million years ago, and it looks more similar to older sauropods. It's a more basal member of Lithosauria and probably evolved from a "ghost lineage," from still undiscovered dinosaurs alongside other known lithosaurids.
- The genus name *Sarmientosaurus* refers to the town of Sarmiento and the administrative department where *Sarmientosaurus* was found.
- The species name *musacchioi* is in honor of Dr. Eduardo Musacchio, who was a scientist and educator at the Universidad Nacional de la Patagonia San Juan Bosco in Argentina.

 Find out more in the I Know Dino *podcast, episode 77, "Tethyshadros."*

Tratayenia rosalesi: "Tratayén"

Take soft steps. *Tratayenia rosalesi* instinctively knows that she must tread lightly to avoid attracting attention. She's a medium-sized megaraptoran, about 29 ft (9 m) long, and she's hungry for fresh meat.

She has to catch her prey by surprise. Though she is large for her habitat, her food is rarely easy to snatch.

Tratayenia has a long tail and an elongated snout full of sharp, serrated teeth. She walks on two powerful legs. Her biggest weapon is in her hands. Her forelimbs are long, and two of the fingers on each hand end in large claws that are 16 in (40 cm) long.

As *Tratayenia* walks, she flexes her claws, ready to attack as soon as she sees something worth eating. Sometimes she finds morsels hiding within the vegetation in water. *Tratayenia* veers toward the nearest stream. She passes the crocodylomorph *Comahuesuchus*.

Though the animal is not a threat to her, *Tratayenia* bares her teeth so it knows she's in charge. *Comahuesuchus* lies down in the shallow water to signal that it means no harm. *Tratayenia* keeps moving.

Tratayenia hears a plop, the sound of something in the water. She turns her head and spots a *Lomalatachelys*. Unfortunately for her, *Lomalatachelys* is a turtle with a protective shell. Not ideal for an easy meal. *Tratayenia* stays still to see if the turtle has noticed her. For a moment, it doesn't. *Tratayenia* watches as the turtle stretches its long, snake-like neck out of its shell to nibble at some food in the water.

Tratayenia takes a small step toward *Lomalatachelys*, but the turtle sees the ripples in the water from her step and retracts its head into the thick shell. *Tratayenia* tries again. Once she's in front of the turtle, she bends down and halfheartedly smacks it with one of her arms. The shell rocks a little. *Tratayenia* decides to move on.

Not far away, *Tratayenia* sees an opportunity: a juvenile *Bonitasaura* busily eating vegetation. *Tratayenia* takes a moment to size up the animal. The young titanosaur is small, maybe even under 10 ft (3 m) long, enough that *Tratayenia* can win in a fight. There are other *Bonitasaura* around, but they are not close enough. If *Tratayenia* attacked, they couldn't band together for defense in time. And, best of all, the juvenile is currently distracted.

Tratayenia sneaks up on her prey. *Bonitasaura* notices her too late, and *Tratayenia* is able to dig her claws into the side of the titanosaur. *Bonitasaura* lets out a loud, pained noise and tries to wiggle away. *Tratayenia* holds fast.

The noise attracts the attention of the nearby *Bonitasaura*, but they soon realize that it's too late for their juvenile and move away from the danger.

Bonitasaura thrashes, kicking up its feet and swinging its relatively short neck and tail. *Tratayenia* takes a bite in her prey's shoulder and enjoys the tender meat. *Bonitasaura* keeps fighting back, but it's bleeding heavily. *Tratayenia* continues to grip her prey until it falls down and stays still.

Facts

- *Tratayenia rosalesi* was a megaraptoran theropod that lived in the Late Cretaceous in what is now Argentina.
- *Tratayenia* was the largest predator in its habitat.
- *Tratayenia* had long, sharp claws that it probably used to hunt prey.
- The genus name *Tratayenia* refers to Tratayén, where the holotype was found.
- The species name *rosalesi* is in honor of Diego Rosales, who found the specimen and did a lot of the preparation work.

 Find out more in the I Know Dino *podcast, episode 175, "Metriacanthosaurus."*

More Dinosaurs From South America

Aoniraptor libertatem

- *Aoniraptor libertatem* was a megaraptoran that lived in the Cretaceous in what is now Argentina.
- The holotype found included hip vertebrae, tail vertebrae, and tail chevrons.
- *Aoniraptor* was about 20 ft (6 m) long.
- The genus name *Aoniraptor* means "southern plunderer."
- The species name *libertatem* means "freedom." *Aoniraptor* was discovered in 2010, on the 200th anniversary of Argentina's declaration of their independence from Spain.

Austroposeidon magnificus

- *Austroposeidon magnificus* was a titanosaur that lived in the Cretaceous in what is now Brazil.
- *Austroposeidon* was about 82 ft (25 m) long and was the biggest dinosaur found in Brazil at the time of its discovery. Based on the sandstone it was found in, it probably was preserved on a floodplain.
- *Austroposeidon* was first found by Llewellyn Ivor Price in 1953 and later described in 2016 by Kamila L.N. Banderia, Felipe Medieros Simbras, Elaine Batista Machado, Diogenes de Almeida Campos, Gustavo R. Oliveira, and Alexander W. A. Kellner.
- The genus name *Austroposeidon* means "southern Poseidon" (Poseidon is the Greek god of earthquakes).
- The species name *magnificus* means "noble" or "great" and refers to the large size of *Austroposeidon*.

 Find out more in the I Know Dino *podcast, episode 99, "Afrovenator."*

Baalsaurus mansillai

- *Baalsaurus mansillai* was a titanosaur that lived in the Late Cretaceous in what is now Patagonia, Argentina.
- Scientists described the right dentary of *Baalsaurus*, which was "L" shaped.
- *Baalsaurus* is estimated to be medium-sized, with a skull length of about 15.7 in (40 cm).
- The genus name *Baalsaurus* refers to the name of the dinosaur site. Baal is also the name of the fertility god from ancient Phoenician and Canaanite lands.
- The species name *mansillai* is in honor of Juan Eduardo Mansilla, a technician at the Geology and Paleontology Museum of the National University of Comahue, who found the fossil.

 Find out more in the I Know Dino *podcast, episode 213, "Qantassaurus."*

Bagualosaurus agudoensis

- *Bagualosaurus agudoensis* was a sauropodomorph that lived in the Late Triassic in what is now Brazil.
- The skull of *Bagualosaurus* was similar to *Plateosaurus*.
- The body of *Bagualosaurus* had features like other early dinosaurs, meaning that its legs and feet weren't prepared to support a lot of weight.
- The genus name *Bagualosaurus* comes from Bagual, a term from southern Brazil that refers to a person or animal of strong build or an untamed horse.
- The species name *agudoensis* refers to Agudo, the town where the dinosaur was found.

 Find out more in the I Know Dino *podcast, episode 184, "Segisaurus."*

Bonapartesaurus rionegrensis

- *Bonapartesaurus rionegrensis* was a saurolophine hadrosaur that lived in the Cretaceous in what is now Río Negro Province, Argentina.
- The fossils were found in an area known for titanosaurs, which "suggests at least two saurolophine dispersal events from North America, one toward South America and another toward Asia, no later than the late Campanian" (within about 10 million years of the Chicxulub impact credited with causing the extinction of non-avian dinosaurs).
- Scientists found about 20 vertebrae, some ribs, an arm, a leg, hip bones, and a nearly complete left foot.
- The genus name *Bonapartesaurus* is in honor of José Fernando Bonaparte, for his contribution to paleontology in Argentina.
- The species name *rionegrensis* refers to the Río Negro Province.

 Find out more in the I Know Dino *podcast, episode 127, "Masiakasaurus."*

Buriolestes schultzi

- *Buriolestes schultzi* was a sauropodomorph that lived in the Triassic in what is now Brazil.
- *Buriolestes* looked like a carnivorous theropod, with serrated, slightly curved teeth, even though it was a sauropodomorph (the group that gave rise to the herbivorous sauropods).
- *Buriolestes* helps show that sauropodomorphs and early dinosaurs in general were carnivorous, and then some dinosaurs eventually became herbivorous.
- The genus name *Buriolestes* means "Buriol's robber." *Buriolestes* was found in the Buriol ravine in Brazil.
- The species name *schultzi* is in honor of paleontologist Cezar Schultz.

Find out more in the I Know Dino *podcast, episode 104, "Archaeopteryx."*

Choconsaurus baileywillisi

- *Choconsaurus baileywillisi* was a titanosaur that lived in the Late Cretaceous in what is now Patagonia, Neuquén Province, Argentina.
- Scientists found vertebrae from the neck and tail and parts of the dinosaur's limbs.
- *Choconsaurus* had some basal characteristics and is the most complete basal titanosaur found so far.
- The genus name *Choconsaurus* refers to Villa El Chocón, where the fossils were found.
- The species name *baileywillisi* is in honor of Bailey Willis, who worked on stratigraphy in the area where it was found in the early 20th century.

 Find out more in the I Know Dino *podcast, episode 154, "Protoceratops."*

Ingentia prima

- *Ingentia prima* was a sauropodomorph that lived in the Late Triassic in what is now Argentina.
- *Ingentia* was about 30 ft (10 m) long.
- *Ingentia* had many hollow bones in the neck, probably to help reduce weight.
- The genus name *Ingentia* means "huge one."
- The species name *prima* means "first."

 Find out more in the I Know Dino *podcast, episode 189, "Lamaceratops."*

Lucianovenator bonoi

- *Lucianovenator bonoi* was a coelophysid neotheropod that lived in the Triassic in what is now San Juan Province, Argentina.
- *Lucianovenator* had a long neck and was skinny and generally small, weighing about 90 lb (40 kg). The dinosaur was also quick and carnivorous.
- *Lucianovenator* was going to be named *Lucianosaurus*, but that name was already taken.
- The genus name *Lucianovenator* means "Luciano's hunter" and is in honor of Luciano Leyes, who reported finding the fossils.
- The species name *bonoi* is in honor of Tulio Abel del Bono, who helped get funding for the dinosaur's excavation.

 Find out more in the I Know Dino *podcast, episode 131, "Gryposaurus."*

Macrocollum itaquii

- *Macrocollum itaquii* was a sauropodomorph that lived in the Late Triassic in what is now Brazil.
- *Macrocollum* is the oldest known long-necked sauropod.
- *Macrocollum* was found in 2012 by Estefânia Temp Müller. She called her paleontologist son Rodrigo to tell him that his uncle had found fossils on his rural property.
- The genus name *Macrocollum* means "long neck."
- The species name *itaquii* is in honor of José Jerundino Machado Itaqui, who helped found the Center for Paleontological Research.

 Find out more in the I Know Dino *podcast, episode 212, "Wuerhosaurus."*

Padillasaurus leivaensis

- *Padillasaurus leivaensis* was a brachiosaurid that lived in the Cretaceous, in what is now Colombia, in the Paja Formation.
- Before *Padillasaurus* was found, only fragments of brachiosaurid fossils had been found in South America, and those fragments were from the Jurassic.
- *Padillasaurus* was medium sized, probably weighing about 10 tons, and was 52-59 ft (16-18 m) long.
- The holotype of *Padillasaurus* is probably of an adult, which is not large for a sauropod. Scientists think this may be because it lived on an island.
- The genus name *Padillasaurus* is in honor of Carlos Padilla Bernardo Bernal, a molecular biologist who co-founded the Center for Paleontological Research in Colombia. The species name *leivaensis* is in honor of Villa de Leyva, the town near where the fossils were found.

Pandoravenator fernandezorum

- *Pandoravenator fernandezorum* was a theropod that lived in the Jurassic in what is now Chubut Province in Patagonia, Argentina.
- *Pandoravenator* was the first Late Jurassic theropod found in Argentina.
- Scientists found tail vertebrae and part of a foot. No *Pandoravenator* skull was found.
- The genus name *Pandoravenator* means "Pandora hunter."
- The species name *fernandezorum* is in honor of the Fernández family, including Daniel Fernández, the late Victoriano Fernández and his daughters and sons (especially Abel), who have helped the Museo Paleontológico Egidio Feruglio for more than 20 years.

Find out more in the I Know Dino *podcast, episode 158, "Camarasaurus."*

Patagotitan mayorum

- *Patagotitan mayorum* was a titanosaur that lived in the Cretaceous in what is now Chubut Province, Patagonia, Argentina.
- A *Patagotitan* replica is on display at the American Museum of Natural History in New York City, United States.
- *Patagotitan* is estimated to be 120 ft (36.5 m) long and weigh 69 tonnes, which may make it the largest land animal, though there is a "±17 tonnes standard error."
- The genus name *Patagotitan* means "Patagonian giant."
- The species name *mayorum* is in honor of the Mayo family for their hospitality during fieldwork at the "La Flecha" ranch.

 Find out more in the I Know Dino *podcast, episode 142, "Alxasaurus."*

Pilmatueia faundezi

- *Pilmatueia faundezi* was a dicraeosaurid sauropod that lived in the Early Cretaceous in what is now Patagonia, Argentina.
- *Pilmatueia* is the earliest known dicraeosaurid from the Cretaceous. Dicraeosauridae is a family of diplodocoids that include *Amargasaurus*.
- *Pilmatueia* had tall spines.
- The genus name *Pilmatueia* refers to the Pilmatué area of Argentina (in Patagonia).
- The species name *faundezi* is in honor of Ramón Faúndez, the manager of the Museo Municipal de Las Lajas, who supported the project.

 Find out more in the I Know Dino *podcast, episode 198, "Alectrosaurus."*

Powellvenator podocitus

- *Powellvenator podocitus* was a coelophysoid neotheropod that lived in the Triassic in what is now La Rioja, Argentina.
- *Powellvenator* was small, quick, and bipedal.
- *Powellvenator* fossils were previously thought to be coelurosaurian and pseudosuchian (a crocodile-like body with dinosaur limbs).
- The genus name *Powellvenator* is in honor of Jaime Eduardo Powell, an Argentine paleontologist.
- The species name *podocitus* means "fast foot" in Latin.

 Find out more in the I Know Dino *podcast, episode 154, "Protoceratops."*

Taurovenator violantei

- *Taurovenator violantei* was a carcharodontosaurid that lived in the Cretaceous in what is now Argentina.
- Only one bone has been found so far of *Taurovenator*: an isolated right postorbital.
- *Taurovenator* had a horn-like structure in its brow.
- The genus name *Taurovenator* means "bull hunter."
- The species name *violantei* is in honor of Enzo Violante, who owned the farm where *Taurovenator* was found.

Thanos simonattoi

- *Thanos simonattoi* was an abelisaur that lived in the Late Cretaceous in what is now Brazil.
- *Thanos* is similar to the carnivorous theropod *Carnotaurus*.
- Based on the single partial vertebra found, *Thanos* was about 18 to 21 ft (5.5 to 6.5 m) long.
- The genus name *Thanos* refers to the Marvel super villain Thanos. *Thanos* is also derived from thánato, which means "death" in Greek.
- The species name *simonattoi* is in honor of Sérgio Simonatto, who found the fossil in 1995.

Find out more in the I Know Dino *podcast, episode 211, "Dracopelta."*

Triunfosaurus leonardii

- *Triunfosaurus leonardii* was a titanosaur that lived in the Cretaceous in what is now northeastern Brazil.
- *Triunfosaurus* lived in the very Early Cretaceous, which makes it potentially the oldest known titanosaur.
- No skull was found, but *Triunfosaurus* is considered to be closely related to *Argentinosaurus* and *Malawisaurus*.
- The genus name *Triunfosaurus* refers to the Triunfo Basin where the dinosaur was found. The Triunfo Basin is mostly known for tracks and tends to preserve bones poorly.
- The species name *leonardii* is in honor of Giuseppe Leonardi, a local paleontologist.

 Find out more in the I Know Dino *podcast, episode 116, "Miragaia."*

Viavenator exxoni

- *Viavenator exxoni* was an abelisaurid that lived in the Cretaceous in what is now Argentina.
- The holotype was about 18 ft (5.5 m) long.
- *Viavenator* probably hunted small- to medium-sized dinosaurs.
- *Viavenator* may have been a transitional dinosaur that links earlier and later abelisaurids.
- The genus name *Viavenator* means "road hunter."

 Find out more in the I Know Dino *podcast, episode 152, "Plateosaurus."*

Resources

Africa

Ledumahadi mafube

- "A Giant Dinosaur from the Earliest Jurassic of South Africa and the Transition to Quadrupedality in Early Sauropodomorphs" on Current Biology (*https://www.cell.com/current-biology/fulltext/S0960-9822(18)30993-X*)

- "Ledumahadi mafube—South Africa's new jurassic giant" on Phys.org (*https://phys.org/news/2018-09-ledumahadi-mafubesouth-africa-jurassic-giant.html*)

Sefapanosaurus zastronensis

- "A new basal sauropodiform from South Africa and the phylogenetic relationships of basal sauropodomorphs" on the Zoological Journal of the Linnean Society (*https://onlinelibrary.wiley.com/doi/abs/10.1111/zoj.12247*)

- "Sefapanosaurus: New Dinosaur Found in South Africa" on Sci-News (*http://www.sci-news.com/paleontology/science-sefapanosaurus-dinosaur-south-africa-02963.html*)

Spinosaurus aegyptiacus

- "Semiaquatic adaptations in a giant predatory dinosaur" on Science (*https://science.sciencemag.org/content/345/6204/1613*)
- "Spinosaurus: The Largest Carnivorous Dinosaur" on Live Science (*https://www.livescience.com/24120-spinosaurus.html*)

More Dinosaurs From Africa

Afromimus tenerensis

- "Early Cretaceous Ornithomimosaurs (Dinosauria: Coelurosauria) From Africa" on Ameghiniana (*http://www.ameghiniana.org.ar/index.php/ameghiniana/article/view/3155*)

Chenanisaurus barbaricus

- "An abelisaurid from the latest Cretaceous (late Maastrichtian) of Morocco, North Africa" on ScienceDirect's Cretaceous Research (*https://www.sciencedirect.com/science/article/pii/S0195667116303706*)

Eucnemesaurus entaxonis

- "A second species of Eucnemesaurus Van Hoepen, 1920 (Dinosauria, Sauropodomorpha): new information on the diversity and evolution of the sauropodomorph fauna of South Africa's lower Elliot Formation (latest Triassic)" on Journal of Vertebrate Paleontology (*https://www.tandfonline.com/doi/full/10.1080/02724634.2015.980504*)
- "New dinosaurs from South Africa shed light on evolution of giant

plant-eaters" on Science Recorder (*https://www.sciencerecorder. com/news/2015/09/18/new-dinosaurs-south-africa-shed-light-evolution-giant-plant-eaters/*)

Mansourasaurus shahinae

🦕 "New Egyptian sauropod reveals Late Cretaceous dinosaur dispersal between Europe and Africa" in Nature Ecology & Evolution (*https://www.nature.com/articles/s41559-017-0455-5*)

Meroktenos thabanensis

🦕 "New material and revision of Melanorosaurus thabanensis, a basal sauropodomorph from the Upper Triassic of Lesotho" on PeerJ (*https://peerj.com/articles/1639/*)

Pulanesaura eocollum

🦕 "A new basal sauropod from the pre-Toarcian Jurassic of South Africa: evidence of niche-partitioning at the sauropodomorph–sauropod boundary?" on Nature (*https://www.nature.com/articles/srep13224*)

Shingopana songwensis

🦕 "The second titanosaurian (Dinosauria: Sauropoda) from the middle Cretaceous Galula Formation, southwestern Tanzania, with remarks on African titanosaurian diversity" on Journal of Vertebrate Paleontology (*https://www.tandfonline.com/doi/full/10.1080/02724634.2017.1343250*)

Antarctica

Morrosaurus antarcticus

- "A new ornithopod (Dinosauria, Ornithischia) from the Upper Cretaceous of Antarctica and its palaeobiogeographical implications" on Cretaceous Research *(https://www.sciencedirect.com/science/article/pii/S0195667115300677)*

- "New plant-eating dinosaur discovered in Antarctica" on Science Recorder (*https://www.sciencerecorder.com/news/2015/10/01/new-plant-eating-dinosaur-discovered-antarctica/*)

Asia

Bayannurosaurus perfectus

- "A large-sized basal ankylopollexian from East Asia, shedding light on early biogeographic history of Iguanodontia" on Science Bulletin (*https://www.sciencedirect.com/science/article/pii/S2095927318301580?via%3Dihub*)

- "Bayannurosaurus" on Wikipedia (*https://en.wikipedia.org/wiki/Bayannurosaurus*)

Caihong juji

- "A bony-crested Jurassic dinosaur with evidence of iridescent plumage highlights complexity in early paravian evolution" on Nature Communications (*https://www.nature.com/articles/s41467-017-02515-y*)

- "New 'Rainbow' Dinosaur May Have Sparkled Like a Hummingbird" on National Geographic (*https://news.nationalgeographic.com/2018/01/new-dinosaur-rainbow-feathers-china-caihong-paleontology-science/*)

Changyuraptor yangi
- "A new raptorial dinosaur with exceptionally long feathering provides insights into dromaeosaurid flight performance" on Nature (*https://www.nature.com/articles/ncomms5382*)
- "Bizarre Dinosaur Had 4 'Wings,' Long Tail Feathers" on Live Science (*https://www.livescience.com/46803-changyuraptor-yangi-dinosaur-longest-feathers.html*)

Corythoraptor jacobsi
- "High diversity of the Ganzhou Oviraptorid Fauna increased by a new 'cassowary-like' crested species" on Nature's Scientific Reports (*https://www.nature.com/articles/s41598-017-05016-6*)
- "Newfound Dino Looks Like the Creepy Love Child of a Turkey and an Ostrich" on Live Science (*https://www.livescience.com/59958-newfound-dinosaur-has-cassowary-like-crest.html*)

Datonglong tianzhenensis
- "A new hadrosauroid dinosaur from the Late Cretaceous of Tianzhen, Shanxi Province, China" on Vertebrata PalAsiatica (*http://www.ivpp.cas.cn/cbw/gjzdwxb/xbwzxz/201602/*

P020160229559242531386.pdf)

🦕 "New hadrosauroid dinosaur found from the late Cretaceous of Shanxi, China" on Phys.org (*https://phys.org/news/2016-03-hadrosauroid-dinosaur-late-cretaceous-shanxi.html*)

Deinocheirus mirificus

🦕 "Resolving the long-standing enigmas of a giant ornithomimosaur Deinocheirus mirificus" on Nature (*https://www.nature.com/articles/nature13874*)

🦕 "Deinocheirus Exposed: Meet the Body Behind the Terrible Hand" on Phenomena, National Geographic (*https://www.nationalgeographic.com/environment/great-energy-challenge/*)

Fukuivenator paradoxus

🦕 "A bizarre theropod from the Early Cretaceous of Japan highlighting mosaic evolution among coelurosaurians" on Nature (*https://www.nature.com/articles/srep20478#f1*)

🦕 "Seventh new dinosaur discovery confirmed in Japan" on Japan Times (*https://www.japantimes.co.jp/article-expired/#.WILuPbYrIk-*)

Halszkaraptor escuilliei

🦕 "Synchrotron scanning reveals amphibious ecomorphology in a new clade of bird-like dinosaurs" on Nature (*https://www.nature.com/articles/nature24679*)

🦕 "Duck-Like Dinosaur Is Among Oddest Fossils Yet Found"

on National Geographic (*https://news.nationalgeographic. com/2017/12/duck-dinosaur-amphibious-halszkaraptor-fossil- mongolia-science/*)

Kulindadromeus zabaikalicus

- "A Jurassic ornithischian dinosaur from Siberia with both feathers and scales" in Science (*https://science.sciencemag.org/ content/345/6195/451*)

- "Siberian Discovery Suggests Almost All Dinosaurs Were Feathered" on National Geographic (*https://news. nationalgeographic.com/news/2014/07/140724-feathered- siberia-dinosaur-scales-science/*)

Qianzhousaurus sinensis

- "A new clade of Asian Late Cretaceous long-snouted tyrannosaurids" on Nature (*https://www.nature.com/articles/ ncomms4788*)

- "Long-snouted tyrannosaur unearthed" on Nature (*https:// www.nature.com/news/long-snouted-tyrannosaur- unearthed-1.15159*)

Qiupanykus zhangi

- "A new alvarezsaurid dinosaur from the Late Cretaceous Qiupa Formation of Luanchuan, Henan Province, central China" on China Geology (*http://chinageology.cgs.cn/article/ doi/10.31035/cg2018005?pageType=cn*)

- "Qiupanykus" on Wikipedia (*https://en.wikipedia.org/wiki/Qiupanykus*)

Serikornis sungei

- "A new Jurassic theropod from China documents a transitional step in the macrostructure of feathers" on The Science of Nature (*https://link.springer.com/article/10.1007/s00114-017-1496-y*)
- "New Feathered Dinosaur Had Four Wings but Couldn't Fly" on National Geographic (*https://news.nationalgeographic.com/2017/08/feathered-dinosaur-four-wings-species-serikornis-science/*)

Tongtianlong limosus

- "A Late Cretaceous diversification of Asian oviraptorid dinosaurs: evidence from a new species preserved in an unusual posture" on Nature (*https://www.nature.com/articles/srep35780*)
- "'Mud Dragon' Dinosaur Unearthed—By Dynamite" on National Geographic (*https://news.nationalgeographic.com/2016/11/dinosaur-oviraptorosaurs-extinction-fossil-birds-mud-dragon/*)

Yi qi

- "A bizarre Jurassic maniraptoran theropod with preserved evidence of membranous wings" on Nature (*https://www.nature.com/articles/nature14423*)
- "Yi qi Is Neat but Might Not Have Been the Black Screaming

Dino-Dragon of Death" on Scientific American (*https://blogs. scientificamerican.com/tetrapod-zoology/yi-qi-is-neat-but-might-not-have-been-the-black-screaming-dino-dragon-of-death/*)

Zhenyuanlong suni

- "A large, short-armed, winged dromaeosaurid (Dinosauria: Theropoda) from the Early Cretaceous of China and its implications for feather evolution" on Nature (*https://www.nature.com/articles/srep11775*)
- "Paleo Profile: Zhenyuanlong suni" on National Geographic (*https://www.nationalgeographic.com/environment/great-energy-challenge/*)

More Dinosaurs From Asia

Aepyornithomimus tugrikinensis

- "First Ornithomimid (Theropoda, Ornithomimosauria) from the Upper Cretaceous Djadokhta Formation of Tögrögiin Shiree, Mongolia" on Nature's Scientific Reports (*https://www.nature.com/articles/s41598-017-05272-6*)

Almas ukhaa

- "Osteology of a new late Cretaceous troodontid specimen from Ukhaa Tolgod, Ömnögovi Aimag, Mongolia." on American Museum of Natural History Research Library (*http://digitallibrary.amnh.org/handle/2246/6818*)

Anhuilong diboensis

🦕 "The second mamenchisaurid dinosaur from the Middle Jurassic of Eastern China" in Historical Biology (*https://www.tandfonline.com/doi/full/10.1080/08912963.2018.1515935*)

Anomalipes zhaoi

🦕 "A new caenagnathid dinosaur from the Upper Cretaceous Wangshi Group of Shandong, China, with comments on size variation among oviraptorosaurs" in Scientific Reports (*https://www.nature.com/articles/s41598-018-23252-2*)

Avimimus nemegtensis

🦕 "Oviraptorosaur anatomy, diversity and ecology in the Nemegt Basin" in Palaeogeography, Palaeoclimatology, Palaeoecology (*https://www.sciencedirect.com/science/article/pii/S0031018217306065?via%3Dihub*)

Bannykus wulatensis

🦕 "Two Early Cretaceous Fossils Document Transitional Stages in Alvarezsaurian Dinosaur Evolution" on Current Biology (*https://www.cell.com/current-biology/fulltext/S0960-9822(18)30987-4*)

Beibeilong sinensis

🦕 "Perinate and eggs of a giant caenagnathid dinosaur from the Late Cretaceous of central China" on Nature Communications

(https://www.nature.com/articles/ncomms14952)

Beipiaognathus jii

- "A new species of compsognathid from the Early Cretaceous Yixian Formation of western Liaoning, China" on CNKI (http://en.cnki.com.cn/Article_en/CJFDTotal-JSDZ201602029.htm)
- "Beipiaognathus" on Wikipedia (https://en.wikipedia.org/wiki/Beipiaognathus)

Choyrodon barsboldi

- "A new iguanodontian (Dinosauria: Ornithopoda) from the Early Cretaceous of Mongolia" in PeerJ (https://peerj.com/articles/5300/)

Crichtonpelta benxiensis

- "Systematics, phylogeny and palaeobiogeography of the ankylosaurid dinosaurs" on Journal of Systematic Palaeontology (https://www.tandfonline.com/doi/full/10.1080/14772019.2015.1059985)

Daliansaurus liaoningensis

- "A New Troodontid Dinosaur from the Lower Cretaceous Yixian Formation of Liaoning Province, China" on Acta Geologica Sinica (http://www.geojournals.cn/dzxben/ch/reader/view_abstract.aspx?file_no=2017endzxb03001&flag=1)

Hualianceratops wucaiwanensis

- "A New Taxon of Basal Ceratopsian from China and the Early

Evolution of Ceratopsia" on PLOS One (*https://journals.plos.org/plosone/article?id=10.1371/journal.pone.0143369*)

Huanansaurus ganzhouensis

🦕 "A New Oviraptorid Dinosaur (Dinosauria: Oviraptorosauria) from the Late Cretaceous of Southern China and Its Paleobiogeographical Implications" on Nature (*https://www.nature.com/articles/srep11490*)

Ischioceratops zhuchengensis

🦕 "A New Leptoceratopsid (Ornithischia, Ceratopsia) with a Unique Ischium from the Upper Cretaceous of Shandong Province, China" on PLOS One (*https://journals.plos.org/plosone/article?id=10.1371/journal.pone.0144148*)

Jianianhualong tengi

🦕 "Mosaic evolution in an asymmetrically feathered troodontid dinosaur with transitional features" on Nature Communications (*https://www.nature.com/articles/ncomms14972*)

Jinguofortis perplexus

🦕 "A new clade of basal Early Cretaceous pygostylian birds and developmental plasticity of the avian shoulder girdle" in Proceedings of the National Academy of Sciences of the United States of America (*https://www.pnas.org/content/115/42/10708*)

Jinyunpelta sinensis

🦕 "The most basal ankylosaurine dinosaur from the Albian–Cenomanian of China, with implications for the evolution of the tail club" in Scientific Reports (*https://www.nature.com/articles/s41598-018-21924-7*)

Koshisaurus katsuyama

🦕 "New basal hadrosauroid (Dinosauria: Ornithopoda) from the Lower Cretaceous Kitadani Formation, Fukui, central Japan" on BioTaxa (*https://biotaxa.org/Zootaxa/article/view/zootaxa.3914.4.3*)

🦕 "Koshisaurus" on Wikipedia (*https://en.wikipedia.org/wiki/Koshisaurus*)

Laiyangosaurus youngi

🦕 "A new saurolophine hadrosaurid (Dinosauria: Ornithopoda) from the Upper Cretaceous of Shandong, China" on Anais da Academia Brasileira de Ciências (*http://www.scielo.br/scielo.php?script=sci_arttext&pid=S0001-37652017005020113*)

Lepidocheirosaurus natatilis

🦕 "The most ancient Ornithomimosaur (Theropoda, Dinosauria), with cover imprints from the Upper Jurassic of Russia" on Paleontological Journal (*https://link.springer.com/article/10.1134%2FS0031030115060039*)

🦕 "The rise of feathered dinosaurs: Kulindadromeus zabaikalicus, the oldest dinosaur with 'feather-like' structures" on PeerJ

(*https://www.researchgate.net/publication/330808943_The_rise_of_feathered_dinosaurs_Kulindadromeus_zabaikalicus_the_oldest_dinosaur_with_'feather-like'_structures*)

Liaoningotitan sinensis

🦕 "A new titanosauriformes dinosaur from Jehol Biota of western Liaoning, China" in Global Geology (*http://sjdz.jlu.edu.cn/EN/abstract/abstract9375.shtml*)

Liaoningvenator curriei

🦕 "A New Troodontid Dinosaur (Liaoningvenator curriei gen. et sp. nov.) from the Early Cretaceous Yixian Formation in Western Liaoning Province" on Acta Geoscientica Sinica (*http://www.cagsbulletin.com/dqxben/ch/reader/view_abstract.aspx?file_no=20170306&flag=1*)

Lingwulong shenqi

🦕 "A new Middle Jurassic diplodocoid suggests an earlier dispersal and diversification of sauropod dinosaurs" in Nature Communications (*https://www.nature.com/articles/s41467-018-05128-1*)

Microenantiornis vulgaris

🦕 "Discovery of a new enantiornithine bird from Lower Cretaceous of western Liaoning, China" in Global Geology (*https://www.xueshu.com/sjdz/201703/30282706.html*)

Mosaiceratops azumai

- "A psittacosaurid-like basal neoceratopsian from the Upper Cretaceous of central China and its implications for basal ceratopsian evolution" on Nature (*https://www.nature.com/articles/srep14190*)
- "Mosaiceratops" on Wikipedia (*https://en.wikipedia.org/wiki/Mosaiceratops*)

Nebulasaurus taito

- "A new basal eusauropod from the Middle Jurassic of Yunnan, China, and faunal compositions and transitions of Asian sauropodomorph dinosaurs" on ACTA Paleontologica Polonica (*https://www.app.pan.pl/article/item/app20120151.html*)
- "Nebulasaurus" on Wikipedia (*https://en.wikipedia.org/wiki/Nebulasaurus*)

Qijianglong guokr

- "A new sauropod dinosaur from the Late Jurassic of China and the diversity, distribution, and relationships of mamenchisaurids" on Journal of Vertebrate Paleontology (*http://www.xinglida.net/pdf/Xing_et_al_2015_Qijianglong.pdf*)
- "Long-necked 'dragon' discovered in China" on University of Alberta (*https://www.folio.ca/long-necked-dragon-discovered-in-china*)

Shuangbaisaurus anlongbaoensis

- "A new crested theropod dinosaur from the Early Jurassic of

Yunnan Province, China" on Institute of Vertebrate Paleontology and Paleoanthropology (*https://www.researchgate.net/publication/316776056_A_new_crested_theropod_dinosaur_from_the_Early_Jurassic_of_Yunnan_Province_China*)

Sibirotitan astrosacralis

- "A new sauropod dinosaur from the Lower Cretaceous Ilek Formation, Western Siberia, Russia" in Geobios (*https://www.sciencedirect.com/science/article/pii/S0016699517301080*)

Sirindhorna khoratensis

- "A New Basal Hadrosauroid Dinosaur from the Lower Cretaceous Khok Kruat Formation in Nakhon Ratchasima Province, Northeastern Thailand" on PLOS One (*https://journals.plos.org/plosone/article?id=10.1371/journal.pone.0145904*)

Tarchia teresae

- "The cranial morphology and taxonomic status of Tarchia (Dinosauria: Ankylosauridae) from the Upper Cretaceous of Mongolia" on Cretaceous Research (*https://www.sciencedirect.com/science/article/pii/S0195667116302646*)

Tengrisaurus starkovi

- "A new lithostrotian titanosaur (Dinosauria, Sauropoda) from the Early Cretaceous of Transbaikalia, Russia" on Biological Communications (*https://www.researchgate.net/publication/316685161_A_new_lithostrotian_titanosaur_*

Dinosauria_Sauropoda_from_the_Early_Cretaceous_of_Transbaikalia_Russia)

Timurlengia euotica

🦕 "New tyrannosaur from the mid-Cretaceous of Uzbekistan clarifies evolution of giant body sizes and advanced senses in tyrant dinosaurs" on Proceedings of the National Academy of Sciences in the United States of America (*https://www.pnas.org/content/113/13/3447.abstract*)

Xingxiulong chengi

🦕 "A new basal sauropodiform dinosaur from the Lower Jurassic of Yunnan Province, China" on Scientific Reports (*https://www.nature.com/articles/srep41881*)

Xiyunykus pengi

🦕 "Two Early Cretaceous Fossils Document Transitional Stages in Alvarezsaurian Dinosaur Evolution" on Current Biology (*https://www.cell.com/current-biology/fulltext/S0960-9822(18)30987-4*)

Yangavis confucii

🦕 "A new confuciusornithid (Aves: Pygostylia) from the Early Cretaceous increases the morphological disparity of the Confuciusornithidae" in Zoological Journal of the Linnean Society (*https://academic.oup.com/zoolinnean/article-abstract/185/2/417/5066665?redirectedFrom=fulltext*)

Yizhousaurus sunae

🦕 "A new sauropodiform dinosaur with a 'sauropodan' skull from the Lower Jurassic Lufeng Formation of Yunnan Province, China" in Scientific Reports (*https://www.nature.com/articles/s41598-018-31874-9*)

Zhongjianosaurus yangi

🦕 "A new tiny dromaeosaurid dinosaur from the Lower Cretaceous Jehol Group of western Liaoning and niche differentiation among the Jehol dromaeosaurids" on Institute of Vertebrate Paleontology and Paleoanthropology (PDF) (*http://www.ivpp.cas.cn/cbw/gjzdwxb/xbwzxz/201704/P020170427357657919644.pdf*)

Zhuchengtitan zangjiazhuangensis

🦕 "A new titanosaurian sauropod from the Late Cretaceous strata of Shandong Province" on Geological Bulletin of China (*http://en.cnki.com.cn/Article_en/CJFDTOTAL-ZQYD201709001.htm*)

Zuoyunlong huangi

🦕 "A second hadrosauroid dinosaur from the early Late Cretaceous of Zuoyun, Shanxi Province, China" on Taylor & Francis Online (*https://www.tandfonline.com/doi/abs/10.1080/08912963.2015.1118688?journalCode=ghbi20*)

Australia

Diluvicursor pickeringi

- "A new small-bodied ornithopod (Dinosauria, Ornithischia) from a deep, high-energy Early Cretaceous river of the Australian–Antarctic rift system" on PeerJ (*https://peerj.com/articles/4113/*)
- "Tiny dinosaur that roamed 'lost world' between Australia and Antarctica identified" on The Guardian (*https://www.theguardian.com/science/2018/jan/14/tiny-dinosaur-that-roamed-lost-world-between-australia-and-antarctica-identified*)

Kunbarrasaurus ieversi

- "Cranial osteology of the ankylosaurian dinosaur formerly known as Minmi sp. (Ornithischia: Thyreophora) from the Lower Cretaceous Allaru Mudstone of Richmond, Queensland, Australia" on PeerJ (*https://peerj.com/articles/1475/*)
- "Australia's new armoured dinosaur revealed" on University of Queensland News (*https://www.uq.edu.au/news/article/2015/12/australia%E2%80%99s-new-armoured-dinosaur-revealed*)

Weewarrasaurus pobeni

- "Ornithopod diversity in the Griman Creek Formation (Cenomanian), New South Wales, Australia" in PeerJ (*https://peerj.com/articles/6008/*)
- "First dinosaur named in NSW in nearly a century after chance discovery" on ABC News (*https://www.abc.net.au/news/2018-*

12-05/weewarra-dinosaur/10583990)

More Dinosaurs From Australia

Savannasaurus elliottorum

- 🦕 "New Australian sauropods shed light on Cretaceous dinosaur palaeobiogeography" on Nature (*https://www.nature.com/articles/srep34467*)

Europe

Dracoraptor hanigani

- 🦕 "The Oldest Jurassic Dinosaur: A Basal Neotheropod from the Hettangian of Great Britain" on PLOS One (*https://journals.plos.org/plosone/article?id=10.1371/journal.pone.0145713*)

- 🦕 "Wales Gets A New Dragon With 200 Million-Year-Old Dinosaur Discovery" on Forbes (*https://www.forbes.com/sites/shaenamontanari/2016/01/20/wales-gets-a-new-dragon-with-200-million-year-old-dinosaur-discovery/#7992b36b461d*)

Morelladon beltrani

- 🦕 "A New Sail-Backed Styracosternan (Dinosauria: Ornithopoda) from the Early Cretaceous of Morella, Spain" on PLOS One (*https://journals.plos.org/plosone/article?id=10.1371/journal.pone.0144167*)

- 🦕 "Dinosaur's Curious Back Sail May Have Aided Migration" on Live Science (*https://www.livescience.com/53122-sail-back-dinosaur-discovered.html*)

Ostromia crassipes

- "Re-evaluation of the Haarlem Archaeopteryx and the radiation of maniraptoran theropod dinosaurs" on BMC Evolutionary Biology (*https://bmcevolbiol.biomedcentral.com/articles/10.1186/s12862-017-1076-y*)
- "Have we lost an Archaeopteryx but gained a new species of theropod dinosaur?" on The Guardian (*https://www.theguardian.com/science/2017/dec/06/archaeopteryx-new-species-therapod-dinosaur-ostromia-crassipes*)

Torvosaurus gurneyi

- "Torvosaurus gurneyi n. sp., the Largest Terrestrial Predator from Europe, and a Proposed Terminology of the Maxilla Anatomy in Nonavian Theropods" on PLOS One (*https://journals.plos.org/plosone/article?id=10.1371/journal.pone.0088905*)
- "Largest Predatory Dinosaur in Europe Found, Was 'Big Bruiser'" on National Geographic (*https://news.nationalgeographic.com/news/2014/03/140305-dinosaurs-biggest-europe-torvosaurus-gurneyi-animals-science/*)

More Dinosaurs From Europe

Adynomosaurus arcanus

- "Adynomosaurus arcanus, a new lambeosaurine dinosaur from the Late Cretaceous Ibero-Armorican Island of the European archipelago" in Cretaceous Research (*https://www.sciencedirect.*

com/science/article/pii/S0195667118303227)

Burianosaurus augustai

- "A basal ornithopod dinosaur from the Cenomanian of the Czech Republic" on Journal of Systematic Palaeontology (*https://www.tandfonline.com/doi/full/10.1080/14772019.2017.1371258*)

- "First Cenomanian dinosaur from Central Europe (Czech Republic)" on Acta Palaeontologica Polonica (PDF) (*http://agro.icm.edu.pl/agro/element/bwmeta1.element.agro-article-4cb3cc29-d9b1-4499-bcdc-be3ca25277f4/c/app50-295.pdf*)

Europatitan eastwoodi

- "Europatitan eastwoodi, a new sauropod from the lower Cretaceous of Iberia in the initial radiation of somphospondylans in Laurasia" on PeerJ (*https://peerj.com/articles/3409/*)

Haestasaurus becklesii

- "The Anatomy and Phylogenetic Relationships of 'Pelorosaurus' becklesii (Neosauropoda, Macronaria) from the Early Cretaceous of England" on PLOS One (*https://journals.plos.org/plosone/article?id=10.1371/journal.pone.0125819*)

Horshamosaurus rudgwickensis

- "A New British Dinosaur is Announced – Horshamosaurus" on Everything Dinosaur (*https://blog.everythingdinosaur.co.uk/blog/_archives/2015/09/08/a-new-british-dinosaur-is-*

announced-horshamosaurus.html)

🦕 "Horshamosaurus" on Wikipedia (*https://en.wikipedia.org/wiki/Horshamosaurus*)

Iguanodon galvensis

🦕 "Perinates of a new species of Iguanodon (Ornithischia: Ornithopoda) from the lower Barremian of Galve (Teruel, Spain)" on Science Direct (*https://www.sciencedirect.com/science/article/pii/S019566711530001X*)

Lohuecotitan pandafilandi

🦕 "A new titanosaur (Dinosauria, Sauropoda) from the Upper Cretaceous of Lo Hueco (Cuenca, Spain)" on Cretaceous Research (*https://www.sciencedirect.com/science/article/pii/S0195667116301513*)

🦕 "Paleo Profile: The Lo Hueco Titan" on Scientific American (*https://blogs.scientificamerican.com/laelaps/paleo-profile-the-lo-hueco-titan/*)

Magnamanus soriaensis

🦕 "Un Nuevo dinosaurio estiracosterno (Ornithopoda: Ankylopollexia) del Cretácico Inferior de España" on Dialnet (*https://dialnet.unirioja.es/servlet/articulo?codigo=5799188*)

🦕 "Soria ya tiene su dinosaurio" on Soria Noticias (*http://sorianoticias.com/noticia/2017-02-01-soria-ya-tiene-su-dinosaurio-37276*)

Matheronodon provincialis

🦕 "Extreme tooth enlargement in a new Late Cretaceous rhabdodontid dinosaur from Southern France" on Nature's Scientific Reports (*https://www.nature.com/articles/s41598-017-13160-2*)

Saltriovenator zanellai

🦕 "The oldest ceratosaurian (Dinosauria: Theropoda), from the Lower Jurassic of Italy, sheds light on the evolution of the three-fingered hand of birds" on PeerJ (*https://peerj.com/articles/5976/*)

Soriatitan golmayensis

🦕 "A new Brachiosauridae Sauropod dinosaur from the lower Cretaceous of Europe (Soria Province, Spain)" on Cretaceous Research (*https://www.sciencedirect.com/science/article/pii/S0195667117301325*)

Volgatitan simbirskiensis

🦕 "The oldest titanosaurian sauropod of the Northern Hemisphere" in Biological Communications (*https://biocomm.spbu.ru/article/view/1077*)

Vouivria damparisensis

🦕 "The earliest known titanosauriform sauropod dinosaur and the evolution of Brachiosauridae" on PeerJ (*https://peerj.com/articles/3217/*)

Wiehenvenator albati

- "A new megalosaurid theropod dinosaur from the late Middle Jurassic (Callovian) of north-western Germany: implications for theropod evolution and faunal turnover in the Jurassic" on Paleontologica Electronica (*https://palaeo-electronica.org/content/2016/1536-german-jurassic-megalosaurid*)

North America

Anzu wyliei

- "A New Large-Bodied Oviraptorosaurian Theropod Dinosaur from the Latest Cretaceous of Western North America" on PLOS One (*https://journals.plos.org/plosone/article?id=10.1371/journal.pone.0092022*)
- "Scientists Discover a Large and Feathered Dinosaur that Once Roamed North America" on Smithsonian (*https://www.smithsonianmag.com/smithsonian-institution/scientists-discover-discover-large-feathered-dinosaur-once-roamed-north-america-180950130*)

Aquilops americanus

- "A Ceratopsian Dinosaur from the Lower Cretaceous of Western North America, and the Biogeography of Neoceratopsia" in PLOS One (*https://journals.plos.org/plosone/article?id=10.1371/journal.pone.0112055*)
- "Bunny-Size Dinosaur Was First Of Its Kind in America" on

National Geographic (*https://news.nationalgeographic.com/news/2014/12/141210-ceratopsian-aquilops-dinosaur-fossil-paleontology-science/*)

Arkansaurus fridayi

- "A new ornithomimosaur from the Lower Cretaceous Trinity Group of Arkansas" in Journal of Vertebrate Paleontology (*https://www.tandfonline.com/doi/abs/10.1080/02724634.2017.1421209?journalCode=ujvp20*)
- "NEW (really old dead) DINOSAUR!!! Arkansaurus fridayi" on dontmesswithdinosaurs.com (*http://dontmesswithdinosaurs.com/?p=2087*)

Borealopelta markmitchelli

- "An Exceptionally Preserved Three-Dimensional Armored Dinosaur Reveals Insights into Coloration and Cretaceous Predator-Prey Dynamics" on Current Biology (*https://www.cell.com/current-biology/fulltext/S0960-9822(17)30808-4*)
- "It's Official: Stunning Fossil Is a New Dinosaur Species" on National Geographic (*https://news.nationalgeographic.com/2017/08/nodosaur-dinosaur-fossil-study-borealopelta-coloration-science/*)

Dakotaraptor steini

- "The first giant raptor (Theropoda: Dromaeosauridae) from the Hell Creek Formation" on KU Paleontological Institute (*https://*

kuscholarworks.ku.edu/bitstream/handle/1808/18764/
DePalma%2014.pdf?sequence=3)

- "Did Dakotaraptor Really Face Off Against Tyrannosaurus?" on National Geographic (https://www.nationalgeographic.com/environment/great-energy-challenge/)

Daspletosaurus horneri

- "A new tyrannosaur with evidence for anagenesis and crocodile-like facial sensory system" on Nature's Scientific Reports (https://www.nature.com/articles/srep44942)

- "Discovery of new predatory dinosaur species gives new insight on their evolution" on ScienceDaily (https://www.sciencedaily.com/releases/2017/03/170330092838.htm)

Dynamoterror dynastes

- "A new tyrannosaurid (Dinosauria: Theropoda) from the Upper Cretaceous Menefee Formation of New Mexico" on PeerJ (https://peerj.com/articles/5749/)

- "A Terror Ruled The Menefee" on dontmesswithdinosaurs.com. (http://dontmesswithdinosaurs.com/?p=2167)

Galeamopus pabsti

- "Osteology of Galeamopus pabsti sp. nov. (Sauropoda: Diplodocidae), with implications for neurocentral closure timing, and the cervico-dorsal transition in diplodocids" on PeerJ (https://peerj.com/articles/3179/)

- "New species of dinosaur increases the already unexpected diversity of 'whiplash dinosaurs'" on Phys.org (*https://phys.org/news/2017-05-species-dinosaur-unexpected-diversity-whiplash.html*)

Nanuqsaurus hoglundi

- "A Diminutive New Tyrannosaur from the Top of the World" on PLOS One (*https://journals.plos.org/plosone/article?id=10.1371/journal.pone.0091287*)
- "New Pygmy Tyrannosaur Found, Roamed the Arctic" on National Geographic (*https://news.nationalgeographic.com/news/2014/03/140313-new-species-dinosaurs-tyrannosaurus-rex-animals-science/*)

Probrachylophosaurus bergi

- "A New Brachylophosaurin Hadrosaur (Dinosauria: Ornithischia) with an Intermediate Nasal Crest from the Campanian Judith River Formation of Northcentral Montana" on PLOS One (*https://journals.plos.org/plosone/article?id=10.1371/journal.pone.0141304*)
- "Getting a Head: 'Superduck' Dinosaur Shows How Dino Crests Evolved" on LiveScience (*https://www.livescience.com/52856-crested-duckbilled-dino-discovered.html*)

Rativates evadens

- "A new ornithomimid theropod from the Dinosaur Park

Formation of Alberta, Canada" on Journal of Vertebrate Paleontology (*https://www.tandfonline.com/doi/abs/10.1080/02724634.2016.1221415?journalCode=ujvp20&*)

🦕 "New Dinosaur Named for Ability to Evade Predators" on Cleveland Museum of Natural History (*https://www.cmnh.org/rativates*)

Regaliceratops peterhewsi

🦕 "A New Horned Dinosaur Reveals Convergent Evolution in Cranial Ornamentation in Ceratopsidae" on Current Biology (*https://www.cell.com/current-biology/fulltext/S0960-9822(15)00492-3*)

🦕 "Newly-Named Horned Dinosaur was a Copycat" on National Geographic (*https://www.nationalgeographic.com/environment/great-energy-challenge/*)

Spiclypeus shipporum

🦕 "Spiclypeus shipporum gen. et sp. nov., a Boldly Audacious New Chasmosaurine Ceratopsid (Dinosauria: Ornithischia) from the Judith River Formation (Upper Cretaceous: Campanian) of Montana, USA" on PLOS One (*https://journals.plos.org/plosone/article?id=10.1371%2Fjournal.pone.0154218*)

🦕 "New Frilly-Necked Dinosaur Identified" on Live Science (*https://www.livescience.com/54788-new-frilly-necked-dinosaur-identified.html*)

Tototlmimus packardensis

- "A new ornithomimid dinosaur from the Upper Cretaceous Packard Shale formation (Cabullona Group) Sonora, México" on Cretaceous Research (*https://www.sciencedirect.com/science/article/pii/S0195667115300562*)
- "Paleo Profile: Mexico's 'Bird Mimic'" on National Geographic (*https://www.nationalgeographic.com/environment/great-energy-challenge/*)

Yehuecauhceratops mudei

- "Mexican ceratopsids: Considerations on their diversity and biogeography" on ScienceDirect (*https://www.sciencedirect.com/science/article/pii/S0895981116302917*)
- "Paleo Profile: Mexico's Ancient Horned Face" on Scientific American (*https://blogs.scientificamerican.com/laelaps/paleo-profile-mexicos-ancient-horned-face/*)

Zuul crurivastator

- "A new ankylosaurine dinosaur from the Judith River Formation of Montana, USA, based on an exceptional skeleton with soft tissue preservation" on The Royal Society Publishing (*https://royalsocietypublishing.org/doi/full/10.1098/rsos.161086*)
- "Zuul, Destroyer of Shins" on Royal Ontario Museum (*https://www.rom.on.ca/en/collections-research/research-community-projects/zuul*)

More Dinosaurs From North America

Acantholipan gonazalezi

- "Paleodiversity of Late Cretaceous Ankylosauria from Mexico and their phylogenetic significance" in Swiss Journal of Palaeontology (*https://link.springer.com/article/10.1007/s13358-018-0153-1*)

Agujaceratops mavericus

- "New specimens of horned dinosaurs from the Aguja Formation of West Texas, and a revision of Agujaceratops" on Journal of Systematic Paleontology (*https://www.tandfonline.com/doi/abs/10.1080/14772019.2016.1210683?journalCode=tjsp20*)

- "Agujaceratops" on Wikipedia (*https://en.wikipedia.org/wiki/Agujaceratops*)

Akainacephalus johnsoni

- "A new southern Laramidian ankylosaurid, Akainacephalus johnsoni gen. et sp. nov., from the upper Campanian Kaiparowits Formation of southern Utah, USA" in PeerJ (*https://peerj.com/articles/5016/*)

Albertavenator curriei

- "A new species of troodontid theropod (Dinosauria: Maniraptora) from the Horseshoe Canyon Formation (Maastrichtian) of Alberta, Canada" on Canadian Journal of Earth Sciences (*https://www.nrcresearchpress.com/doi/10.1139/cjes-2017-0034#*.

XPIaVtNKgk9)

Alcovasaurus longispinus

- 🦕 "The plated dinosaur Stegosaurus longispinus Gilmore, 1914 (Dinosauria: Ornithischia; Upper Jurassic, western USA), type species of Alcovasaurus n. gen." on Neues Jahrbuch für Geologie und Paläontologie (*https://www.researchgate.net/publication/293328275_The_plated_dinosaur_Stegosaurus_longispinus_Gilmore_1914_Dinosauria_Ornithischia_Upper_Jurassic_western_USA_type_species_of_Alcovasaurus_n_gen*)
- 🦕 "Alcovasaurus" on Wikipedia (*https://en.wikipedia.org/wiki/Alcovasaurus*)

Anodontosaurus inceptus

- 🦕 "Revised systematics of the armoured dinosaur Euoplocephalus and its allies" in Neues Jahrbuch für Geologie und Paläontologie - Abhandlungen (*https://www.ingentaconnect.com/content/schweiz/njbgeol/2018/00000287/00000003/art00002*)
- 🦕 "Anodontosaurus" on Wikipedia (*https://en.wikipedia.org/wiki/Anodontosaurus*)

Apatoraptor pennatus

- 🦕 "A new caenagnathid (Dinosauria: Oviraptorosauria) from the Horseshoe Canyon Formation of Alberta, Canada, and a reevaluation of the relationships of Caenagnathidae" on Journal of Vertebrate Paleontology (*https://www.tandfonline.com/doi/abs*

/10.1080/02724634.2016.1160910?journalCode=ujvp20)

Boreonykus certekorum

- "A high-latitude dromaeosaurid, Boreonykus certekorum, gen. et sp. nov. (Theropoda), from the upper Campanian Wapiti Formation, west-central Alberta" on Journal of Vertebrate Paleontology (*https://www.tandfonline.com/doi/full/10.1080/02724634.2015.1034359*)

Crittendenceratops krzyzanowskii

- "A New Ceratopsid Dinosaur (Centrosaurinae: Nasutoceratopsini) From the Fort Crittenden Formation, Upper Cretaceous (Campanian) of Arizona" in the New Mexico Museum of Natural History and Science Bulletin (*https://www.researchgate.net/publication/328637301_A_NEW_CERATOPSID_DINOSAUR_CENTROSAURINAE_NASUTOCERATOPSINI_FROM_THE_FORT_CRITTENDEN_FORMATION_UPPER_CRETACEOUS_CAMPANIAN_OF_ARIZONA*)

Dryosaurus elderae

- "A Photo Documentation of Bipedal Ornithischian Dinosaurs from the Upper Jurassic Morrison Formation, USA" in Geology of the Intermountain West (*https://www.utahgeology.org/wp-content/uploads/2018/08/GIW2018-v05-pp167-107-Carpenter-print.pdf*)

Eotrachodon orientalis

- "A primitive hadrosaurid from southeastern North America and the origin and early evolution of 'duck-billed' dinosaurs" on Journal of Vertebrate Paleontology (*https://www.tandfonline.com/doi/abs/10.1080/02724634.2015.1054495?journalCode=ujvp20&*)

- "Anatomy and osteohistology of the basal hadrosaurid dinosaur Eotrachodon from the uppermost Santonian (Cretaceous) of southern Appalachia" on PeerJ (*https://peerj.com/articles/1872/*)

Foraminacephale brevis

- "Cranial variation and systematics of Foraminacephale brevis gen. nov. and the diversity of pachycephalosaurid dinosaurs (Ornithischia: Cerapoda) in the Belly River Group of Alberta, Canada" on Zoological Journal of the Linnean Society (*https://onlinelibrary.wiley.com/doi/abs/10.1111/zoj.12465*)

- "Foraminacephale" on Wikipedia *(https://en.wikipedia.org/wiki/Foraminacephale)*

Galeamopus hayi

- "A specimen-level phylogenetic analysis and taxonomic revision of Diplodocidae (Dinosauria, Sauropoda)" on PeerJ

Gastonia lorriemcwhinneyae

- "Redescription of Gastonia burgei (Dinosauria: Ankylosauria,

Polacanthidae), and description of a new species" on Neues Jahrbuch für Geologie und Paläontologie (*https://www.researchgate.net/publication/308878540_Redescription_of_Gastonia_burgei_Dinosauria_Ankylosauria_Polacanthidae_and_description_of_a_new_species*)

- "Gastonia (dinosaur)" on Wikipedia (*https://en.wikipedia.org/wiki/Gastonia_(dinosaur)*)

Gryposaurus alsatei

- "Hadrosaurian dinosaurs from the Maastrichtian Javelina Formation, Big Bend National Park, Texas" on Journal of Paleontology (*https://www.researchgate.net/publication/304364183_Hadrosaurian_dinosaurs_from_the_Maastrichtian_Javelina_Formation_Big_Bend_National_Park_Texas*)

Invictarx zephyri

- "A new nodosaurid ankylosaur (Dinosauria: Thyreophora) from the Upper Cretaceous Menefee Formation of New Mexico" in PeerJ (*https://peerj.com/articles/5435/*)

Latenivenatrix mcmasterae

- "Troodontids (Theropoda) from the Dinosaur Park Formation, Alberta, with a description of a unique new taxon: implications for deinonychosaur diversity in North America" on Canadian Journal of Earth Sciences (*https://www.nrcresearchpress.com/doi/*

pdf/10.1139/cjes-2017-0031)

Lepidus praecisio

- "The early fossil record of dinosaurs in North America: A new neotheropod from the base of the Upper Triassic Dockum Group of Texas" on Acta Paleontologica Polonica (*http://app.pan.pl/article/item/app001432014.html*)

- "Paleo Profile: Lepidus praecisio" on National Geographic (*https://www.nationalgeographic.com/environment/great-energy-challenge/*)

Maraapunisaurus fragillimus

- "Maraapunisaurus Fragillimus, N.G. (Formerly Amphicoelias Fragillimus), A Basal Rebbachisaurid From the Morrison Formation (Upper Jurassic) of Colorado" in Geology of the Intermountain West (*https://www.utahgeology.org/wp-content/uploads/2018/10/GIW2018-v05-pp227-244-Carpenter-screen.pdf*)

Machairoceratops cronusi

- "A New Centrosaurine Ceratopsid, Machairoceratops cronusi gen et sp. nov., from the Upper Sand Member of the Wahweap Formation (Middle Campanian), Southern Utah" on PLOS One (*https://journals.plos.org/plosone/article?id=10.1371/journal.pone.0154403*)

Mierasaurus bobyoungi

- "Descendants of the Jurassic turiasaurs from Iberia found refuge in the Early Cretaceous of western USA" on Nature's Scientific Reports (*https://www.nature.com/articles/s41598-017-14677-2*)

Platypelta coombsi
- "Revised systematics of the armoured dinosaur Euoplocephalus and its allies" in Neues Jahrbuch für Geologie und Paläontologie - Abhandlungen (*https://www.ingentaconnect.com/content/schweiz/njbgeol/2018/00000287/00000003/art00002%3bjsessionid=255o75lqc3tip.x-ic-live-01*)

Saurornitholestes sullivani
- "A new dromaeosaurid (Theropoda: Dromaeosauridae) from the Late Cretaceous of New Mexico" on Academia.edu (*https://www.academia.edu/12172255/A_new_dromaeosaurid_Theropoda_Dromaeosauridae_from_the_Late_Cretaceous_of_New_Mexico_B_and_W_*)
- "Saurornitholestes sullivani: New Dinosaur Discovered in New Mexico" on Sci-News (*http://www.sci-news.com/paleontology/science-saurornitholestes-sullivani-dinosaur-02791.html*)

Scolosaurus thronus
- "Revised systematics of the armoured dinosaur Euoplocephalus and its allies" in Neues Jahrbuch für Geologie und Paläontologie - Abhandlungen (*https://www.ingentaconnect.com/content/*

schweiz/njbgcol/2018/00000287/00000003/art00002%3bj sessionid=255o75lqc3tip.x-ic-live-01)

Ugrunaaluk kuukpikensis

🦕 "A new Arctic hadrosaurid from the Prince Creek Formation (lower Maastrichtian) of northern Alaska" on Acta Palaontologica Polonica (*https://www.app.pan.pl/article/item/app001522015.html*)

Wendiceratops pinhornensis

🦕 "Cranial Anatomy of Wendiceratops pinhornensis gen. et sp. nov., a Centrosaurine Ceratopsid (Dinosauria: Ornithischia) from the Oldman Formation (Campanian), Alberta, Canada, and the Evolution of Ceratopsid Nasal Ornamentation" on PLOS One (*https://journals.plos.org/plosone/article?id=10.1371/journal.pone.0130007*)

South America

Chilesaurus diegosuarezi

🦕 "An enigmatic plant-eating theropod from the Late Jurassic period of Chile" on Nature (*https://www.nature.com/articles/nature14307*)

🦕 "Meet Chilesaurus, a New Raptor-Like Dinosaur With a Vegetarian Diet" on Smithsonian Mag (*https://www.smithsonianmag.com/science-nature/meet-chilesaurus-new-raptor-dinosaur-vegetarian-diet-180955101/?no-ist*)

Dreadnoughtus schrani

- "A Gigantic, Exceptionally Complete Titanosaurian Sauropod Dinosaur from Southern Patagonia, Argentina" on Nature (*https://www.nature.com/articles/srep06196*)
- "Argentine Dinosaur Was an Estimated 130,000 Pounds, and Still Growing" on New York Times (*https://www.nytimes.com/2014/09/05/science/dinosaur-dreadnoughtus-discovery.html?_r=1*)

Gualicho shinyae

- "An Unusual New Theropod with a Didactyl Manus from the Upper Cretaceous of Patagonia, Argentina" on PLOS One (*https://journals.plos.org/plosone/article?id=info%3Adoi%2F10.1371%2Fjournal.pone.0157793*)
- "Meet Gualicho shinyae, the puny-armed distant relative of T. rex" on The Guardian (*https://www.theguardian.com/science/2016/jul/13/meet-gualicho-shinyae-the-puny-armed-distant-relative-of-t-rex*)

Isaberrysaura mollensis

- "A new primitive Neornithischian dinosaur from the Jurassic of Patagonia with gut contents" on Nature's Scientific Reports (*https://www.nature.com/articles/srep42778*)
- "Paleo Profile: Isabel Berry's Dinosaur" on Scientific American (*https://blogs.scientificamerican.com/laelaps/paleo-profile-*

isabel-berrys-dinosaurs/)

Lavocatisaurus agrioensis

🦕 "A new rebbachisaurid sauropod from the Aptian–Albian, Lower Cretaceous Rayoso Formation, Neuquén, Argentina" on Acta Palaeontologica Polonica (*https://www.app.pan.pl/article/item/app005242018.html*)

🦕 "New Species of Long-Necked Dinosaur Discovered" on Sci-News (*http://www.sci-news.com/paleontology/lavocatisaurus-agrioensis-dinosaur-06631.html*)

Murusraptor barrosaensis

🦕 "A New Megaraptoran Dinosaur (Dinosauria, Theropoda, Megaraptoridae) from the Late Cretaceous of Patagonia" on PLOS One (*https://journals.plos.org/plosone/article?id=10.1371/journal.pone.0157973*)

🦕 "Murusraptor barrosaensis likely a megaraptorid 'Giant Thief'" on University of Alberta (*https://www.ualberta.ca/science/science-news/2016/july/murusraptor-barrosaensis*)

Notocolossus gonzalezparejasi

🦕 "A gigantic new dinosaur from Argentina and the evolution of the sauropod hind foot" on Nature (*https://www.nature.com/articles/srep19165*)

🦕 "Carnegie Museum scientist helps unearth new dinosaur" on Pittsburgh Post-Gazette (*https://www.post-gazette.com/ae/art-*

architecture/2016/01/18/Carnegie-Museum-scientist-part-of-discovery-of-new-gigantic-dinosaur/stories/201601180159)

Sarmientosaurus musacchioi

- "A Basal Lithostrotian Titanosaur (Dinosauria: Sauropoda) with a Complete Skull: Implications for the Evolution and Paleobiology of Titanosauria" on PLOS One (https://journals.plos.org/plosone/article?id=10.1371/journal.pone.0151661)
- "New Droopy Dinosaur Hung Its Head Like an Enormous Eeyore" on National Geographic (https://news.nationalgeographic.com/2016/04/160426-new-dinosaur-species-skull-titanosaur-senses/)

Tratayenia rosalesi

- "A new megaraptoran theropod dinosaur from the Upper Cretaceous Bajo de la Carpa Formation of northwestern Patagonia" on Cretaceous Research (https://www.sciencedirect.com/science/article/pii/S0195667118300806)
- "This Truck-Size Dinosaur Terrorized Prey with Razor-Sharp 'Meat Hooks'" on Live Science (https://www.livescience.com/62164-dinosaur-sported-meat-hook-claws.html)

More Dinosaurs From South America

Aoniraptor libertatem

- "New theropod fauna from the Upper Cretaceous (Huincul Formation) of northwestern Patagonia, Argentina" on Research

Gate (*https://www.researchgate.net/publication/304013683_NEW_THEROPOD_FAUNA_FROM_THE_UPPER_CRETACEOUS_HUINCUL_FORMATION_OF_NORTHWESTERN_PATAGONIA_ARGENTINA*)

🦕 "Aoniraptor" on Wikipedia (*https://en.wikipedia.org/wiki/Aoniraptor*)

Austroposeidon magnificus

🦕 "A New Giant Titanosauria (Dinosauria: Sauropoda) from the Late Cretaceous Bauru Group, Brazil" on PLOS One (*https://journals.plos.org/plosone/article?id=10.1371/journal.pone.0163373*)

Baalsaurus mansillai

🦕 "Baalsaurus mansillai gen. et sp. nov. a new titanosaurian sauropod (Late Cretaceous) from Neuquén, Patagonia, Argentina" in SciELO (*http://www.scielo.br/scielo.php?script=sci_arttext&pid=S0001-37652018005018110&lng=en&tlng=en*)

Bagualosaurus agudoensis

🦕 "A new dinosaur (Saurischia: Sauropodomorpha) from the Late Triassic of Brazil provides insights on the evolution of sauropodomorph body plan" on Zoological Journal of the Linnean Society (*https://academic.oup.com/zoolinnean/advance-article-abstract/doi/10.1093/zoolinnean/zly028/5003418?redirectedFrom=fulltext*)

Bonapartesaurus rionegrensis

🦕 "Bonapartesaurus rionegrensis, a new hadrosaurine dinosaur from South America: implications for phylogenetic and biogeographic relations with North America" on Journal of Vertebrate Paleontology (*https://www.tandfonline.com/doi/abs/10.1080/02724634.2017.1289381?journalCode=ujvp20&*)

Buriolestes schultzi

🦕 "A Unique Late Triassic Dinosauromorph Assemblage Reveals Dinosaur Ancestral Anatomy and Diet" on Current Biology (*https://www.cell.com/current-biology/fulltext/S0960-9822(16)31124-1*)

Choconsaurus baileywillisi

🦕 "A new titanosaur sauropod from the Upper Cretaceous of Patagonia, Neuquén Province, Argentina --- Preprint" on Ameghiniana (*http://www.ameghiniana.org.ar/index.php/ameghiniana/article/view/3051*)

Ingentia prima

🦕 "An early trend towards gigantism in Triassic sauropodomorph dinosaurs" in Nature Ecology & Evolution (*https://www.nature.com/articles/s41559-018-0599-y*)

Lucianovenator bonoi

🦕 "A Late Norian-Rhaetian Coelophysid Neotheropod (Dinosauria, Saurischia) From the Quebrada Del Barro Formation,

Northwestern Argentina" --- Preprint on Ameghiniana (*https://bioone.org/journals/Ameghiniana/volume-54/issue-5/AMGH.09.04.2017.3065/A-Late-NorianRhaetian-Coelophysid-Neotheropod-Dinosauria-Saurischia-from-the-Quebrada/10.5710/AMGH.09.04.2017.3065.short*)

Macrocollum itaquii

🦕 "U-Pb age constraints on dinosaur rise from south Brazil" in Gondwana Research (*https://www.sciencedirect.com/science/article/pii/S1342937X18300327?via%3Dihub*)

Padillasaurus leivaensis

🦕 "A new Early Cretaceous brachiosaurid (Dinosauria, Neosauropoda) from northwestern Gondwana (Villa de Leiva, Colombia)" on Journal of Vertebrate Paleontology (*https://www.tandfonline.com/doi/abs/10.1080/02724634.2015.980505?journalCode=ujvp20*)

🦕 "Científicos descubren el primer dinosaurio en suelo colombiano" on Scientific American Español (*https://www.scientificamerican.com/espanol/noticias/cientificos-descubren-el-primer-dinosaurio-en-suelo-colombiano/*)

Pandoravenator fernandezorum

🦕 "A Theropod Dinosaur From The Late Jurassic Cañadón Calcáreo Formation Of Central Patagonia, And The Evolution Of The Theropod Tarsus" on Ameghiniana (*https://www.researchgate.*

net/publication/321166616_A_Theropod_Dinosaur_from_ the_Late_Jurassic_Canadon_Calcareo_Formation_of_Central_ Patagonia_and_the_Evolution_of_the_Theropod_Tarsus)

Patagotitan mayorum

- "A new giant titanosaur sheds light on body mass evolution among sauropod dinosaurs" on Proceedings of the Royal Society B (*https://royalsocietypublishing.org/doi/full/10.1098/ rspb.2017.1219*)

Pilmatueia faundezi

- "A new dicraeosaurid sauropod from the Lower Cretaceous (Mulichinco Formation, Valanginian, Neuquén Basin) of Argentina" in Cretaceous Research (*https://www.sciencedirect. com/science/article/pii/S0195667118300405?via%3Dihub*)

Powellvenator podocitus

- "A New Early Coelophysoid Neotheropod From the Late Triassic of Northwestern Argentina" on Ameghiniana (*http://www. ameghiniana.org.ar/index.php/ameghiniana/article/view/3100*)

Taurovenator violantei

- "New Theropod Fauna from the Upper Cretaceous (Huincul Formation) of Northwestern Patagonia, Argentina" on Research Gate (*https://www.researchgate.net/publication/304013683_ NEW_THEROPOD_FAUNA_FROM_THE_UPPER_ CRETACEOUS_HUINCUL_FORMATION_OF_*

NORTHWESTERN_PATAGONIA_ARGENTINA)
- "Taurovenator" on Wikipedia (*https://en.wikipedia.org/wiki/Taurovenator*)

Thanos simonattoi
- "A new Abelisauridae (Dinosauria: Theropoda) from São José do Rio Preto Formation, Upper Cretaceous of Brazil and comments on the Bauru Group fauna" in Historical Biology (*https://www.tandfonline.com/doi/full/10.1080/08912963.2018.1546700*)

Triunfosaurus leonardii
- "A new basal titanosaur (Dinosauria, Sauropoda) from the Lower Cretaceous of Brazil" on Journal of South American Earth Sciences (*https://www.sciencedirect.com/science/article/pii/S0895981116301584*)

Viavenator exxoni
- "A new brachyrostran with hypertrophied axial structures reveals an unexpected radiation of latest Cretaceous abelisaurids" on Cretaceous Research (*https://www.sciencedirect.com/science/article/pii/S0195667115301439*)

Index

Africa	1
Ledumahadi mafube	2
Sefapanosaurus zastronensis	6
Spinosaurus aegyptiacus	10
More Dinosaurs From Africa	14
Afromimus tenerensis	15
Chenanisaurus barbaricus	16
Eucnemesaurus entaxonis	17
Mansourasaurus shahinae	18
Meroktenos thabanensis	19
Pulanesaura eocollum	20
Shingopana songwensis	21
Antarctica	22
Morrosaurus antarcticus	23
Asia	24
Bayannurosaurus perfectus	25
Caihong juji	29
Changyuraptor yangi	33
Corythoraptor jacobsi	37

Datonglong tianzhenensis	42
Deinocheirus mirificus	46
Fukuivenator paradoxus	50
Halszkaraptor escuillici	54
Kulindadromeus zabaikalicus	58
Qianzhousaurus sinensis	62
Qiupanykus zhangi	66
Serikornis sungei	70
Tongtianlong limosus	74
Yi qi	78
Zhenyuanlong suni	82
More Dinosaurs From Asia	86
Aepyornithomimus tugrikinensis	87
Almas ukhaa	88
Anhuilong diboensis	89
Anomalipes zhaoi	90
Avimimus nemegtensis	91
Bannykus wulatensis	92
Beibeilong sinensis	93
Beipiaognathus jii	94
Choyrodon barsboldi	95
Crichtonpelta benxiensis	96
Daliansaurus liaoningensis	97

Hualianceratops wucaiwanensis	98
Huanansaurus ganzhouensis	99
Ischioceratops zhuchengensis	100
Jianianhualong tengi	102
Jinguofortis perplexus	103
Jinyunpelta sinensis	104
Koshisaurus katsuyama	105
Laiyangosaurus youngi	106
Lepidocheirosaurus natatilis	107
Liaoningotitan sinensis	108
Liaoningvenator curriei	109
Lingwulong shenqi	110
Microenantiornis vulgaris	111
Mosaiceratops azumai	112
Nebulasaurus taito	113
Qijianglong guokr	114
Shuangbaisaurus anlongbaoensis	115
Sibirotitan astrosacralis	116
Sirindhorna khoratensis	117
Tarchia teresae	118
Tengrisaurus starkovi	119
Timurlengia euotica	120
Xingxiulong chengi	121

Xiyunykus pengi	122
Yangavis confucii	123
Yizhousaurus sunae	124
Zhongjianosaurus yangi	125
Zhuchengtitan zangjiazhuangensis	126
Zuoyunlong huangi	127
Australia	128
Diluvicursor pickeringi	129
Kunbarrasaurus ieversi	133
Weewarrasaurus pobeni	137
More Dinosaurs From Australia	141
Savannasaurus elliottorum	142
Europe	143
Dracoraptor hanigani	144
Morelladon beltrani	148
Ostromia crassipes	152
Torvosaurus gurneyi	156
More Dinosaurs From Europe	160
Adynomosaurus arcanus	161
Burianosaurus augustai	162
Europatitan eastwoodi	163
Haestasaurus becklesii	164
Horshamosaurus rudgwickensis	165

Iguanodon galvensis	166
Lohuecotitan pandafilandi	167
Magnamanus soriaensis	168
Matheronodon provincialis	169
Saltriovenator zanellai	170
Soriatitan golmayensis	171
Volgatitan simbirskiensis	172
Vouivria damparisensis	173
Wiehenvenator albati	174
North America	175
Anzu wyliei	176
Aquilops americanus	180
Arkansaurus fridayi	184
Borealopelta markmitchelli	188
Dakotaraptor steini	193
Daspletosaurus horneri	197
Dynamoterror dynastes	201
Galeamopus pabsti	205
Nanuqsaurus hoglundi	209
Probrachylophosaurus bergi	213
Rativates evadens	218
Regaliceratops peterhewsi	222
Spiclypeus shipporum	228

Tototlmimus packardensis	232
Yehuecauhceratops mudei	236
Zuul crurivastator	240
More Dinosaurs From North America	244
Acantholipan gonazalezi	245
Agujaceratops mavericus	246
Akainacephalus johnsoni	247
Albertavenator curriei	248
Alcovasaurus longispinus	249
Anodontosaurus inceptus	250
Apatoraptor pennatus	251
Boreonykus certekorum	252
Crittendenceratops krzyzanowskii	253
Dryosaurus elderae	254
Eotrachodon orientalis	255
Foraminacephale brevis	256
Galeamopus hayi	257
Gastonia lorriemcwhinneyae	258
Gryposaurus alsatei	259
Invictarx zephyri	260
Latenivenatrix mcmasterae	261
Lepidus praecisio	262
Maraapunisaurus fragillimus	263

Machairoceratops cronusi	264
Mierasaurus bobyoungi	265
Platypelta coombsi	266
Saurornitholestes sullivani	267
Scolosaurus thronus	268
Ugrunaaluk kuukpikensis	269
Wendiceratops pinhornensis	270
South America	271
Chilesaurus diegosuarezi	272
Dreadnoughtus schrani	276
Gualicho shinyae	280
Isaberrysaura mollensis	284
Lavocatisaurus agrioensis	288
Murusraptor barrosaensis	292
Notocolossus gonzalezparejasi	296
Sarmientosaurus musacchioi	301
Tratayenia rosalesi	306
More Dinosaurs From South America	310
Aoniraptor libertatem	311
Austroposeidon magnificus	312
Baalsaurus mansillai	313
Bagualosaurus agudoensis	314
Bonapartesaurus rionegrensis	315

Buriolestes schultzi	316
Choconsaurus baileywillisi	317
Ingentia prima	318
Lucianovenator bonoi	319
Macrocollum itaquii	320
Padillasaurus leivaensis	321
Pandoravenator fernandezorum	322
Patagotitan mayorum	323
Pilmatueia faundezi	324
Powellvenator podocitus	325
Taurovenator violantei	326
Thanos simonattoi	327
Triunfosaurus leonardii	328
Viavenator exxoni	329
Resources	330

About

Sabrina is a writer and podcaster. She loves nerdy things, like technical specs and dinosaurs, especially sauropods. When she's not writing, she's podcasting with her husband at *I Know Dino* (iknowdino.com), a weekly show about dinosaurs.

Thank you for reading! If you liked what you just read, then please consider leaving a review. Even if it's only a few sentences, it would make a big difference and be greatly appreciated.

books2read.com/50dinosaurtales

For Dinosaur Enthusiasts

Are you really into dinosaurs? Sign up to the *I Know Dino* mailing list for news, updates, and special offers on all upcoming dinosaur books.

iknowdino.com/subscribe

Connect With Sabrina via *I Know Dino*

Website: iknowdino.com
Apple Podcasts: bit.ly/iknowdino
Instagram: @iknowdino
YouTube: youtube.com/c/iknowdino
Facebook: facebook.com/iknowdino
Twitter: @IKnowDino
TikTok: @IKnowDino
Tumblr: iknowdino.tumblr.com
Pinterest: pinterest.com/iknowdino
LinkedIn: linkedin.com/company/i-know-dino
Patreon: patreon.com/iknowdino

More
I Know Dino
Books

Keep Your Dinosaurs Here

Sabrina Ricci

100 creative journal prompts for dinosaur enthusiasts

What Happened to *Brontosaurus*?

written by Sabrina Ricci   illustrated by Gagyi Palffy Andrea

Made in the USA
Monee, IL
02 April 2022

7342fdc5-427b-40bc-9716-fa6f31b434ddR01